TEMPTED

Sex, Drama, and Indecision…
Will Temptation Win?

Ameehsal MindSpeaka

For information contact:

MindSpeaka@gmail.com
http://www.MindSpeaka.com

PierceWright@gmail.com
http://www.PierceWright.com

Book and Cover design by L. D. Pierce
Photography by Kandi Huggins and Michael Daniels
Book Formatting by Derek Murphy @Creativindie

ISBN-13: 978-1-7337252-0-0

First Edition: April 2019

10 9 8 7 6 5 4 3 2 1

Dedicated to Damita A.W. McCartha. You live on every day through me.

CONTENTS

aaliyah

Chapter 1

Had you told me that I would see the end of Xavier and me, I would've told you, you were lying against God. We were a match made in Heaven. If there was such a thing as an Earth Angel, he was definitely mine. At least, that is what I thought up until I got this unexpected call from him.

I sat on the phone and listened as I heard Xavier's voice tell me, "I slept with someone else. I'm sorry."

Realization quickly crept in. He was telling me he cheated on me. I was floored. "Sorry? But ... but, how? How?" I cried into the phone, already feeling the tears sliding down my face, "How?"

"It just happened," he replied like it was no big deal. I sat on the other end of the phone feeling my world fall apart. It hadn't even been a week since I last saw him. How could so much change in just a week? This obviously was some failed joke. This couldn't possibly be true. Xavier loves me, is in love with me, and I with him. There's no way he would do this to me.

"You are joking, right? This has to be a joke."

"I'm not joking."

"Don't play, Xavier. I'm not laughing."

"Neither am I, Aaliyah. I'm not playing any games, just telling you the truth. I slept with someone else."

I yelled into the phone, "YOU CAN'T BE SERIOUS! YOU CANNOT BE SERIOUS RIGHT NOW!" He answered my anger with silence. I sat there and thought about everything we had been through; all the ups and downs since freshman year. The last thing I wanted was to lose everything I felt we were building together.

Forcing the words out, I sniffled into the phone and said, "Baby, I love you. Whatever this is you are feeling or going through, we can work it out. You still love me, don't you? There is nothing we can't get through together." Again I was met with silence in reply. "Baby, did you hear me? You do still love me, don't you," I asked into the receiver. "XAVIER?!?"

"Yeah, what's up?" he finally replied as if he had been distracted by something else the whole time.

"*What's up?* I just asked you if you love me. I said we can work this out."

"Look, Aaliyah, I don't know if I want to work it out."

"What is that supposed to mean? Are you trying to break up with me?"

"Look, man, I don't know. Maybe. They say things happen for a reason. Maybe this is why. Maybe it's time to call it quits."

"*You don't know?* How don't you know, Xavier? *And call it quits?* Really? Are you serious?" I demanded. My cool was coming completely undone all over again. At the rate I was going, I didn't know how much longer I could keep it together.

"We've been going through a lot lately, and I think it might be better if we just went our separate ways." Sounding as if he had reached some goal or accomplishment, he continued, "There. I said it."

Like a flash flood, the tears came and I could not stop them. I cried into the phone again, "ARE YOU SERIOUS? YOU CANNOT BE SERIOUS! ARE YOU SERIOUSLY THROWING US AWAY?" I tried pleading with him, "Every couple has problems, Baby. We can fix this. I still love you and don't want to lose you. We all make mistakes, so please, Baby, I will ..."

He cut me off in mid-sentence, "I love you, too, but I don't think this is going to work out for us, Aaliyah. To be honest, this wasn't a mistake. I've been thinking about ending it for a minute but didn't. Now I realize I just really want to see what else is out there. Maybe you should think about doing the same."

I continued to cry, begging with him to reconsider, "Baby, I don't want to see other people. I want to see you! We've built so much together. Why would you want to throw all of that away?" Trying to make sense of it all, I continued, "You are right, we have been going through it lately, so I can see why you've been thinking those things. How about we both take some time and sleep on it? With everything that had been going on and has happened, we are both getting emotional, making it hard to think clearly. Let's sleep on it and then when we are less emotional we can discuss it with clearer minds."

Thinking on my feet, I thought of an alternative, anything to save my relationship, I added, "Or I can just come back later this week so we can sit down and talk about this. I don't mind making the drive. Anything to show you I am for real about us and doing what I can to save us."

"No, that's not necessary. Stay there. You coming down here won't change anything." He paused and I could swear I heard a female's voice in the background.

"You cheated on me, yet I'm begging to stay with you, and you have the audacity to have someone there with you in the background? Really? Who's that, Xavier? Who's with you right now?"

"No one," he quickly responded before adding, "Umm, look, Aaliyah, I have to go. Be easy." Seconds later, he was gone.

In the darkness, I could see my cell phone light up as the disconnection became final, then dim and die down again. I sat there holding the rest of my tears hostage, threatening death to any that tried to escape. Looking at the digital clock on my nightstand, I saw it was close to midnight. Everyone in the house was sleeping.

Even though I knew I was in no condition to drive, I grabbed my keys and headed for the door. As soon as I got in the car and turned the ignition on, my lips turned down and the tears fell again. With each tear I cried, the intensity picked up and my moans of agony got louder and louder. No matter how loud I got, though, I could still barely hear myself over the blaring music.

As I continued to sob, I thought to myself, "*I need to learn to turn the radio down before I get out the car.*" The station I had left it on had the smooth R&B melodies of Mary J. Blige playing through my speakers. Her words invaded my thoughts as she sang about not crying anymore because he was never worth her tears. The perfect soundtrack to what I was going through at that moment.

"Yeah," I told myself, "Xavier isn't worth my tears. I know there is better out there." My attempt at building myself back up to make me feel better slowed my tears down as I began singing with Mary J. Blige with every emotion I had inside of me.

Putting the car in reverse, I backed out the driveway and started heading for the highway. There is only one place to go in New Jersey at this hour and that was New York. Well, that isn't really New Jersey, but it was close enough. I got on the 95 north and headed toward the bridge, on my way to the city that never sleeps.

About thirty minutes later I was cruising through the streets of New York City. People were out having fun while I drove around feeling sorry for myself. A couple crossed in front of me as I stopped at a red light, laughing and holding hands and it just made me want to cry all over again. Determined not to, I sped off at the changing of the light and headed toward the Village. From what I understood, the Village was where gay men and women gathered. I never stayed out and about long enough to find out. The Village wasn't really my scene, but that was where the best novelty stores were. Porn and sex toys fascinated me and usually took my mind off my troubles.

I was lucky to find a parking space close to a place called *The Pink Pussy*. It looked like a fairly new spot, well, new to me since I hadn't been in the Village since my first year in college. The establishment was bright, with pink neon lights all around, and took up the whole corner of the block. In the windows were mannequins dressed in leather costumes with colorful boas and leather whips for accessories. On various boxes were pornos, vibrators, and lubricants of varying sizes strategically placed between them. Looking at this setup, I just knew I would find something to take my mind off my current situation.

Walking in, I headed straight to where I could find the leather, which was usually where you would find the whips. I looked at the different kinds and ran my fingers through the ones with multiple strands. I smiled at the feel of the leather.   It has long been a fantasy of mine to incorporate leather into my sessions of lovemaking, but Xavier wasn't into that type of thing.   The thought of Xavier reminded me that he had just broken up with me over the phone. It made me frown, so I moved on to another section of the store trying to leave the negativity behind me.

I decided to stop at a wall filled with nothing but dildos of every shape, size, and color you could think of and started looking at them.

"Can I help you?" someone asked from behind me. I turned around, ready to say I was just looking when I saw a female. She had spiked, jet black hair, tattoos and spiked bracelets on both arms, a piercing in her eyebrow and lip, a tight T-shirt with a band I had never heard of on it, fairly tight blue jeans held up with a black leather belt, shoes that looked like slide-on Keds, and a welcoming smile. She was tall, probably 5'8" and her skin was the color of cooled mocha. Her eyes were hazel with a hint of green. How I had noticed all of that in those few seconds, I don't know, but I did.

I fumbled over my words as I said, "Umm, no ... I think ... I think I am good."

She smiled harder as she told me, "Well, if you need anything, and I do mean anything, let me know. The name is Jess." With that, she smiled, turned around, and walked away to another part of the establishment. I stared at her back as she disappeared around a corner and wondered why the hell I was staring so hard at her. Closing my eyes and laughing to myself, I refocused and started looking at the display of dildos in front of me again. Once I felt I had seen enough, I moved to the vibrators and figured I would buy myself a new one since I didn't know the next time I was going to be getting any.

I picked up a toy called the "Dolphin," which had a little blue dolphin on it. The label stated that it had multiple speeds and was waterproof. As I continued reading the box, someone said, "That is a good one if you are going to be alone, but I doubt you would need something like that." I turned around to find Jess standing right behind me.

"You shouldn't just walk up on people like that," I told her as I jumped a little.

"I apologize," she stated, "though it is my job to make sure that our customer is finding everything she may want, need, or both," she said smiling at me. Her eyes flashed and my knees slightly buckled.

"Well," I began, recapturing my composure, "you should still use more tact when approaching people from behind. And why would you say that anyway?"

"Believe me," she grinned, "I do." She paused to let the statement sink in before stating, "But, to answer your question, I doubt you have to satisfy yourself."

"You are quite forward, aren't you?"

"No. I just rarely hold my tongue," she said, smiling at me again.

"Well, maybe I do not mind self-love," I stated, turning my attention back to the box I had in my hand.

"Indeed, there is nothing wrong with handling business for yourself. If that is what you are going for, then I would recommend the Dolphin. With brand new batteries, it has a bit of a kick to it." Jess grinned again, as she took the box from my hand. "Follow me and I will give you a demonstration."

I didn't move. I looked at her like she was crazy, then told her, "I don't know what you have in mind, but I don't get down like that."

Realizing the possible implications of her words, she turned around and laughed. "I apologize for the misunderstanding. I am only going to put batteries in it so you can see the various speeds in order to make a more informed decision on whether or not to buy the Dolphin." As she said the name of the toy, she raised the box up in her right hand. I automatically felt flush and stupid for insinuating such a thing.

Catching up to where she had stopped, I said, "I apologize. I didn't mean anything by it. I just have gone through a lot tonight."

She waved it off, "It's not a problem. I am not easily offended."

"That's good," I said, relieved. "I am sure being gay you have people saying some really out the way things to you all the time." She stopped in her tracks, looked at me, laughed to herself, and then continued walking. I asked, "Did I say something funny?"

Walking behind the counter with the register, she continued to laugh. She pulled out a box of AA batteries and put it on the counter. She looked me dead in my eyes and I cowered away from her glare. "Ma'am, how do you know I am gay?"

"I ... I ... I," I stumbled out but didn't know what else to say, other than to apologize for my comment. "I apologize. I just assumed ..."

She cut me off, "You make a lot of assumptions, you know that?" She smiled at me as she began taking the Dolphin out of the box and inserting the batteries into the white hand-held controller.

"I really didn't mean anything by it," I said as I lowered my eyes. I didn't want to chance her seeing me on the brink of tears. I was already emotional due to what happened earlier, and now I was also frustrated at myself for passing judgment when I hate when someone does it to me.

"It's cool," Jess said calmly. "I am gay, but I do not think being gay is any harder than being straight. Everyone faces adversity; sexuality is just one of the many. You still have race, religion, and other issues that create barriers between us. So I am gay. It is what it is. I refuse to let it be my crutch." She paused as I heard her snap the back of the controller back into place. "Okay. Ready to give it a feel?"

I looked up to see her smiling as if she wasn't even fazed by my pre-judgment, holding the Dolphin out to me. I put my finger to the tip and automatically became aroused from the gentle feel of the material. "What is this?"

Checking the box, she said, "Regular old silicone. You like?"

"Yes. It's really soft."

"Yeah? Let me turn it on and see how you like the vibration."

She turned it on and I was sold. "Oh, yes," I moaned, "I like that."

She laughed, "Great! Would you like me to add some batteries, too?"

"Wait, I didn't say I was getting it."

"You're not?"

She turned the vibrator back on and I caved, "Okay, yes, I am going to get it," I semi-blushed.

Smiling she asked again, "Would you like some batteries, too?"

"Yes, that would be good," I told her, feeling a little bashful about my excitement over a toy.

"Awesome! Will this be all for you, or would you like to keep looking?" She just kept smiling at me, and I felt my stomach twirl as butterflies flew around inside it.

"I think I am done for tonight."

"Aww, no porn to go with your new toy?"

I blushed, "No, I think I am good."

Jess smiled at me as she gave me the damage and I handed her my debit card. "May I see some ID?"

"Oh, yeah, of course." I handed her my license and she looked it over.

"Aaliyah, huh? Can you sing like her?"

"Yeah, Aaliyah, but, no, I can't sing like her. I wish I could."

"Oh well. You're still as cute as she was." She handed me a slip of paper with a pen, "Can I get your autograph?" I smiled at her, signed the slip and handed it back. As she was handing me my bag, she said, "Thank you for shopping at *The Pink Pussy*. Hope to see you again."

I smiled, said "Thank-you," and took my bag. As I was heading to the door, I turned around and ran smack into her stare. I stuttered but was able to get out, "I apologize, again, for my comment earlier."

She replied, "It's not a problem. You are cool with me. Be safe."

Feeling silly, I nodded and bolted out of the store, making a bee-line to my car. Once I got in my car, I hit my steering wheel, cursing myself for running out the store like a coward. Honestly, what was I running from? Surely, not another female? Coming to terms with what was done being done, I put my key in the ignition and headed back over the bridge on my way home.

jess

Chapter 2

I watched her until I couldn't see her through the glass door anymore. She wasn't really the type of girl I was usually into, but something about her sparked my interest. All of my exes were fashion model types, tall and skinny. She wasn't that at all, not to say that she wasn't cute. I found her to be very attractive, actually. She was roughly 5'5" or 5'6" in the heels she wore. She had loose fitted jeans on that became taut around her high, rounded backside, and a semi-see-through white blouse with a modest amount of c-cup cleavage showing. Her hair was layered with brown highlights, her eyes were almond shaped and dark brown, and her skin was the shade of brown that could easily cause her to be mistaken for redbone on a bright sunny day. To top it all off, she had the same name as my only celebrity crush, Aaliyah. Indeed, she was attractive.

"I am surprised you didn't get her number," my co-worker and best friend, Ty, said appearing out of thin air.

"Where did you come from? And what for? She isn't even gay."

He laughed, "That never stopped you before."

"Yeah? Maybe that was the problem."

"Yeah, whatever J. I am going to the back to watch some porn. Call me if you need me."

"Hey, don't be back there jacking off. And if you do, make sure you clean up after yourself," I said laughing.

He threw up his hands in a "W" and said, "Whatever," before giving me the middle finger and walking away. I smiled and watched him disappear down the hallway leading to the viewing areas. As my smile relaxed, I sat there at the counter just a little dazed. He was right. Whether a woman was gay, bi, or even straight, if I wanted her, I knew I could have her. It's not that I am cocky, I just know too well that it is a matter of approach. I'm not even sure what stopped me from going after her, though. It was more than obvious she was curious, yet I hesitated in acknowledging her interest and I have no idea why.

I decided not to lose any sleep over the matter and looked at the time. There was still an hour left before I should get ready to close up shop. Thinking about what I could do to occupy my time, I remembered that there were some inventory sheets I'd been putting off completing. With so much time left and nothing to fill it with, I decided the best thing to do at work was work. Aaliyah had been the most excitement in the store all night, and with her gone, that was all there was left to do.

I pulled out the stack hidden behind the counter and started reading through the paperwork. It was busy work that wasn't really keeping my attention at all. I was still thinking about this girl who I am sure I will never see again. Even with that knowledge, my focus was shot.

There was no reason to keep things going, so I decided to call it a night early. It was one of the few perks of being the owner of *The Pink Pussy*. I didn't have to work the floor or late night shifts, either, but I found it kept me humble and closer to those who kept me out of the poor house. Not too long ago, the *Voice of the Village* had a feature article on me and my business. I am one of the youngest, successful business owners here in the Village.   What can I say? I am blessed.

I locked the main entrance before heading to the back to get Ty so we could go home. Closing up an hour earlier than usual would probably save me more money on electricity before making me any. "Come on, Ty. We're getting out of here," I said as I approached one of the three video viewing areas.

"Yes, Ma'am! I was wondering when you were going to wrap it up. There is nobody out here tonight." He got up and turned the video of a guy receiving head from two other guys off and followed me out the room. "Tonight has been a drag."

"I know," I agreed with him as we made it back to the front of the store. "Want to hit up *Lollipops* tonight?"

"No," he said rolling his eyes, "I am not in the mood for *fish*."

I laughed and told him, "Well, I DEFINITELY am always in the mood for a good fish dinner!" He fake gagged at my comment while I just continued to laugh. I turned off the lights and locked the door to the store, taking in the cool breeze passing by outside. "Tonight is a good night to be out and about. Sure you don't want to tag along?"

"I am good," Ty said, "I think I am gonna just go home and relax tonight." He leaned in and hugged me, "You be safe out there, though. You know those felines would love to get their claws in you."

Embracing him the same, I said, "Awww, don't worry about me. I'm a big girl. I can handle myself."

He mumbled, "It's not you I am worried about you handling."

"I heard that!" I said, pushing him off me and laughing.

"Don't act like it's not true, J."

"Haha, you think you know, huh?"

"Think? I am way past that stage with you, honey."

"A'ight, you're right. I'll be careful."

"Good. Call me when you get in. Better yet, text me and I'll get it when I wake up."

"I got you." Hugging him again I told him, "Love you. Text

me when you get home."

"A'ight." We let go of the embrace and headed in opposite directions to our cars. There is a parking lot connected to *The Pink Pussy*, but we usually parked close to the front when we worked the late shift.

I got into my Ashton Martin, looked myself over in my rearview mirror, concluded I was fine and headed down to *Lollipops*. I checked my watch. At 1 am, the club would just be getting started.

After parking in the parking garage adjacent to the club, I walked to the VIP line. I can be a bit impatient so waiting wasn't something I liked to do. Once the guard was finished searching me, I gave the girl directly inside the doorway my money and walked into the spot. As usual, the crowd was thick. *Lollipops* never disappointed. With three levels, each with lounge areas for general conversation, private rooms for a more intimate setting, and full bars with bartenders who knew every drink you could think of, it is no wonder *Lollipops* was THEE place to be seen in the Lesbian Community.

Avoiding the crowd at the main floor bar, I went to the second floor to order a Long Island Iced Tea, my drink of choice when I want to loosen up fairly quickly. Tipping the bartender, I posted up on one of the empty barstools and sipped my drink. While sipping my drink and taking up surveillance of the crowd, I felt a presence slide up next to me.

"Hi," the woman's voice said in my ear, "I don't mean to bother you, but don't I know you?"

Turning in my chair to face her, I grinned, internally sighing with relief at the brown skin beauty that was standing there. "Oh," I asked her, "Where do you think you know me from?"

"Don't you work at *The Pink Pussy*?"

"Yes, I do," I answered, smiling at her.

"I thought that was you! I was in there last week, just ... uhh ... looking, when I saw you. I wanted to speak, but you were busy."

"Well, we are speaking now."

She blushed, "Yes."

"Can I get you a drink?"

"Oh, no. No thank-you. I am the DD tonight, so no drinks for me."

"Ah, that's good. Making sure your friends get home safely. How sweet." I took a sip of my drink before asking, "So what's your name?"

"Jordyn, but most of my friends just call me J."

"What a coincidence. Most of my friends call me J, too." She smiled seeming to relax a little. Taking a chance I asked, "Would you like to go sit in the lounge and get better acquainted?"

Looking over her shoulder, at who I couldn't tell, she replied, "Sure," with a smile.

I grabbed my drink and she followed me to the lounge across from the bar. Most of the seats lined up against the wall were taken, but we were able to find a free spot near the back end of the room. Easily we fell into conversation. As time went by, I sipped on my drink and Jordyn told me about herself and how she had just moved to New York from California. I asked her if she was enjoying N.Y. She said it was different here and that it would still take some getting used to. I told her meeting the right people would help with that. She smiled and blushed a little.

Our conversation had to go on for at least an hour before one of her friends came up and stole her attention from me. Excusing herself, she got up to speak to her friend. They spoke briefly before Jordyn came back and told me she had to go. "I really enjoyed talking to you, but one of my friends has had way too much to drink."

"I understand. You should probably get her home."

"Yeah. Ummm, can I ... can I get your number so we can talk again sometime?"

"Sure. 555-1204, that's a 917 area code."

She smiled, "Thanks. Would you like mine?"

"No. I'll wait for you to call me."

"Oh, ok." She smiled. I smiled back.

From a short distance, her friend called out to her. "J, we have to go. Tonya is already outside with Kristen walking to the car."

To her friend she said, "All right," then turned her attention back to me. "It was a pleasure meeting you ... just J?"

"Jess, but J is fine too," I said with a wink.

"Ok," she blushed.

"C'mon Jordyn," her friend beckoned.

"I have to go," she blurted as she snapped out of her trance. "Have a good night Jess."

"You too. Be safe out there on the road," I told her before she disappeared out the lounge following her friend's exit. Looking at the empty glass in my hand, I tried to decide whether or not I should get another drink. I concluded the one was enough and that it would probably just be best for me to call it a night, too. Getting up, I took the glass, placed it on a table and exited the room.

"Well, well, well, didn't expect to see you here, Gorgeous." I turned to see my ex, and sometimes bedmate, Mieko. Tall and exotic Mieko. She was everything I ever asked for in a woman. Beautiful, sexy, intelligent, determined and accomplished. She didn't need me for anything, Ms. Independent in the flesh. And that was what made me fall for her and grow so attached to her. Unfortunately, her lifestyle did not allow for her to be around all the time and that put a strain on us. I like being around my lady and she just couldn't always be there. Rather than have her choose between her career and me, I removed myself. She hated me for it but later grew to understand. From time to time we'll get together and it will seem like old times, hence her still being my bedmate, but we know we are not together. So she does her own thing and I do mine.

"Mieko. I see you are back in town. Looking gorgeous yourself, I might add. When did you get back?"

She grinned, "This evening. Only here for a few days. A few shots for a couple of magazines, and then I am gone."

"You are always gone," I said to her with a sly grin.

"Yes, but I will always be sure to come back and make time for you." The words slid off her tongue like sweet honey, commanding my full and unbridled attention. Smiling back at me slyly herself, she asked, "You have any plans after you leave here?"

"What did you have in mind?" She cupped my ear, whispering in her desires. Grinning fully I told her, "I think I can help you with that."

"Good. My hotel isn't too far from here. Let's go."

"Whoa, Mi-Mi! Right now? How do you know I am ready to leave? You said plans for after the club."

"Don't play, Baby. You and I both know you don't stay at the club all night. Besides, I am sure you won't regret leaving now."

I smiled at her. "Oh yeah?"

"Have I ever disappointed you?"

Having a flashback in my mind, I wanted to bring up the time she stood me up for dinner on my birthday for a casting party she just couldn't miss, but I decided not to take it there. Instead, I smiled and said, "All right. Let's go."

With that, she grabbed my hand and led me outside. "Did you drive or ride your bike tonight?"

"I drove."

"I will wait for you in my limo. Follow it to the hotel."

"A'ight." I went to the garage, got in my car and headed down to the main street where Meiko was waiting for me. As I drove down, I texted Ty, "Mi-Mi's back," telling him Mieko was back in town. That was enough to let him know I would probably be out all night. Reaching the street, I pulled up to the side of the limo and rolled my window down. Mieko rolled down her window and told me to follow her. I did, knowing that it was going to be a good night.

aaliyah

Chapter 3

"Oh my god! Oh my god! I'm cuming!" I moaned to myself as I pressed the vibrator against my clit and felt my release. I had found that the best time to masturbate was in the morning after everybody had already left for work. Since buying the Dolphin, this had become my morning routine. Wake up. Masturbate. Shower. Wash my sheets. Watch TV. Sleep. Repeat.

As my orgasm rushed out of me, I pressed the toy harder against my clit until I just couldn't take it anymore, riding the ending waves of my orgasm. Laying there in my aftermath, I dropped the vibrator and stared at the ceiling. Even though the release was good, I was having to really concentrate just to have a decent orgasm anymore, because truthfully, my body craved the real thing. I was still missing Xavier and hadn't found anyone to replace him, even if just for the summer. There weren't any distractions worth having here in Jersey.

So frustrated, I rolled out bed and started to gather the sheets.

I threw them all in a pile at the foot of my bed and walked to the bathroom to wash my toy, and then myself. After a refreshing shower, I decided that I was going to get out of the house, even if it killed me. With that in mind, I took my bedding down to the laundry room to put them in the wash. On my way back to my room I got a new sheet set for my bed. I made up my bed and pulled out some clothes to put on for the day.

At about 9 in the morning, I left the house with no idea of where I was going. I just hopped in my car and drove. Since moving to Atlanta for college, I had lost track of most of the friends I had in Jersey. All except Tina. One could pretty much say that she's my best friend. We met our junior year of high school, the year she transferred into the school. We didn't necessarily hit it off from the start due to our different understandings on life, but we eventually grew close and damn near inseparable. The fact I left Jersey for college was what broke us apart. She stayed here for school. I didn't want to leave my sister from another mister, but I just couldn't stay here. Even so, we remained close despite the distance.

Hoping that Tina was home, I turned into someone's driveway and started heading in the opposite direction I was going on Union so that I was heading toward Downtown. To get to Tina's house I would have to take Route 4. Just to be sure she'd be home before I left town though, I called her on my cell. "Hello," she answered on the first ring.

"Hey, Tina! I can't believe you are actually home! That's good, though. I am coming to get you."

"What's up, Liyah! Girllllll, it's about time you called me, although you could have called my cellphone! I was beginning to think you didn't love me anymore," she laughed into the phone. Tina's mom believed in keeping a house phone just in case of an emergency. I have yet to change her main number in my phone to her cell number, so my phone automatically calls her house.

"Oh hush!" I laughed with her. "Naw, you know since Xavier and I broke up, I have been playing hermit crab, hiding away from the world."

"I know! But Girl, you need to get over that! We are too young to get hung up over other people. C'est la vie!"

"Yeah, yeah ... but you know how ..."

"Un-un," she cut me off, already knowing I was about to start talking about my love for Xavier and trying to figure out where we went wrong. "Don't even go there! Next topic. So, where are we going?"

I smiled at how well my friend knew me and answered, "I don't even know, but I am on my way to your house. I'm on Route 4 now."

"Ok, cool. Umm, want to go to New York? We can go have an early lunch and walk around. We are bound to find *something* to do in N.Y. We can even take the bus up."

"You know what," I responded, "that sounds good. I can save me some money on gas because gas prices are ridiculous!" I laughed into the phone.

"I know that's right," Tina agreed with me. "A'ight. I'll see you in a few. By the time you get here, I should have found my bus schedule and know what time the bus is coming."

"All right then. Sounds like a plan." We hung up and I already felt better about deciding to get up and get out. Tina could always be depended on to help turn a frown upside down. It was her free spirit and lack of tolerance for bullshit, I think, that kept us friends, even with me moving away.

There wasn't much traffic on the roads, for the most part, except around the exits to the malls. I was able to get to her exit in no time. Thinking about what I had in my purse, I realized I didn't have much cash on me. You have to have cash to get on the bus, so I decided to stop at a bank to get some out. These days, I rarely ever carried cash on me. It is all about the plastic. If someone was to rob me, debit cards are easier to track and replace then cash.

As I pulled up, Tina walked on the porch to greet me. I parked my car and headed up the steps where she grabbed me in a major bear hug. "Girlll, I have missed you so much!" she exclaimed as she rocked me side to side.

"Tina, stop! I saw you the last time I was home." I broke from her hug and smiled. "But I've missed you, too. Is mom home?"

"Nah, she's at work. I didn't have to go in today, so I am glad you called. Otherwise, I would've been sitting here bored to death!" We laughed and walked into the house.

Tina informed me that, "The bus won't come for another hour, so we can chill for a second." Chilling must've been code for giving me the third degree because we spent the next half hour discussing what happened between Xavier and me. I told her that he just called me out the blue after I arrived in Jersey and broke up with me. Tina sympathized with me, and then told me I needed to let it go. For the rest of the day I was not allowed to mention Xavier, or our failed relationship, at all.

"All right," I said, "I get it. Today will be about getting up and getting out."

"Exactly! I am serious, Liyah. We will fight in the middle of New York. I'm not playing."

"I know, I know," I giggled. Looking at my watch I asked, "Isn't it time for us to go catch the bus?"

"Yeah, let's go out there now. You never know with these bus drivers these days. Especially NJ Transit bus drivers. They just make up their own schedules." We both laughed at her joke. With that, we got up and headed out the door. Within minutes we saw the bus come rolling down the street.

On the bus, we played more catch up without the mention of my former. Tina told me about her last school year at 'Willie P.,' also known as, William Paterson University. She'd had a run in with a few girls from the school over he said, she said. Even almost got kicked out over it, but they settled just to put her on probation. If anything else was to happen, though, she'd have to find another institution of higher learning to complete her studies.

"I'm not beat, though," Tina said. "I only have one more year and then I will have my degree. After that, I am getting the hell on!"

"Wow, we really are about to graduate, huh?"

"Yeah, Liyah. We about to leave Easy Street and head straight for Economic Crash Boulevard," she laughed.

"Ugh, don't remind me of that."

"It is what it is. Nothing we can do but make the best of the situation."

"I hope by then something is done to put the economy back on track."

"You and me, both. I'll never have my own place at this rate. Gonna be paying my mom rent for the rest of my life."

I laughed, "There is nothing like having your own."

"I believe it." We continued to chat about this and that and other random happenings. The ride to Port Authority on 42nd Street ended up taking close to an hour, but we finally made it. We hopped off the bus and started heading to the street. Looking around, the closest restaurant was Burger King on the corner. Neither of us was trying to eat that, so we decided to just walk around for a while and see if we saw anything else we might like.

We came across Chevys Fresh Mex. Both of us enjoy Mexican food, so we decided to stop and get a table. I ordered a quesadilla. Tina went with a steak fajita. We both had a margarita and water while we waited. Didn't take long for the food to come, but that could've been because it was still early and the lunch rush hadn't seemed to start yet. In silence, we consumed our food. Neither of us was much for talking when it came to eating. Yet, another reason why our friendship held so strong. Even with our differences, it was just some similarities we had that were key to us. We were both serious about our food and tended to be focused when eating. We knew talking could wait until we were done.

Upon finishing her fajita, Tina asked, "So what you want to get into?"

"I'm not sure. I just wanted to get out of the house. Masturbating every day starts to get boring at some point," I said whipping salsa mixed with sour cream from my lips.

She busted out laughing. "Oh shit! I know you didn't just say that!"

"I am so serious, T. I know you remember how I am. I am wearing the hell out of some batteries," I admitted, laughing along with her.

"Dang, Liyah. That bad, huh?"

"Yeah. I have looked for a better alternative, but there is nothing going on, on my side of town."

"I feel you on that. I've been pretty solo myself these days. All the pickings seemed to have been picked over to the point of being spoiled."

"True. So Duracell and Energizer are the men in my life."

"Haha, it's gonna be all right." She looked around, "I wonder where our waiter is with the check so we can at least be in motion while we decide what to do with the rest of our day."

As if he heard us calling, he showed up and asked, "Would you ladies like dessert?"

"No," I answered. "We would just like the check." He gave us both our checks before disappearing again. "You got it, T?"

"Yup, I got it." She placed her money with her check. I opted to use my debit card to pay for my meal. He came back, completed the transaction of payment, and we went about our business.

Walking in the direction of Port Authority, we decided to head down to the Pier. By this point, it was a bit crowded since the lunch rush had kicked into gear and was causing some traffic. I had to hold onto Tina's shirt just to keep up with her as she slipped through the various people, headed for the A Train. She moved like she was use to this. I fumbled around behind her like a lost child, now being so far removed from the days when I had to depend on public transportation and slither through crowds of people all seeming to be going in the opposite direction from you. We ended up making it on the train right before the doors closed.

The train ride wasn't as long as the bus ride, but we still had to walk from the train to the Pier. We talked about random stuff like cars, new movies, and school, as we weaved through people on the sidewalks heading to the Pier. When we got there, we sat on a bench overlooking the ocean. I took it all in, enjoying being anywhere but cooped up in my bedroom. "It's a really nice day," I said, taking note of the clear blue sky, calm ocean, and cool breeze sweeping over us.

"Yeah. I love it out here. I tend to come out once or twice a month just to chill and write," Tina said, leaning back on the bench.

"Do you come up here by yourself?"

"Yeah. Why not?"

"Just asking," I said, looking around us. From left to right you could see men holding hands and kissing other men, as well as women holding hands and kissing other women. I also noticed that a nice number of the females out and about were dressed like boys. It wasn't anything I ever really understood or could grasp. I figured if you wanted to be with a female, fine, that is your business, but what was the point if you were going to date someone who looked just like a boy? I just didn't get it. Why not date a man?

"You wouldn't?" Tina asked, snapping me back and away from my thoughts.

"Wouldn't what?" I asked still thinking about girls dressing up like boys and these girls seeming to like that sort of thing.

"Come up here by yourself?"

"No. Not just to sit out in the open." I scooted closer to her and whispered, "I heard people come out here to get picked up and whatnot."

She sat up and looked at me, "What are you talking about?"

"I mean, like, you know, girls by girls and guys by guys."

Busting out laughing she said, "Girlllll, ain't nobody going to try to take your cookies!"

I looked at her like she was crazy, "I'm not trying to say that. I mean, I know, but I am just saying. I don't want to put myself out there like I am when I'm not."

"Liyah, are you for real? Just because you are a female doesn't mean they want you. There are plenty of lesbian and bi chicks to go around whereas no one needs to stalk a straight chick."

"How you know?" I asked, curious to know her answer.

"Haha, because I do."

"Whatever T," I said, dismissing her lack of an answer.

"Just believe I do." I rolled my eyes at her and looked away. At that moment I saw a ghost. Tina stopped laughing and asked, "What's wrong with you?" noticing my dead gaze. Following it to see what I was looking at, she zoned in on what I was staring at, or better yet, who. "You know her?" she asked, seeming a bit disgusted.

I responded, "No, not exactly."

"And what does that mean?"

"I mean, I met her when I brought my last toy. She worked at the store I got it from. I only saw her that one time."

"Oh. Good."

"Why you say that?" I asked, curious and wondering if Tina somehow knew this girl.

"Because she's not anyone you want to know." Just then, she walked toward us. Under her breath, Tina cursed, "Dammit." She was acting really suspicious, but with the female quickly approaching where we were, I figured I'd give her the third degree later.

I watched as she drew near, taking in her look, yet again. Her hair was still in a spiked do, though it looked a bit longer. She had on a lime green polo and some long, green and white plaid shorts with those white shoes that looked like slide on Keds. She had a white T-shirt under her polo, with the sleeves slightly rolled up to expose her tattoos. I noticed myself staring at her details again and forced myself to stop.

"Well, well, well, fancy seeing you here," she said to me. Turning her attention to my friend, she asked, "And how are you, Tina?"

Tina mumbled, "Sup."

"Oh, don't be like that. I know you are not still holding a grudge against me," she asked. From where I was sitting, she seemed sincere.

"What do you want, Jesstina?" she responded, sounding a bit irritated.

"Nothing much more than to say hello to an old friend," Jess replied.

I watched the interaction, feeling the tension building up between them. Not knowing what to say or really wanting to say anything, I opted to stay out of it and keep my mouth shut. Even so, I wanted to know what was going on and how they knew each other, but remained silent, knowing that was a discussion that Tina and I would have to have later. Jess turned to me, "Aaliyah, right?"

I smiled and answered, "Yeah, that's me. I am surprised you remembered."

"I loved Aaliyah, so, you having the same name as her made it easy." She winked at me and I could tell Tina was not happy with Jess flirting with me. Oddly enough, though, it was making me blush a little and I knew that needed to stop.

"Umm, well," I stumbled out, "cool." Wanting to stop the dialogue before it became even more tense and uncomfortable. I tried pushing Jess along telling her, "Well, it was nice seeing you again."

Luckily, she took the hint. "Indeed, it was," she said to me, still smiling. Then she turned to Tina and told her, "You shouldn't be so mean. No hard feelings, right? We are still friends. I have no issues with you." Tina just rolled her eyes at her. Jess smiled, "Take care, Tina."

"Yeah, whatever," she huffed in reply. Jess just continued smiling as she walked away.

Once Jess was out of earshot, I looked at my friend filled with curiosity, "What was that all about?"

She waved me off, "Nothing to worry about, Liyah."

"Umm, T, that didn't sound like nothing."

"For real, she's nobody."

"So why do I feel like you two know each other fairly well?"

She exploded, "Because she's my ex! Damn!"

"YOUR WHAT?!?" I exclaimed.

"Jess is my ex."

I didn't know what to say. As far as I knew, Tina was just like me, straight. She had never mentioned females before in all the years we've been friends. Not liking them, anyway. I felt thrown off. "Wait. You're gay?" I asked astonished with this new information.

She sighed, "Something like that."

"Something like that? Are you bi?"

"No, I'm not bi."

"Then what are you? C'mon Tina. Stop beating around the bush."

"I like chicks."

"Like, seriously?"

"Like, yeah," she mocked my tone. "I came out shortly after high school."

"Wow." I sat there with my mouth wide open. I was at a loss for words.

"You're not gonna start acting weird toward me, are you?"

I wanted to say I would never treat her any different from how I did before she had said anything, that as long as she was happy, I was happy for her, but I was still in shock over the whole situation. "This is a lot to take in, Tina."

"Does that mean yeah? Look, I didn't want to tell you in the first place."

"I don't mean it like that. Just," I looked away, "I'm just shocked. This is a lot to be finding out."

"Well, if you don't want to be friends anymore, that's cool. You wouldn't be the first one," she said as she stood up. "Ready to go?"

I looked up at her, panicking, not knowing what to say. I finally answered, "Umm, yeah." I really wanted to tell her that her sexuality didn't matter to me. Wanted to tell her that she should've told me sooner and no matter what, we would always be friends. I should've said so many things, but I didn't say anything. I just walked with her in silence.

When we got to the train, I looked at her, but she didn't even notice. Tina looked like she was somewhere else.   Maybe reliving what went wrong between her and Jess. Maybe she was cursing Jess for showing up like that. Maybe she was cussing me for not supporting her when I am supposed to be her best friend. Maybe she was cussing all of us who walked away when she decided to open up and be real with us. She could've been thinking anything. Taking a deep breath, sucking in all my inhibitions, I grabbed her hand and told her, "I'm not going anywhere. You are my sister and I've got your back."

aaliyah

Chapter 4

Since that day in New York, Tina and I haven't seen much of each other. It honestly felt like she was avoiding me, but it could have truly been that I have been busy. I got a summer job at the mall selling retail, taking on as many hours as possible. This summer had already started off rough, but I wasn't trying to allow it to dictate how it would ultimately end. I figured I'd just work to keep my mind off of everything while saving some money for the forthcoming semester. Seemed like a foolproof idea to me.

Finishing up another long day, I said good-bye to my coworkers and headed to my car. As late as it was, there were still plenty of cars in the parking lot. I weaved through the rows until I found my little Jetta, got in, gave her some juice, and headed toward the highway. Even with my ultimate plan being to submerge myself in work and nothing else, I had the next day off. For the first time in a while, I was filled with extra energy and really felt like going out. Looking at my cell, I scrolled through my contacts, hitting talk once I got to who I was looking for.

"Hello," a voice answered after the third or fourth ring.

"T! I can't believe you answered! What's up?" I pretty much screamed into the phone. I really wasn't expecting Tina to answer my call. She could be stubborn as a mule, which I knew something about because I'm the same way.

"Aaliyah?"

"Yeah. What's up? I just got off work and have the day off tomorrow. What are you getting into tonight?"

"Wassup," she hesitated, "I'm actually about to head out with some friends."

I was a bit disappointed to hear that, and I don't think I did a great job masking it in my voice. "Oh. I was going to ask if you wanted to chill tonight since I don't have work tomorrow. I thought it might be cool to chill with my best friend since we haven't in a while."

"Oh, my bad. I mean, you should've called me earlier. I already have plans now."

"I couldn't. I was at work."

"Oh."

"Yeah," I paused. The silence was beginning to become awkward, so I said, "Well, have fun and be safe."

"A'ight." We hung up and I felt alone. Tina was my only real friend and she already had plans. I wish she'd invited me, but she was probably still upset about what happened at the pier. I started thinking about that and how I should've said something or responded differently. My reaction was kind-of too little, too late. If I hadn't taken so long, she probably would've asked me to go with her tonight. Then again, maybe she wouldn't have. I am sure her other friends are gay, and I'm not. Not really the crowd I want to hang out with either. Maybe it was for the best she didn't invite me.

The thoughts just continued to run around my mind as I entered the city of Paterson. Like any other night, the city was alive. Lights from gas stations, corner stores, and chicken places illuminated the street ways. Like flies to neon lights, a lot of people were out under these lights. A lot of men, women, and children running around as if it wasn't nearing 11 at night. I drove past it all heading to my home on Union Ave, close to Totowa, where there wasn't as much activity.

When I got in, no one was home. The family had driven to Georgia for a week and left me alone. My work schedule wouldn't permit a weeklong trip, so I opted to stay back. I picked up the mail from the floor as I entered through the front door and threw it on the table directly to the left of the entryway. I walked into the living room, plopped on the sofa and turned the TV on. *Lifetime* appeared on the screen showing some dramatization. I'd missed most of it, but I was sure it would end with some woman finding strength within her struggle to succeed and help others fulfill their dreams of a better life, or something close to it. That is pretty much how *Lifetime* movies always ended. Happy endings all around. Supposedly reality, but not any reality I've ever witnessed. I didn't see those type of endings around my way.

I changed the channel to see what else was on. Finding nothing of interest, I decided to raid the cupboards and just watch a DVD.

In the kitchen, I gathered a bowl of kettle corn popcorn, the only kind I eat, and a glass of White Zinfandel, which my mom kept plenty of in the house. She said it relaxes her and helps her unwind. That is exactly what I needed to do, unwind. I put in my favorite movie, *Meet Joe Black*, turned the lights off and cuddled with the throw blanket on the sofa. Already, I was feeling better. I sipped my glass of wine and pressed play on the remote.

Sometime after death made its grand entrance and exit in the film, I fell asleep. I woke up to the sun shining through the den and the title screen of *Meet Joe Black* watching me. Yawning and stretching from a cramped sleep on the sofa, I turned the TV and DVD player off and headed up to my room, running from the sun. My room had thick shades to assist in blocking the sun out because of my love of the dark. Must be the nocturnal being within, but the sun and I never really got along. With no real plans, I crawled into my waiting bed and went back to sleep.

Around noon I woke up again, reaching in my nightstand for

my Dolphin. Hadn't had much time to get my rocks off since I got my job, so a little TLC was definitely appreciated. I prepped myself to play, only to find that the batteries were dead. I cursed under my breath and searched the bed for my remote. I found my remote, opening the back to steal the batteries. Just my luck, my remote used AAA batteries. My toy required AA. Sucking my teeth in, I put a pair of sweats and a T-shirt on. I took a quick minute to brush my hair into a ponytail and headed to the store.

Corner stores around my way rip you off, charging way too much for convenience, so I hopped in my car and headed to K-Mart. I got there in record time, grabbed a pack of AA batteries, and got in line to finish the transaction. As the cashier was ringing up my transaction, I realized I left my wallet at home on my dresser. I didn't have anything.

"Shit," I cursed, frustrated and loud enough for both the person behind me and the cashier to hear me.

"Is there a problem, Ma'am?" the cashier asked.

I smiled, "It seems I have forgotten my wallet."

"Would you like us to hold these while you go get it?"

"Umm," I said, before cursing myself again.

"Just add it to my items. I will get them for her," the person behind me said.

Turning to face them, I said, "I couldn't. You don't have to do that."

"I insist," he offered with a smile.

"That will be $25.96, Sir," the cashier told the stranger before accepting two twenty dollar bills from him. "Your change is $14.04. Thank you for shopping at K-Mart and have a good day!"

Walking toward the exit, he handed me the batteries. "I think these are yours."

"Umm, thank-you, but you really didn't have to do that," I said, remembering I didn't brush my teeth and trying to keep my distance so he didn't smell my morning breath.

"It was my pleasure to help a beautiful woman like yourself," he said, flashing me his pearly whites again. That's when I noticed his dark mocha skin, pretty brown eyes and long lashes to complete his baby face. His hair was short, midnight black waves across his head. He was dressed in dark blue jeans and a dark blue, short sleeve polo that was accentuating his muscular and defined physique.

I blushed, lowering my face to hide my smile and continue blocking my breath. "How can I repay you, when I don't even know your name?"

"Kevin. My name is Kevin. And you can repay me by accompanying me to get something to eat so we can get to know each other better if you are not in a hurry."

I looked down at my appearance and felt a little embarrassed about running out the house in a simple T-shirt and sweats. It must've shown on my face because he said, "Don't worry about what you have on. You still look gorgeous."

I blushed again. No matter what he said about my appearance, though, I didn't want to go out looking like who did it and ran. I needed to hygiene badly, so taking him up on that offer was a no-go. I asked, "Can I take a rain check?"

"If that is what you would like ... ummm ... what is your name again?" he asked flashing me those pearly whites.

"Aaliyah. You know, like the singer."

"Aaliyah, huh? I like it. So, Ms. Aaliyah, may I call you for the rain check?"

"Oh, yeah! Sure." I gave him my number then waved the batteries in the air, "You really didn't have to buy these for me, but I do appreciate it."

"A gentleman always helps a lady in distress, even if only for a pack of batteries," he winked at me.

Feeling myself turning bright red, I told him it was a pleasure meeting him, but that I had to go. He said the same, and I was off, speeding to get to my car. Once I got in my car, I screamed my excitement about finally meeting someone, and a good looking someone at that. Calming myself down, I put my little Jetta in gear and headed out the parking lot for the highway back home.

I turned the radio on blast, singing about my sweet thang being my everything along with Mary J. Blige. She was always hitting the nail on the head for me.   There wasn't anything anyone could do to take me off my high.

It felt like I floated home, as I pulled into the driveway and turned the music down. I heard the beep from my cell phone as soon as I turned the car off, letting me know I had missed a call. I grabbed my cell phone and looked at the screen. New voicemail. I dialed my voicemail up while getting out the car, being sure not to leave my batteries.

Just as I was opening the front door, Tina's voice started flowing through the speaker. "Aaliyah? Look, my bad for the way things have been between us lately. Just, I didn't expect you to act like that. I mean, you're my best friend, so, you know, I just thought you would be cool with it all." She paused. "Well, at least cooler than that. I know it's a lot and I didn't give you time to digest it, but now that I have stopped being mad and thought about it from your view, I guess I was wrong for not trusting you enough to tell you myself, rather than because seeing my ex frustrated me. So, my ..."

The phone hung up and the next voicemail message queued up and began, "My bad. The message cut off on me. Let me hurry up before it does it again. My bad about the way things have been lately and for acting distant last night. You're my best friend. We need to squash this distance. Cool?" I could hear her smile as she asked that. "Cool. So, a couple of my friends and I are going out again tonight. I'm inviting you. It's a gay spot in New York. I know you're straight, but just to chill. You don't have to do any..." The phone cut off on her again.

"Dammit! A'ight. Look, Liyah, if you wanna go be at my crib by 10 tonight and we will go from there. A'ight? Cool." She hung up. There were no more new messages after that. Ten was kind-of late to go out to New York when I knew I had to work the next day. But, this is my best friend and we did need to get past this.

I decided it would be better to go. Work wasn't until 11 in the morning the next day anyway, so I should be fine.

I got to Tina's in about five minutes to ten. I decided to dress in a manner that I felt would not bring too much attention to myself. I had on a simple pair of skinny jeans and a burgundy blouse with short, puffy sleeves. The blouse was long enough to cover my backside which I knew usually brought unwanted attention my way. I accented it all with a black belt and black pumps. My accessory ensemble was usually minimal, so I only had a few silver bangles on with a pair of studded earrings. I pulled my hair back in a bun, leaving my bang down enough to swoop over my right eye.

Tina answered the door with a smile, "I'm glad you came, Liyah." She hugged me and told me, "My bad about everything."

"No. I apologize for acting the way I did. I didn't mean anything by it."

"I know, I know. I just was so frustrated with Jesstina showing up and everything."

"It's cool. We're cool," I smiled at her.

Someone from inside asked, "Ya'll could come inside. We not gonna bite her T." The person's comment was followed by laughter.

Tina smiled and said, "That's Shawn. Pay her no mind. She thinks she's a comedian."

From inside I heard the same voice respond, "You must do, too, 'cause your ass is always laughing." The laughter came again and then a female appeared at the door. "Hello. I apologize for T's rudeness, but I am Shawn, and over there on the sofa is Briana, and the chick wrapped around her is Pamela." She moved out the way so I could see who she was pointing to.

"Hello," I said walking into the house.

"Hey!" That was the one Shawn called Pamela. "You can just call me Pam." She was dressed in a long, flowing dress with open toe heels on. The dress was made of linen and in shades of brown that worked well with her flawless brown skin. Her hair was pulled back in a ponytail, braided down her back. She had wooden Bohemian earrings in her ears and bracelets on both arms. To complement the dip in the front of her dress, she wore a wooden cross on a thin black rope. She smiled at me as if she was flirting. I smiled an awkward smile back.

The one named Briana looked at me, then said a stiff, "Hey." She didn't seem like she cared for me too much as she sat next to Pamela in black slacks and a brown button down shirt, the two top buttons undone exposing a little bit of cleavage. She had on suspenders that also accentuated her breast and black heels that strapped around her ankles. Her hair was pulled back into a bun similar to mine. Next to her sat a felt black hat with a silk brown ribbon to match her top wrapped around it, above the rim. Her presence was dominating and made me a little uncomfortable. I didn't like how she seemed to be looking me up and down in disgust.

Tina spoke, "Now that we are all here, we can go catch the bus. It should be here soon. Ya'll ready?"

"Yeah, let's get going," Shawn said grabbing her jacket off the arm of one of the chairs. I actually got a better look of her then, than I did when I first got there. She was dressed like a man in Sean Jean jeans, a button down red and black shirt of the same namesake, both looking too big for her frame. In her ears she had medium sized diamond studs, or maybe they were cubic zirconium, a thick silver chain around her neck and a flashy watch around her wrist. The jacket she picked up was an oversized black leather bomber jacket and her sneakers were Jordans that matched her outfit to a T. Her hair was dreaded with auburn tips. Aside from being dressed like a man, I could tell Shawn was an attractive female. Guys probably still hit on her regardless to her appearance.

I turned around and headed back out the door and waited for everyone on the curb. Tina came out first with Shawn behind her. Shawn kept moving past her to the curb and stood next to me. Briana came out next holding Pamela's hand as she helped her down the steps. Tina locked the door, met us all on the curb and started walking toward the bus stop.

While walking to the bus stop they talked about random people who were out last night and who they were dealing with now. I just walked and listened, since I had no idea who they were talking about. Shawn tried to pull me into the conversation, asking me random things about myself. I politely answered, but still didn't say much. I really didn't have any input into the various conversations they had going on anyway.

We waited about ten minutes before the bus finally came. It was late but didn't seem to faze anyone. The conversations just kept going with random questions about me as well as my opinion on this and that every now and then. For the most part, though, I just was there taking it all in and listening.

When we got to New York, we hopped on the train for about two stops, then we were back on the street heading toward a building with the name *Lollipops* in neon lights on it. It looked like an old three-level warehouse to me, but obviously, it was more because there were long lines on either side of the entrance. One of the lines wrapped all the way around the side of the building.

"DAAAMMMNNN!! Is everybody here tonight?!?" Tina exclaimed laughing.

Pamela responded, "Girllllll, you know how it is during Pride. Everybody comes out trying to be seen." They all laughed but I just looked. It kind of reminded me of how Atlanta gets around Labor Day weekend. I would see all these men and women down on Peachtree Street, some men looking better than females, some females dressed like men. I've seen it all before, but I usually just kept away to avoid being suspected of being interested. Now here I was in New York about to participate in their festivities. I stood closer to Tina.

"So, what ya'll wanna do? Wanna get on that long ass line or go through VIP?" Briana asked.

"You know better. We don't wait as long as we got Tina 'I know every-damn-body' with us," Shawn said. More laughter. I've never seen anybody laugh as much as they did.

"True, true," Tina said, waving everybody to follow her as she walked straight to the entrance, by-passing all those waiting on the lines. "Hey Biggie," she said to the guard, "I got four with me. " This guy who really did look like Biggie Smalls turned to her like he was about to curse her and yell that she get on line like everybody else.

Then he smiled. They obviously knew each other well, because he responded to her in a familiar tone, "A'ight Tiny. When you go in tell Sofi at the register you here with the B.S. and she should let you through. You know we got some strippers coming through."

I thought to myself, "*Tiny?*" questioning how he referenced Tina.

"Word?!?" she responded. "Who the main attraction tonight?"

Listening to them interact, my thoughts continued "*Hmm, guess that's something between them.*"

"You know we got some locals coming through, but the main attraction tonight is Whiplash."

"For real?" Shawn chimed in getting excited.

"A'ight Biggie. You see these other bitches in line getting upset cause we holding everything up. I'll get at you later."

"A'ight Tiny." As soon as we walked past, his demeanor went back to being that of someone you didn't want to get into an altercation with. I know I wouldn't mess with him, that's for sure. We walked to the register and Tina told the female there what the guard told her to say. She looked at us all, then stamped the back of our hands and let us in.

As we walked through the threshold of the entrance my eyes grew, taking in the scene of the club. There were women everywhere of every shade of the rainbow bumping and grinding on one another, and from what I could tell, the few men present weren't interested, so it wasn't for them. Again I stuck a little closer to Tina. She suggested we all get a drink to start the night off right. Shawn offered to get me a drink. Normally I would have declined, but I needed something to calm my nerves. I told her I would like an apple martini. She turned to the bar to get our drink orders. I wasn't even sure why I was acting crazy because none of the females there were paying me any mind, yet I did stay close to the group.

We were able to find an open booth and sat down with our drinks. Eventually, Pamela and Briana made their way to the dance floor to join the other free spirits moving to the beat of the music. Shawn excused herself when she saw someone she knew and Tina was asked to dance by someone. Tina would've stayed with me, but I told her to go and enjoy herself. She said she'd be back after one song. I waved her off and told her to have fun.

When she left, I sunk deeper into the booth and just watched. "Aaliyah right?" someone asked.

I looked up to see Jess standing there. How she snuck up on me, I couldn't begin to explain, other than I had to have been seriously focused or deep in thought. I smiled slightly, "Jess, right?"

"Yeah, fancy seeing you in a place like this."

"Yeah. T invited me out."

"Oh? And she left you here alone? There are predators, you know?"

I smiled, "I can handle myself. I'm a big girl." I looked at Jess, and as always, her style caught my attention. Tonight her hair was slicked straight back, curling up a little at the nape of her neck. She had on a white T-shirt with another random band on it, a black vest over it and boot cut jeans. To accentuate it all, she wore black boots, a thick belt with a broken heart as the buckle, and a black tie. She had her spiked bracelets on and all her piercings. Normally that would look a mess to me, but everything she wore just seemed to work for her.

"Okay *big girl*. Don't let a bigger girl come and get you," she smiled.

I laughed at her. "I will be ok..."

"Jess, you want to dance?" Some female asked cutting me off. Before I could stop myself, I cut my eyes at her. She did the same to me.

"Yes, I will dance with you. Give me a second," she said to the other female. She took a step back but didn't go far. Turning her attention to me, Jess said, "Well, I hope you enjoy the rest of your night. Maybe I can get a dance with you later?" she smiled and winked at me.

"I see your dance card is already full," I shot back, trying to hide my jealousy. Jess just walked away smiling. When she got to the female waiting for her, the female wrapped her arm around her as if to claim ownership. I swear I do not know why, but that upset me. I took the rest of my drink to the head and decided that I would need another one before I lost it. Getting up out of the booth, I went to the bar, ordered me a Long Island Iced Tea and let the alcohol help calm my green-eyed monster.

jess

Chapter 5

I looked back to see if Aaliyah was watching after I walked away, but was caught off guard by Jordyn wrapping her arm around mine. "Whoa, Miss," I said as I released myself from her hold. "We can dance, but don't get the wrong idea. We are not on a date. You can do your thing because I know I am going to do mine."

Jordyn frowned at me. "Why did you even invite me out?"

"Hold up now. Pump your brakes, Love. You called and asked if I knew what was going on for Pride. I told you about *Lollipops* being the hot spot and that you should come through."

"Exactly. You said I should come through."

"There wasn't any underlining meaning. I meant exactly what I said, come through to the club and enjoy yourself. Not lock yourself under me all night. It's Pride. You should be out enjoying it, just as I plan to."

"Why are you even tripping?"

"Because obviously you are!" I shouted out of frustration. This was no good. I felt myself getting outside my element, so I took a deep breath before telling her, "Look, if this is how it is going to be, let me apologize now because that's not what I'm looking for. Not at this point." I paused for a second for her reaction. When no words came, I made up my mind it was time to exit stage left. I told her, "I have to go," and politely excused myself, leaving Jordyn standing there with her mouth open. I was sure that once my back was turned she started cursing my name but it no longer mattered. I no longer cared. I wasn't about to have her thinking it was something going on between us when there wasn't. Best to let that ride now and be thankful I dodged a bullet.

Needing some room to move around, I went up to the second floor and got myself a drink. I sipped on my Long Island and watched various women come into my line of sight then disappear. Without warning, Tina appeared. She was off in a corner sitting with some female, smiling and laughing. For a minute I let her memory infiltrate my mind. Her attitude didn't match her appearance. She looked like Vanessa Williams during her reign as a beauty queen, but had a mental like Rah Digga. She was a pit-bull in a skirt like they use to call Eve. There weren't too many times I could remember her biting her tongue, not even in compromise. That was our biggest issue. It had to always be her way and I couldn't deal with it. I told her that. Nothing changed. Shortly thereafter I just stopped talking to her altogether.

Eventually, I started seeing someone else. I guess Tina thought I just needed breathing space. She didn't expect me to really move on. I couldn't see how she wouldn't expect it when I always felt her pushing me to it. Even so, never imagined she'd take it that bad. Never imagined the girl would go to her school. Never imagined it would go as far as it did. I did a lot to help keep her from getting kicked out of the school, but she doesn't know that. I felt like the altercation between Tina and the other female was my fault. She doesn't know I talked to the school board on her behalf and even gave a monetary donation in her name. And she never will. She's not supposed to. I don't want her to.

Tina happened to look my way and her smile instantly turned into a scowl. I took that as my queue to move on. Getting up, I placed the empty glass on the bar and headed back downstairs. The crowd was pressed close to the stage as Whiplash performed, pulling females on stage to embarrass them. She reminded me of D.C.'s Bad Girl Oohzee. Both could get it at the end of the day if you asked me. I smiled at my inner thoughts as I made my way to the bathroom.

The line wasn't long since everyone was trying to get a glance at Whiplash. I was able to move in and out fairly quickly. As I was exiting the bathroom, I caught a glimpse of Aaliyah leaving the club. Sliding through the crowd, I decided to follow her and talk to her without an audience watching my every move this time.

I walked outside to catch up to her but found someone else had beaten me to it and was already talking to her. Trying to play it off, I walked a little ways in the opposite direction and took out my phone. Pretending to be on the phone, I eavesdropped on her conversation. "Thank-you for the offer, but I'll be fine," she told the other person.

"Are you sure? It's pretty late and the city isn't the safest at night," her companion stated.

"I will be ok. I called an uber anyway. It should be here soon."

"Are you sure?"

"Yeah, I am sure," she smiled at the other female.

My stomach turned and I wasn't even sure why. I don't even know this girl. On top of that, she is linked to Tina. Honestly, just standing out here like this so I could talk to her was a little crazy, but here I was, hoping to get a turn. I thought to myself, *"Dude, what the hell is wrong with you? Go back inside and stop this foolishness."*

Interrupting my thoughts, I heard the other female say, "A'ight. Will you at least take my number and call me to let me know you made it home?"

"Okay. I can do that. What is your number?" She reached for Aaliyah's phone, to put in her number I assumed. She took her phone back and told the other female it was nice meeting her, and the female stated the same. Seeming to try and reassure her friend of her safety, Aaliyah said, "I'll be ok, and I have your number now, so I will call to let you know I made it in." She waved her phone in the air. Then she smiled, as a last-ditch effort to reassure the other female that she'd be all right. Reluctantly the female finally went back inside.

I was beginning to think she would never leave. I watched to make sure she went all the way in the club before I approached Aaliyah. Aaliyah wrapped her arms around herself and rubbed them. Walking in her direction I said, "Seems like somebody may be a little cold."

She responded, "Just a little," before turning toward me with a smile. When she realized it was me, though, she frowned. "What are you doing out here?"

I waved my phone in the air, "Making a call. Why are you out here?"

"I'm waiting on my uber." In a frustrated whisper, she mumbled, "I wish it would get here already."

"May I ask, where are you heading?"

"Home."

"Where is home?"

"Jersey."

"You are going to take an uber all the way to Jersey? At this hour?"

"Yeah. What's wrong with that?" she asked, coming off a little defensive.

"Nothing," I smiled. "It's just a little late and that's a long way to travel, and a pretty penny to pay later."

"What other choice do I have? T isn't ready to go. I refuse to walk the streets and ride public transportation by myself. So, uber it is."

I offered, "I can take you."

"Thank-you, but no thank-you. Uber will get me there just fine."

"That's unsafe. Let me take you. I don't bite unless tempted by a willing participant," I smiled, trying to be humorous. She just frowned harder at me. "I'm serious. It is the least I can do for a friend of Tina's." Aaliyah looked at me again like I was crazy. "I promise I just want to ensure you get home safely. Nothing more. Nothing less."

As if she was thinking it over in her head, she finally answered, "Okay." I told her my car was in the garage next door. She reluctantly followed me to my car as if she was having second thoughts. When we got to the car, I opened the passenger side door and let her in, closing the door behind her. Then I ran to the driver side and put the car in gear before she had a chance to change her mind and hop out.

Pulling out of the garage, I asked what the best route was to get her home. Aaliyah said to take the Washington Bridge into New Jersey heading for Teaneck. She asked if I knew how to get to Teaneck. I told her I did because Tina lives out there. She said, "Good," because that was where she was going.

The ride was quiet, aside from the radio playing. Aaliyah mumbled something, but I couldn't quite understand what she'd said, so I asked, "What did you just say?"

She replied, "I probably shouldn't be here."

"Here where? With me? I assure you my intentions are pure."

"I just really shouldn't be here," she said, shaking her head, not really talking to me.

"We are almost there. After I drop you off, you don't have to ever see me again."

She kept talking as if my words were falling on deaf ears, "It's crazy. This whole situation is crazy. I don't even understand it."

"It's not that bad. Just a friend giving a friend of a friend a ride home." Out the corner of my eye, I could see her turn to me. "What?" I asked in response. "I would never disrespect you. Please know this about me. I know you are not into females, so I would never press that issue with you. I just saw you out there and didn't think it was necessary for you to take a cab when I was free to take you. If you have been to one Pride celebration, you have been to them all. It's just the same people every year. I was on my way out soon, anyway, so it is not like you have taken me from the party or anything," I told her, watching for her exit sign.

She sighed a sigh of frustration, "It's not that simple. A

situation such as this has never presented itself before, and it has me so confused."

"Hey, if you need to talk, I am available. I have no plans other than to go home, so I can listen if you need a good ear. I've been told I am a good listener." Again I felt her eyes looking at me. She shook her head; then turned to look out the window. I really didn't know what was going on with her, so I just let the music fill the space between us. An old Sade song was on the radio. Kiss of Life. The sultry sound of Sade rang through the speakers, seeming to get louder as the silence between Aaliyah and me grew.

I turned onto Tina's block and slowed down a bit. Seeing nowhere to pull up to in front of her house, I slid into the first available spot past it. I turned off the ignition, and looked at Aaliyah, "Well, I got you here all in one piece. I apologize I couldn't get you here sooner, but it has been a pleasure. I would love to be friends, nothing more than that, but I understand if you don't want to." She just sat there fidgeting, like she was trying to get her thoughts together.

Barely above a whisper, she said, "I've never done this before."

"Done what? It's just friendship, I prom...," before I could finish my sentence, she leaned into me, placing her lips against mine. Shock covered my face, but as she continued, determined to be embraced, I received her. I pulled her closer to me and took her tongue into my mouth. She allowed me to take her into me, pulling my tongue in her own. Together our tongues danced against one another, her taste being that of mango and passion fruit. I wanted to devour her. Suck her dry of all her essence. But, as if reality snuck up on her, she suddenly pulled away from me, gathered her belongings, and jumped out the car, slamming the door behind her.

Recovering from the abrupt end of our kiss, I wiped my window and watched her race to a vehicle a few cars behind mine. Lights turned on as the car came to life, backed out of the space, and zoomed past me.

I watched as Aaliyah turned left headed back towards the highway. I licked my lips, still tasting her there. I whispered to myself, "Damn. What was that?" as I put my car in gear and headed in the opposite direction. I didn't know what to think of what had just happened, and even a part of me believed I dreamt it. Traces of her scent, though, let me know this wasn't a fantasy I conjured up.

Needing someone to tell about what just happened, I called Ty. By the time his overdue for an update ring back got to the middle of Destiny's Child's *Cater to You*, he picked up. "Where are you at, Jess? I've been calling your ass all night."

"I was at *Lollipops*."

"Okay. So, you couldn't answer my call because ...?" he asked waiting for my reply.

I continued, "I saw Aaliyah there."

"Aaliyah?" He repeated. There was a pause like he was thinking, "Wait. The chick from a couple of weeks ago? The straight chick?"

"It's been more than a month, but yeah, her. She was at *Lollipops* tonight."

I could hear the disbelief in his voice when he stated more than asked, "I thought she was straight."

"She is. She was there with Tina."

"Tina, Tina?"

"Yeah."

"Your ex, Tina?"

"Yeah."

"How in the world does she know Tina? Your ex, Tina?"

"They are friends, I guess. A week or so after she came to the store, I saw her at the Pier with Tina."

"She is straight but friends with Tina? Are you sure she's straight?"

"Yeah. She let me know as much the night I first met her. Tina and Aaliyah are only friends."

"Damn, Boo. Small world."

"Yeah, and she was at *Lollipops*. I saw her sitting alone and went to speak to her, but this other female named Jordyn needed some attention and was blocking. I ended up having to leave her alone. She was looking for more than what I was offering her."

"Okay. So, that's why you didn't answer my calls? Because you were macking?"

"No. Aaliyah was standing outside waiting for an uber and I offered her a ride home. After some convincing, she finally allowed me to bring her back to Jersey."

"You're in Jersey?"

"Yeah. Well, not really anymore. I'm about to get on the Bridge headed back to New York."

"Okay, so you dropped her off. Still not seeing why you ignored my calls. I called more than once."

"Yeah, but that's not it."

"Then what is it, Jess? I swear you always go around the block just to get across the street."

"She kissed me."

He laughed, "You sure you don't mean you tried to kiss her and she pushed your ass away?"

"I am being serious Ty. She kissed me. I was in the middle of telling her something and she just came out of nowhere and kissed me. And ... and I kissed her back. I pulled her closer to me and took her into me."

"Damn, Boo," he said. I could hear his smile through the phone. "So? Then what happened?"

"She stopped and ran away from me. I saw car lights go on and fly past me while I was still in park."

He laughed again, "Haha. You scared the poor child."

"But she kissed me. I didn't initiate it. I was talking about us being friends, and she kissed me. I mean, I am not going to lie. It was beautiful! I mean, her kiss was so passionate. She was so sweet and I wanted to take her right then and there."

From the other end of the line, I heard him mumble, "Freak."

"Why you say that?"

"You are going to try and pop that girl's cherry, aren't you?"

"No, for real. I wasn't trying to be nasty. It's something about her that I can't explain. I like her. This kiss just makes me want her more than I think I already did."

"Sounds like you both got a thing for each other. You don't hear about too many heteros kissing family unless they're curious."

"Yeah, but this ... I don't think it's the same. There is something about Aaliyah I just can't put my finger on yet."

"Are you sure you even want to go there again? You remember the last time you turned a straight girl out. I am surprised Tina didn't go Left Eye on you," he laughed into the receiver. "Now she's like Queen of the Lesbians," he continued, still laughing.

I wasn't amused, "Very funny, Ty."

"I know it is," he continued laughing. "So *Love Struck*, does that mean you're not gonna come hang out with the bois tonight? You know they love your gay ass."

I smiled, "No, we can still hang out. I think I need a few drinks anyway. Where are you all at?"

"*The Bois Club*. It's packed as hell in here tonight, too, so hurry up before they stop letting people in."

"Give me about 20 minutes and I will be there."

"All right, we'll see you when you get here."

"Yup, love you."

"Love you, too."

aaliyah

Chapter 6

I still don't know why I did that. It has been a couple of weeks
since it happened, but I still cannot believe I kissed Jess that night.
That was so unlike me. When I realized what was going on, what I
was doing, I got as far away from her as possible. I ran home,
speeding the whole way. Thank goodness the cops seemed to be
preoccupied that night because I made it home without being
pulled over. My thoughts of disbelief kept my pedal to the metal.

When I got home, I went and showered like I had done
something dirty and needed to wash it off, but no matter how much
I washed and scrubbed, I still smelt her scent on me. It was like she
had sunk deep into my pores. I brushed. I flossed. Yet, I still felt
her tongue touching mine like it was an everyday norm. I could
feel her grip around me as our kiss got deeper and deeper.

How ridiculous of me to not only be thinking of another female
so much but in an intimate way for a moment we had because I
instigated it. Let alone how Jess took the kiss. Honestly, I bet she

probably didn't even think about it. She probably had a good laugh about this crazy straight chic and has since gone on about her business. At least I knew Tina would never know about it and I would never have to explain to her why I kissed her ex. She couldn't stand her, and that was a saving grace for me in this jacked up situation I kind of put myself into.

Trying to shake my thoughts, yet again for what seemed like the fiftieth time since it all happened, I called myself reading a book. There was no way I was going to be able to calm my thoughts without a distraction, but the book wasn't helping me at all. I mean, I'm not gay. Not even remotely, but Jess was on my mind. Something about her makes me say the hell with my life's script; I want to travel that road. But I can't. That's not me. This isn't me.

I really wish I understood what in the world was going on with me. Did Xavier breaking up with me actually cause me so much damage that now I am showing some type of signs of interest in women? He couldn't have hurt me *that* bad. There's no way. I am seriously tripping and going through a phase. It's got to be a phase.

Even if it is, though, since that night, I have been battling with myself and my feelings or rather, trying to figure out exactly what my feelings are. I've never gone through this before. I've never been interested in a female before. This is foreign to me, and frankly, I rather not go through this. My choice is to continue being normal. I like guys, not girls. That is the norm, and I am normal. "Right," I agreed with myself out loud, "I am normal."

"Aaliyah, right?" I heard the question, and jumped, half expecting it to be Jess. That is the way she first greeted me when I was with Tina. But when I looked up, a handsome guy was there standing in front of me instead. I had never seen him before. I am sure I would've remembered his face. I am usually pretty good with faces, but his was drawing a blank.

I straightened up from the leaning position I was in next to the cash register on the counter, put my book under it, and answered, "Yes?" At first I was curious to know how he knew my name, but then I remembered it was on my nametag. "May I help you?"

"You know Tina Joseph, right?" he asked as if he was pacing himself.

"Maybe, who are you and why are you asking?" I quizzed, taking up a slightly defensive stance wondering how he knew Tina.

"I'm just making sure I have the right person before I continue. So, do you know Tina?"

"And if I do? What is it you want to continue with?" I further questioned him. The more he spoke, the more I was puzzled by what he was trying to get at. The more puzzled I became, the more on guard I became.

"Do you have about fifteen minutes?" he asked. I just looked at him for a second. He was absolutely gorgeous, that couldn't be denied. At least 6 feet tall, he had chestnut brown skin, grey eyes, with midnight black hair braided down his back. Honestly, he was beyond gorgeous, drawing the attention of the other female employees and many of the female shoppers in the store.

Yes, he was definitely eye-catching, but this conversation was more awkward than initial hellos between a girl and a boy from where I was standing. For starters, he was asking me about my gay best friend. His asking about Tina directly had thrown me off completely. Honestly, he had thrown me off and intrigued me at the same time. I wanted to know what exactly he had on his mind to discuss, and how he knew my best friend.

"Yeah, I think I can take a break." I told my supervisor I was taking my break. She waved me off and said to go ahead since it was slow. It was usually slow on Sunday in the morning. People were either sleeping in from a late night at the club, or at church praising the Lord. I was at work trying desperately to outrun my thoughts of Jess. It was a battle I had been losing before this stranger appeared, although the stranger was doing better at distracting my thoughts than the book I had been reading.

We walked outside my job and started heading toward the food court. He began, "I know you probably don't remember me, but I work at *The Pink Pussy*."

I heard my voice raise a decibel or two, "Really?"

"Yes."

Getting my vocals under control, I told him, "You are right, I don't remember you. I only remember a female that works there. The one who helped me the night I was there." Trying to think back, my mind was a blank on whether there were others in the store or not. I told him, "It didn't seem like anyone else was there."

"Yeah, it was pretty dead that night, but I saw you. I was off to the side."

"Okay. So how do you know Tina? You asked me about her," I stated, getting to the point of this whole ordeal. I didn't want the small talk or evasive dialogue anymore. I wanted to know why he was here and what he wanted.

"She used to date Jess, the female who helped you that night."

Hearing her name made me visibly blush. I tried to turn my head, hoping he didn't notice. I let out a calming breath and asked, "How do you know about that?"

"Jess is my best friend. We've been best friends since we were kids and talk about everything. I know who Tina is."

"You talk?" I asked him, knowing this was going down a very different path than my expectations. *Does Jess talk about me? Does he know about the kiss? Is that why he's here? Did she send him?* My thoughts were just racing with questions.

"Yes, and we have talked about you. She won't admit it openly, but she likes you."

I was floored. Even though I didn't know what to expect, I definitely wasn't expecting that. He was making it extremely hard to keep my cool. "How are you so sure of that?" I asked too eager for information. Trying to save face, I continued, "I mean, I don't even get down like that. I ... I don't do stuff like that."

"Well, regardless to whether you do or don't, she has got it bad for you and you messed her up when you kissed her."

I cursed to myself. He did know, and hearing it said out loud rushed blood through my veins as I became flush with remembrance, replaying it all in my head. "She told you that?" I squealed. I could smell her again and even feel her touch. Without thinking, I touched my lips as if her lips were there on mine.

Shaking my head to snap me back to reality, I told him, "That was a mistake. I shouldn't have done that. You can tell her that I apologize. I don't know what came over me." I needed to get away from him. He was making matters worse, causing me to literally regurgitate the memory of that night in my head. A night that I wish never happened, but, deep down, craved it would happen again.

"You can tell her that yourself."

"I have no way of doing that. I don't know her like that."

"But you did kiss her, right?" He looked at me questioningly. I didn't respond. "Okay. Anyway, here is her number." He handed me a business card. I looked at it, realizing it was a business card for *The Pink Pussy*. I read her name in my head, Jesstina Rodriguez, CEO. I looked at him again, eyes big in disbelief. He said, "If you want to apologize to her, call her. Her cell phone number is on there, too." I looked at him, dumbfounded. "It's been about fifteen minutes. I think you have to get back to work." I still didn't respond. I just kept looking at the business card in my hand. When I didn't reply he added, "It was a pleasure, Love."

Before he turned to walk away, I asked, "CEO?"

"Yes, Boo," he smiled and winked, for the first time showing a hint of what might be his true self. I was amazed because the whole time I thought he was definitely straight. I figured him and Jess chased females together, you know, like each other's wingman. He was so attractive, and the scene in the store proves females would easily fall for him. I would have never taken him to be gay. Then again, I really couldn't assume he was gay just because of what he had just said. I really should have learned my lesson from doing that to Jess, although I was right.

As my thoughts consumed me, he turned and continued down the corridor. "Wait! Did she send you?" I shouted in his direction. He just kept walking away. By the time I realized I didn't even ask him his name, he was gone. I looked the card over again, whispering her name to myself. She owned *The Pink Pussy*, but she couldn't be that much older than me. I stuffed the card in my back pocket and headed back to the job to sit behind the register again. So many thoughts were running through my head, and thanks to this stranger, they were mostly of Jess again. I was finding it hard to escape her. *Extremely* hard.

Sundays were generally laid back and relaxed, that is why I didn't mind working on them. After my encounter with the stranger, I spent the following few hours behind the register ringing customers up and sending them on their way. At two I decided to take my lunch. I went to the food court to get a pizza and people watch, but there wasn't much to see. The eye candy was lacking more than usual. Some of the guys I saw looked way too young while others just looked like they were trying too hard. Either way, they definitely were not what I was looking for or needed in my life. Continuing my lunch, I ate and kept watching everyone who passed my sector of vision.

In the middle of taking a bite of my pizza, I noticed Tina's friend Shawn. She was on her phone not too far from where I was sitting. I turned away from her so she didn't notice me. Before everything happened between Jess and I that night, I had promised Shawn I'd call her when I made it in. Seeing her now made me realize I never called. I was so messed up after the kiss that I didn't remember to. I try to be a woman of my word but fell short that night.

I kept my head low hoping she didn't see me when I heard a male voice ask, "Who are you hiding from?"

Was this not my day or something? Because when I looked up, Kevin was standing in front of me. I hadn't called him either since he bought my batteries for me at K-Mart. I stuttered, "Kevin. Hi." I smiled with obvious embarrassment.

He laughed, "Oh, you do remember me? So, am I ever going to receive a call from the elusive Aaliyah? You still owe me a rain check."

"I do, huh?"

Kevin smiled at me with his whiter than white teeth and said, "Yes, you do. So, why not today? What do you have going on?"

"Well, right now I'm actually working. I'm just on my lunch break at the moment."

"I see. Well, what about when you get off?"

I smiled knowing that saying no wasn't a real option, especially since I did owe him, and I actually didn't want to say no. "That should be fine. I didn't have any plans other than going home and probably curling up tonight with this book I've been reading."

"That sounds enlightening. What are you reading?"

"Oh, it's nothing. Just some poetry I picked up randomly by this unknown poet that calls herself MindSpeaka. The book's title is *Emotional Development*."

"MindSpeaka, eh? Is she any good?"

"I like her stuff. I can relate to a lot of it."

"I might need to check her out," he smiled at me.

"Yeah," I smiled back at him.

"So, what time would you like to meet up?"

"Umm, I get off a little later than usual tonight. I am closing. We should be done by seven, so you can meet me outside at about then at the food court entrance."

"All right then, seven it is. I will be there."

"I look forward to it, but I need to get back to the store. My lunch is pretty much over."

"Not a problem. I will see you at seven." I got up to take my tray to the garbage. He also got up and gave me a hug. "See you then Ms. Aaliyah." I blushed as I released myself from his hug and walked away headed back to work. Inside I was excited about seeing Kevin later, but because I felt his eyes watching me walk away, I didn't turn around and kept stepping like I wasn't fazed.

The rest of the day went by fast. Before I knew it, we were closing up shop. As I rung up the last customer and thanked her for shopping with us, one of my co-workers waited at the gate to escort her out. My supervisor had been standing by with her key so we could go through the cycle of closing the register out. While I counted money, others put out any re-stock that needed to be done. Even though it was a slow day, we were still able to reach our sales goal for the day, and I was even able to meet quota on new credit card accounts. Aside from the morning, it was a good day at work.

My co-workers invited me out to Dave & Buster's, but I declined. Normally I might have gone with them. I love Dave & Buster's teriyaki steak and TNT, their special Long Islands. I have tons of the souvenir glasses at home. I also love playing skid ball and race car games. I would get so intense when racing like I was a real racecar driver, but I already had plans, so there would be no racing for me tonight. We all walked to the food court exit together, discussing the day, and then went our separate ways.

Scanning the parking lot, I noticed Kevin heading my way. He had changed from the t-shirt and jeans he had on earlier to a pair of dark slacks and a nice V-neck sweater with the sleeves slightly pushed up. His hair looked freshly cut and he was wearing a silver chain and watch. As he approached me he smiled. I couldn't help but smile back at him. When he got to me, he hugged me and asked, "So, where would you like to go to eat?"

Getting use to his warm embrace, I responded, "I don't know. I really didn't think about it."

He let me go and said, "They have this nice diner on Route 4 heading toward Paterson. How does that sound?"

"You mean the Coach House?" I asked, a little sad the hug ended so soon.

"Yes. Is that okay?"

"Yeah," I smiled. "My Aunt and I went there for lunch once. I really like the atmosphere and there are a lot of good choices on the menu."

"Great!" he exclaimed, "Do you want to go in my car?"

"Oh, no, I don't want to leave my car here in the parking lot. I can meet you up there in fifteen minutes or so. Is that good?"

"Sure, as long as you are really going to show up," he joked.

"I will be there, I promise."

"Okay, well I will see you there in fifteen."

"Cool," I said before turning and heading toward my car.

I turned to see Kevin standing there watching me. "I'm just making sure you make it to your car all right." I smiled at how considerate he was being and continued to my car. Not until I got in and turned the ignition on did he start heading to his own car. I shifted into gear and headed for the highway. Looking in my rearview, I could see Kevin behind me in a black BMW. Most brothers didn't ride in that kind of style unless they participated in illegal activities. I prayed he just happened to be blessed; otherwise, I would have to let him go.

Back in the day I had dealt with a guy who was a hustler, in the business of street pharmaceuticals. I had to be 15, maybe 16 then. Anthony ran through the streets of the East side of Paterson, selling everything from crack to e-pills, but his main line of business was marijuana, also known as Mary Jane, better known as weed. There were plenty of times the cops stopped him when we would be walking to or from his area. I loved him, but that life wasn't for me. Even so, he knew that I would ride or die for him. Lucky for me, he wanted more for me.

Anthony suggested that I leave Jersey for college. I was willing to stay local to be with him, but he pretty much demanded that I get out of the trap Paterson's street life was. At first I thought it was some other girl, but I later realized and understood how much he really loved me.

A year or so after I had left for college, I came home to the news that he and his girlfriend had been shot to death at point-blank range. They were in front of his girlfriend's apartment building when they were gunned down. I was told that the police said it was drug-related. I cried more than my heart could take. That could've been me. Anthony knew what the possibility was for a future with him, so he had pushed me away to save me.

I felt a tear leave my eye in remembrance. I looked at myself in my rearview mirror and wiped the tear away. Telling myself to think happy thoughts, I pushed Anthony out my mind and focused on the man following behind me. There was no way he was into that nonsense. Kevin didn't look the type.

I pulled into Coach House Diner's parking lot and found it hard to find a spot, let alone parking spots close together. A little ways to the right of the establishment I was able to find a spot and headed toward the door to wait for Kevin. Seconds after I reached the entrance, he showed up behind me. We walked in and were

able to get a booth by a window. It was already dark out, but the
street lights outside lit the surrounding area up and shown into the
window like mini moons. Our waiter came and got our drink
orders, then disappeared to get them.

Kevin looked at me and smiled. I turned away as I felt myself
blush. "So, Miss Aaliyah, how have you been? I always wondered
what the batteries were for."

I blushed, fully embarrassed. "I have been okay. Working," I
stated, intentionally ignoring his reference to the batteries.

"I see. So you work at the mall?"

"Yeah, but it is just a summer job. I go back to Atlanta for the
fall semester in August."

"Oh? You are in college?"

"Yes, I am. I start my senior year this fall." Just the thought of
being a senior made me beam from ear to ear. I was excited about
returning back to campus as a returning senior. Not a junior,
sophomore, or newbie freshman, but a senior.

"Which school? Are you in the AU?"

"Yeah. I attend Morris Brown College, though it wasn't
necessarily my first choice."

"Oh?"

"Yeah. The school of my choice didn't accept me," I said, with
overtones of hostility in my voice, "but Good Old Morris Brown
did." It had been three years and I was still bitter about not getting
my first choice. I continued, "I have managed to maintain a 3.9
GPA, despite all the distractions the AUC has to offer. I have my
eye on the prize."

"Sorry to hear that you didn't get into your first choice. I also
commend you on keeping your GPA so high. I attended
Morehouse, myself, and it was definitely not easy to ignore the, uh,
distractions," he said with a grin.

Before I could ask him about going to Morehouse and those
said distractions, the waiter came back with our drinks. He asked,
"Are you ready to place your order?"

I hadn't even looked at the menu. I picked it up and gave it a
quick glance over. I found the wraps and decided to go with a

chipotle wrap they had, requesting some chipotle on the side. Kevin said that sounded good and ordered one for himself, too. Our waiter took our orders and menus, and then he was gone again.

I started back in on the conversation we had been having, "So, Morehouse, huh? I don't recall ever seeing you there, but it could be those distractions," I smirked at him. "I have been to a few functions as a date for a male friend of mine who attends Morehouse."

Kevin ignored my comment and said, "No. I graduated some years ago."

"Oh? How old are you?"

"32. How old are you?"

"21."

"Oh?" he sat back.

"Yes. Is that a problem?"

"Not with me, if it isn't with you," he smiled, leaning back in. "So, what do you study?"

"I major in business administration. I plan to go into business for myself one day, but for now, I pray that once I graduate, somebody already established will hire me. I want to work in the music industry, so I am looking at Atlantic Records or Def Jam. I have done side work for both in the realms of promotions."

"That sounds interesting. I went to school for dentistry. My practice is located in Florida. I am up here on vacation visiting family."

"Knew there had to be a reason why your teeth looked so perfect. Hard to be a dentist and not have a beautiful smile." He smiled at me and for the first time, I saw hints of a dimple in his left cheek.

"Very true," he agreed. Our waiter came back with our food, and most conversation ceased as we ate our meal. We stopped every now and then for small talk, but we both were mostly focused on eating. My appetite was in rare form because I ate everything, including the fries on the side.

We continued our conversation once we were finished eating,

discussing growing up in the North and attending school in the South. We talked about the difference between the two and why he decided to go to Florida instead of coming back home to establish his practice. Kevin was adamant that there wasn't anything for him in Jersey. I agreed, knowing that I would probably avoid coming back to Jersey, even if only to move to New York to pursue my career aspirations.

He shared some of his old college stories with me and some of the things they use to get away with in the AU. I couldn't stop laughing as he recounted times when they would play pranks on incoming freshmen, initiating them into the Morehouse brotherhood. In my mind, I was thankful for his company and hoping we could do this again. He could be the distraction I had been looking for.

Looking at my watch, I realized that it was getting close to nine at night. I let Kevin know as much and we settled our bill and headed for the exit. He walked me to my car and told me that he had a wonderful evening. I told him the feeling was mutual, knowing that I really wasn't ready for the night to end just yet. He expressed he would like to see me again, so I gave him my number so we could make arrangements for another encounter.

We sat outside next to my car for a minute, just smiling at each other when Kevin pulled me toward him and kissed me. My eyes opened wide at the surprise contact, but slowly relaxed close as I kissed him back. It was sweet and spicy from the chipotle we had both enjoyed for dinner. Pulling away, I smiled and blushed at him. In the dim light around my car, I saw him smiling back at me.

I told him I had to be on my way and unlocked the doors to my car with the wireless key lock. He agreed and said he needed to get back home, too. He helped me into my car, closing the door behind me. I rolled down my window and told him again how much I enjoyed my evening. Kevin said he really enjoyed my company and would be calling soon. I turned my ignition and lights on and backed out of the parking spot. He stood by and watched me drive to the highway and then into traffic.

The whole ride home, I smiled and relived our evening

together. I was glad that Kevin came to the mall. He was the perfect distraction.

jess

Chapter 7

"Damn," I mumbled under my breath.

"What's up," Ty asked me. I looked and nodded my head toward outside the store. He followed my stare and saw what was causing my frustration. "Damn, J. Did you put it on her or something?"

"No! I haven't even touched the girl, but she's been driving me insane since I walked away from her at the club during Pride." *She* was Jordyn. Since that night at the club, she had been stalking me at the store. I never dealt well with drama, especially drama that could be avoided. I looked at Jordyn as avoidable drama, so I evaded her like the plague every time she tried to catch up with me.

"She comes around here like you laid it on her."

"I promise you I never touched her. Not a handshake. Not a kiss. And definitely not sex." Looking out the storefront, I watched Jordyn making her way across the street. "Ty, can you cover for me? I'm really not in the mood for this today."

"Yeah, I'll cover, but only if you give me Saturday night off."

"Damn, that's blackmail!"

He giggled as he agreed, "Yes, it is. So, can I get the night off, or should I point a red arrow in your direction."

"Yeah, yeah, yeah," I said, rushing the conversation. She was getting closer by the second. "Yeah, take Saturday off, just cover for me."

"A'ight," he said, smiling at his backhanded win. I really didn't have time to put too much thought into whether or not Ty being off Saturday was feasible. Jordyn was approaching too fast for all of that. I walked out the main area of the store where most of our products were located, headed toward the video viewing area and closed myself behind the door of my office.

The bells over the doorway began to ring, announcing that Jordyn had walked in. "Welcome to *The Pink Pussy*. Can I help you with anything?" Ty asked her once she was in the store. I could barely hear their conversation through the closed door of the office, so I cracked it a little so I could listen in on what was said between them.

"Yeah. Is Jess working today?" she asked him.

"I'm sorry, but she's not here."

Sounding frustrated, she asked, "Well, do you know when she will be here?"

"I am sorry ma'am, but it is not our policy to tell the work schedule of our employees. Your best bet is to ask her yourself."

"I have been trying to do that, but she won't answer my fucking calls," Jordyn told Ty in an irritated tone.

"I am sorry, ma'am. Would you like to leave a message for me to pass on to her?"

Blowing air, she said, "Yeah, can you tell her that Jordyn is looking for her and to please call me? Tell her I am sorry for what happened the other night. I want to start over. Can you tell her that for me?" She actually sounded sincere and for a minute I felt sorry for hiding from her.

"Okay. I will leave this message for her. Is there anything else I can help you with?"

Defeated, Jordyn answered, "No. That'll be it. Thanks."

"Not a problem. Thanks for coming to *The Pink Pussy*," Ty retorted out of habit.

"Yeah," Jordyn said, seemingly unsatisfied with her findings. I listened closely, waiting for the bells to ring over the door announcing her departure, the same way they announced her arrival. After I heard them, I waited a few minutes more before coming out; you couldn't be too careful.

Once I was sure the coast was clear, I came out the office exclaiming, "Ty, you are a lifesaver! Thanks!"

"Mmhmm, just don't forget you gave me Saturday night off."

"Yeah, yeah, yeah. I won't forget."

"You know, she seemed really heartbroken you weren't here. You *sure* you didn't hit it and try to quit it?"

"Positive, Ty." I thought about how Jordyn was sounding right before she left. "She did sound sincere, huh? Maybe I should hear her out."

"That's all on you whether you do or not, J." He shook his head at me and smiled. "You drive these girls crazy like you got the Maidus touch or something."

Ty laughed at his own joke while I just looked at him, contemplating the truth in his words. Women I thought of as friends often ended up confessing their affection towards me. Even if I showed them no interest. As for the women I actually dated, many of them I could call today and they would be willing to kick it. Of course, Tina wasn't one of those women. Brushing it off, I said, "Whatever, Ty."

"I know. It's whatever I say," he winked at me. Ignoring his comment, I went over by the straps and started lining boxes back up.

After a long day, Ty and I said our 'I love yous' and 'goodbyes', and parted ways. I thought about whether I should go to the bar or just call it a night, as I approached my motorcycle. My 2017 Kawasaki Ninja ZX-10R reminded me of Reptile from Mortal Combat, my favorite fighter from back in the day. With an enhanced power transmission and torque control, it was easily ready to race, but I never did that. Racing wasn't and isn't my style. Smiling at my accomplishments in life, I went with the latter and headed in the direction of home.

I pulled up to my two story home with a finished basement and hit the button on my keys for the garage to open. I parked my bike next to my Ashton Martin that was covered and cold. Lately I had been riding my bike more than my car since my bike gave me more freedom on the road, and flexibility when I needed a quick escape from trouble of all kinds. Never being a motorcycle enthusiast, I surprised myself when I got my bike and learned how to ride it. Of course, I have messed it up a time or two from dropping it, but you would never be able to tell that now. I honestly should have started with something smaller, but I'm stubborn. Either way, I figured it out, a pretty penny later, but I did figure it out.

Pressing the button for my garage door to close, I walked into the house. The garage was directly connected to the kitchen. Noticing I forgot to leave my gloves in my helmet, I tossed them on the kitchen counter so I wouldn't forget them when I was leaving out again.

Anyone who loved cooking would love my kitchen. It seemed too big for only one person with its stainless steel appliances, black granite counters and an island that doubled as a chopping block with an additional sink. The ovens were separate from the six range stove top with a chef's hood above it, and sunk into a wall where you could roast a duck in one while baking a marble cake in the other. There were plenty of cabinets and additional counter space all around, as well as a wine cooler in the bottom of the island. Yes, anyone who loved to cook would love my kitchen the way I use to.

When I was with Mieko I use to cook for her all the time. Back then she was still new at being a model, thinking carrots and celery were all she could eat if she wanted to last in the industry. I nurtured her and showed her that with the right combinations of grains, meats, vegetables, and spices, she could eat like a fat kid, yet still look like the supermodel she would always be in my eyes. Thinking about all of that made me miss her. I always missed her, but as things are now we would never work. Turning the light off, I moved on from the kitchen, leaving it and her memory behind, and headed for the study.

My study was my room of complete solace. One of the three walls housed a floor to ceiling window with an oversized oak desk in front of it. Two chairs were strategically placed around a small coffee table that invited leisure in front of the desk. The other two walls in the space were filled with books of all kinds. Most people did not know about the literary side of me. I loved to read. I would read books of various subject matters, both fiction and nonfiction alike. Some of my favorite writers included Aristotle and Freud. As sexually charged as Freud's theories were, there was a lot of truth behind them. Many females I dated thought intellect was sexy, but could never hold a conversation with me on those subjects.

One of my favorite books of all time, though, was "The Fire Next Time," by James Baldwin. Even in these suspected modern times, I can superimpose his words from the '60s over the current structure of today. Being a woman always discovering myself and my place in this world, I thoroughly enjoyed Alice Walker's "The Color Purple." After reading the book, seeing the movie and going to the play on Broadway, I am convinced that the book is the best depiction because it communicated more in-depth and complete expression and knowledge. Knowledge is power, and the most pertinent of information could always be found between the covers of a book.

Not all books I read are like the ones Baldwin or Walker wrote, though. I do like a good Zane or Fiona Zedde, who happens to be one of the better lesbian writers out there, novel.

I decided to re-read my favorite novel by Fiona Zedde, "Every Dark Desire." A part of me always felt like her character Silvija and I had a lot in common. I mean, I wasn't a vampire or sexing as many females as she seemed to be. It was all about her cool demeanor and appeal to the ladies that I felt most in tune with.

I don't think I got too far into the book before I had fallen asleep dreaming in one of the plush chairs in the study. In my dream, I was still in my study, still sitting in the same chair, breathing heavy with my eyes rolled in the back of my head from the sheer pleasure I was feeling between my thighs. Whatever was going on, I knew I didn't want it to stop. Eyes still closed and rolling, I thrust myself up into the most skilled tongue I had ever felt and let out a deep moan.

Finding it hard to contain myself, I reached for whoever was giving me the best cunnilingus I had ever had in my life's head and felt my hands sink into her hair as I pushed her into me. The feeling was amazing. I felt tears stream down my face as my orgasm started to roll off my tongue into the atmosphere. I moaned so deeply and long as I felt the rush of ecstasy leave my body. Limp and weak, I opened my eyes to look at the woman who had left me more than done.

To my disbelief, I saw a pair of almond-shaped dark brown eyes smiling up at me. As the recognition of Aaliyah kneeling there before me was coming through more clearly, loud singing abruptly awakened me from my dream. I heard Boyz II Men singing about their mother knowing that they loved her and automatically knew who was calling. Answering the phone still recovering from my dream I said, "Hey Mom. Something wrong?" I looked at the wall clock near the desk and saw that it was five in the morning. It was actually normal for my mother to be up and about around this time.

"Jesstina Rodriguez? Hello?"

"Mom, mom," I cut her off, "I'm here. Is everything all right?"

"Hey Baby. I'm just calling to check up on you. You know you could come around once and a while to see me. What? Do you not miss your mother?"

She was laying her guilt trip on thick this morning. I rubbed my face with my free hand. "Yes, I miss you, Mom. I will come and see you on Sunday. How about that?"

"That is all I want is to see my Baby," I could hear her smiling through the phone over getting what she wanted. I wondered if she put my brother Jamaal through the same thing whenever she called him. Believe me, I love my mother, but she likes a lot of attention. I smiled to myself and thought, *Yeah, but I do too. I must get it from my momma.* As I was giggling to myself, I heard my mother calling me.

"Jesstina? Jesstina! Did you hear what I said about my arthritis?"

Jumping back into the conversation, I asked her, "What's wrong with your arthritis?"

"It's been acting up lately. I feel it all in my hands and in my back. I feel it the most when I am out in my garden."

"Have you seen the doctor about it, Mom?"

"That old fool doesn't know what he's talking about."

"Mom, go see your doctor. He's not a fool. He's been going through your health hiccups since they began. Do you want me to go with you?"

"Would you Baby? I'll go if you go with me." My mother is like that, a drama queen to start, but sweet and innocent once she is getting her way. I really love that woman.

"Okay, I'll go with you. Just tell me when and I will be there."

"Thank-you Baby. Well, let me go ahead and start cleaning my house. I love you, Baby. Don't forget you said you are coming by Sunday. I will cook and we can have dinner together. Maybe I can get your brother over here too."

"That would be great, Mom. I love you, too. I'll talk to you later."

"Okay Baby." Our conversation was disconnected and I laid the phone on my lap and put my head back. In the middle of me having one of my best wet dreams to-date, my mother would call. That would only happen to me. I looked down to my lap and shuddered with the remembrance of Aaliyah being there in my dream. That could have only been a dream, even though it felt so real.

Thinking I might be wet, I felt myself and felt the dampness in-between my thighs. Realizing I came in my sleep, I decided to get up and take a shower before dragging myself to bed. I wasn't a morning person, thus why I worked afternoon and late night shifts.

Climbing up to the second level where my master bedroom and private bath were located, I stripped out of my clothes. I hopped in the shower, washed all the important parts, then went straight to my king size bed, still wet, and fell back to sleep like I had never even been awake.

The rest of the week was too busy for me to even revisit my dream to consider its true meaning. *The Pink Pussy* had a new shipment of toys come in, some I had ordered for the first time. I prided myself on knowing every item we sold as if I used them all myself. Studying every product and knowing the key selling points for each made it easier to get the customer to close the deal and buy.

By the time Saturday night rolled in, I was beat. I came in expecting to see Ty, forgetting I gave him the night off. When I got to the store and saw the door was still locked, remembrance kicked in and I realized I didn't schedule anyone in his place to cover the shift with me. I silently cursed myself as I opened up and walked to the private office. I retrieved the register drawer from the safe and came back to the counter with the register. *Maybe it will be a slow night*, I thought to myself. If it was, I wouldn't have too much to worry about.

An hour into the shift, I was behind the counter watching one of the DVDs kept stored there just for slow nights, like this one was turning out to be, and glancing at the video monitors that were set up over the front and back entrances. The porno was more watching me than I watching it while I sat reading the novel I had begun earlier in the week. Every so often I took a quick look at the monitors to ensure security, and then went back to reading. As I was turning to the next page in the book, I heard the bells over the door go off. I glimpsed at the monitor but only saw enough to know it was a female.

Jumping up, I extended a greeting to my customer, "Welcome to *The Pink Pussy*. Anything particular I can help," I stopped mid-sentence when I saw Jordyn standing in front of me. "What's up Jordyn?" I awkwardly asked, this being the first time we had been face-to-face since Pride.

She looked at me like she wanted to slap me, but instead she asked, "How have you been Jess? I've tried to catch up with you, but have not been too lucky."

"Yeah. My bad. I have been busy. We've had a lot of new shipments come in. I have been working to get familiar with them and stock them."

"Yeah, that does sound busy," she said, looking off in the distance.

"Oh. I got your message from earlier this week. Sorry you missed me."

"Yeah."

"So, how can I help you? Looking for a video, toy, or anything?" I asked, trying to lighten the mood a little, but keeping it strictly business.

"No, I just came to see you, I mean, to see if you would be here. But, I wasn't expecting much, and now that you are here," she paused, "I don't know what to say. I mean, I did know. I wanted to cuss you out. I wanted to apologize. I went through an extreme thought process to prepare me for what I would say and do when I finally got to speak to you, and yet, I am not prepared."

"Look, Jordyn, my bad about how everything happened at the club, but I'm really not ready for any commitments. I am chilling right now, having fun, and living life. I didn't want you to think it was something more than what it was, and before you did, I knew I had to leave you alone." As I said the last three words, I witnessed her cringe. Trying to lessen the visible blow to her ego, I said, "I mean, I think you are cool people. I really do."

"No. Thanks for your honesty. I respect you more for it," she said, looking distant again.

"Thanks." Attempting to lighten the mood again, I asked her, "So how have you been? You're looking good." And she really was. Jordyn's hair was pulled into a simple slipknot ponytail, hanging a little past her shoulders. She had on a fitted striped button-down shirt with the sleeves rolled up to her elbows, a pair of faded blue jeans, and some black Air Force Ones. She seemed shorter, but I figured that was because she didn't have heels on like the previous times we'd been around each other. From what I could see, she didn't have any make-up on. To be honest, she really didn't need it, for her brown skin was flawless. Her whole look was so laid back. That was attractive to me. Thinking to myself and my latest attractions, I wondered if my stint with strictly model types was coming to an end. I knew better than that. Model chicks would probably remain my weakness, but there was always room for variety. I smiled.

She smiled, "Thank-you. I have been well, for the most part. New York is a lot more different from California than I initially estimated. I am still getting use to those differences."

"Care to share? It's not like I have a lot of customers tonight," I said looking around *The Pink Pussy*. I invited her to sit behind the counter with me, completely forgetting about the porno that was playing until I saw her eyes widen from the action on the screen.

"Oh," I told her, "I wasn't really watching that. I was actually reading." She gave me that "yeah right" look, but played along as if she believed me. I showed her my book to further prove my point and she told me she had heard of the author but has yet to read any of her work. I told Jordyn if she wanted, I could let her borrow one of my books to see if she gets hooked or not. She said that would be cool, so I told her I would have it for her in the next week.

We talked about how she felt New York females were close-minded and self-centered. She was use to a more diverse community that was more geared toward working together, rather than against each other. I told her that not everyone is in constant battle, it's just a mentality that trust was limited and that though there were so many of us, the community was small and so and so use to get down, but now so and so get down, creating more unnecessary drama. I also told her I tend to stay away from that because I was never one for drama. Jordyn agreed, stating that she had never seen so many senseless altercations in her life before Pride. I smiled, understanding completely.

Conversation between us flowed so easily, just like it did the first night we met. This was the woman I liked, the one who was just chill and could talk a good dialogue. Not the woman I had met at the club during Pride. The more we talked, the more drawn to her I became. The hours I thought would just creep on, flew by faster than expected. Before I knew it, it was quitting time. A few people had stopped in, but while I handled business taking care of the customers, Jordyn sat and waited for my return, and now it was time to close up shop.

I got up and locked the door so no one else would come in while I was ensuring that everything in the back was locked and put away. Jordyn said she'd wait for me to finish so I wouldn't be locking up alone. I thought that was sweet. Actually, when you got past the move she pulled at the club, she was awesome company and I liked her. She was genuine and that was like finding a diamond in the rough in our community. Those who showed the most promise usually ended up being the most scandalous. I knew that all too well, thus, why I wasn't trying to get caught up at the moment.

I went into the private office to take care of all the financial matters, counting the night's earnings and balancing the checkbooks. Not too bad for only a few items sold. Even though it was extremely slow, we were still able to make quota. I had left the office door cracked so I could listen for Jordyn if she needed anything while I was completing the accounting data for the night. Walking out the office, I bumped into her standing there, almost knocking her clear over. "Whoa!" I exclaimed. "Sorry about that Jordyn," I apologized and started to maneuver around her. She moved with me and blocked my path. I looked at her, "What's up? Everything okay?"

"Jess, can I ask you something?"

"Sure. You've kept me company all night, and for that, I am grateful, so you can ask me whatever you want." Instead of asking me a question, she stood on her toes and kissed me quickly on my lips. I looked at her, not sure what to do next. I guess she noticed my hesitation and the slight shock and confusion on my face. She stood on her toes again and kissed me, this time staying there prolonging our connection.

Slowly my guard dropped and my mind relaxed. I started to kiss her back. Wrapping my arms around her waist bending down into her lips, I held her against me. The intensity of our kiss grew, as did the ache in-between my thighs. Regardless of me not being able to analyze my dream, the damage had been done. Since the dream, I had longed for the touch of another woman. With each tangoed dance of our tongues, I felt myself become wetter and wetter.

Taking the chance, I slid my hands under Jordyn's shirt. She didn't protest. I pulled away from her lips, looking into her eyes and asked, "Are you sure you want to do this?" because by this point I was sure that unless she told me no, we were going to cross the point of no return.

Without hesitation, she said, "Yes." That was all I needed. I pulled her into the office with me and began undressing her. I unbuttoned her shirt and let it drop to the floor, revealing her cream-colored silk bra. The swell of her breast rose with the tempo of her heart's beat, inviting me to place kisses on the exposed flesh. I took her right breast out of her bra, placed her hard nipple into my mouth and began sucking on it as I fumbled with the clasp of her bra to release the other one. Her breath grew deeper with anticipation. Jordyn rubbed her hands through my hair and ran her nails down the nape of my neck. That drove me crazy. I bit down on her nipple a little causing her to gasp from the unexpected roughness.

Returning my lips to hers, I began to undo Jordyn's jeans and pull them down to her ankles. One by one, she stepped out of her jeans and kicked them to the side. I slid my hand down to her wetness and teased her clit through her silk panties. Her lips were swollen and ready. I pushed the material to the side and continued to play with her clit, every now and then teasing her hole with my fingers. She moaned and shuddered as I kept her on her feet. Taking two fingers, I pushed inside her and filled her up. She grabbed the back of my neck and dug her nails into my skin as I moved my fingers in and out of her once hollow cave at a restrained pace.

When I felt she was ready, I stuck another finger in her and picked up the pace. On cue, her labored breathing quickened with the quickness of my fingers. By this point, she had flung her head back limp leaving her neck accessible for me to suck on, so I did just that. With my free hand and arm, I kept her up and from trying to get away from me. As Jordyn's orgasm came strong and she released her liquid all over my fingers, I laid her on the sofa, my bed when I was too tired to take that ride home, so she could regain some control of her body.

Jordyn laid there in her afterglow, trying to remove her soak panties, while I stripped myself down to match her attire. Looking at her goddess of a body spread on the sofa, I got on top of her and intertwined our legs so that our clits were touching. I damn near came right then from the electricity I felt when our lower lips kissed. I kissed Jordyn on her lips and slowly started rubbing our clits together. I licked the edges of her mouth down to her neck where I began to suck on her again. She cooed while grabbing my butt and holding my pelvis as close to her body as she could without restricting our movement. We moaned in unison as our grinds moved in perfect harmony with one another.

I supported myself on the arm and back of the sofa to give me more leverage, enjoying the view of Jordyn's "ugly" faces. She was feeling so good and making it hard for me to prolong my orgasm. She held onto me, her legs now wrapped around one of mine, slightly gripping it. Our slow grind picked up speed as both of us started to moan and grunt louder and louder. I felt myself slamming my stiffened clit into her clit harder and harder. The adrenaline rush had me fucking her like I was strapped. I tried to calm down, but it was too late and she wasn't trying to stop me anyway. Not until we both reached our orgasmic peak, forcefully pushing our clits into one another's, did I finally stop to a full pause. I came hard and long, needing the release more than Jordyn knew.

We lingered on the sofa in each other's' arms for a while, allowing the AC to cool us back down. Her hair was wild and free, no longer in a slipknot ponytail. I smoothed her hair down, kissing her on her forehead, enjoying the moment. Looking at the time, I mentioned to her that we both probably needed to get up and get ready to go. We dressed slowly and in silence. I tried to push my hair back to looking somewhat decent, while she did the same with hers.

I locked up and stepped away from the door with my hands in my jean pockets. Jordyn looked at me and said, "You think we can do this again sometimes. No strings attached. Just good conversation, and if it's all right with you, maybe benefits afterward."

I tried to shield my smile as I said, "If that's what you want. I mean, I really enjoyed your company tonight. And I mean that. The conversation was outstanding, and the sex was a *very* nice surprise. Besides, I owe you a book."

She smiled, "You do. When would you like me to come by and pick it up?"

"Well, I am busy tomorrow. I am going to spend the day with my mother, but maybe Monday night. Is that cool?"

"Awww, that's sweet spending time with your mom."

"Yeah. Gotta show mom much love when I can," I smiled. "So Monday?"

"Monday should be fine."

"Cool. Then I will see you on Monday." I walked Jordyn to her car and kissed her on her lips before helping her get in.

She rolled down her window, "Jess, I know you're not looking for a commitment, but I really did enjoy being with you tonight. I know you said to come by Monday, but if you start feeling awkward about what went down between us tonight and don't want me to come by, just call and let me know. And if on the other hand *I* start having regrets, I will do the same. Is that all right with you?"

"That would be fine, but I really do enjoy talking to you, so I hope if you do have regrets, we can talk about it and if possible, continue developing our friendship. We don't have to have sex."

"Good. I mean, I want that, too," she smiled impishly, "but I don't want to get caught up when I already know where you stand."

"I understand. Whatever you decide, it will be okay." I smiled to reassure her that my words were sincere. She seemed satisfied. Seconds later her car started up and she was waving good-bye. I watched her drive away smiling at the pleasant surprise she was and hoping that, that wasn't the last time we experienced one another.

aaliyah

Chapter 8

Kevin and I had been dating ever since we went to Coach House that Sunday. Most of my free time was spent with him and I couldn't be any happier. Everything seemed so perfect, within reason, of course. Nothing in the world could bother me anymore. Not even Xavier when he called me the other day. I guess his relationship with that other female was over and now he was trying to get me back.

My cell phone rang and an Atlanta number flashed across the screen. It looked so familiar but I couldn't place it in my mind where I knew it from. I answered, "Hello?"

"Hello? Hello? Aaliyah?" a familiar voice asked.

"This is her. May I ask who's calling?"

"Aaliyah, it's me. Xavier." I heard him say his name and for a split second, I felt the butterflies I use to always feel when I was with him or heard his voice over the phone. In the next second, though, I remembered how he dumped me at the beginning of the summer and all the resentment I felt toward him rolled into my being and laid thick in my tone.

"What do you want Xavier?"

"Hey 'Liyah, Baby. I've been thinking about you and just wanted to call and check up on you."

"Is that right? Well, I am fine, thanks."

"I miss you." I looked at my phone in disbelief. Surely he couldn't be serious after what he put me through.

"Do you, Xavier?" I asked, "Because you sure didn't seem like you missed me or was even concerned about me when you decided to break my heart. As a matter of fact, it seemed like you were already preoccupied with someone else!" I screamed into the phone, losing my cool.

"It wasn't like that. I mean, yeah, I told you I wanted to see what else was out there, but I realized I would never find a woman like you. No woman can treat me like you do."

"Yeah, that *was* true. I guess you never know what you've got 'til it's gone, huh?" Xavier didn't respond. "Look, I have to go. I have a date."

"A date? Who you fucking behind my back Aaliyah?" he demanded.

"Excuse me? Who I'm *fucking* is hardly any of your business. Xavier, you left *me*. I didn't leave you. I begged you to stay with me, but you still *left* ME!" I screamed. "So don't try to stake claim now. What did you say? Oh, I remember." I mocked him, "*I want to see what else is out there. Maybe you should think about doing the same.* Well, I took your advice and have found someone who is more of a man then you will ever be. As a matter of fact, I need to get off the phone with you because he should be here any minute." I hung up without waiting for a reply. I could hear Xavier screaming and cursing my name as my cell phone closed shut.

He's tried calling back a few times since, but I just ignored the calls and erased the voicemails the moment I heard his voice. I told Kevin about Xavier's calls and he simply laughed telling me that one man's loss was a better man's gain before planting a kiss upon my lips. I smiled knowing that I wasn't missing anything not having Xavier in my life.

The summer was beginning to wind down and soon I would have to go back to Atlanta for the fall semester. I decided to take a night away from Kevin to spend time with Tina. I called him to tell him I wanted to spend time with my best friend and he completely understood. He said the time from me would give him time to catch up with some of his friends he had been neglecting. I smiled to myself with the same understanding. We said our goodbyes and got off the phone to head to our separate activities.

I called Tina up to tell her I would be at her house in an hour. As soon as I hung up, I took a quick shower before getting dressed to leave the house. We were going to David & Buster's on 42nd Street in New York, so I decided to wear a pair of jeans and a light blue Baby-T with the word "Blessed" in white across my chest. I grabbed a jean jacket to put on to fight the cold that would come later and some blue and white Nike running shoes. I wore a pair of silver hoop earrings, my silver chain with a small cross charm and my silver Fossil watch with the blue face. I brushed my hair into a simple ponytail with a swooping bang covering a portion of my right eye. Throwing on some Versace Red Jeans and lip gloss, I grabbed my bag and headed to my car to get on the highway.

About twenty minutes later than I had planned, I pulled up to Tina's house. "Damn Liyah! We about to miss the bus waiting on you," Tina said walking toward me.

"My bad, T. I thought I had time to take a quick shower. I didn't know I was going to run into traffic on the way here," I told her.

"Are you ready? We need to start walking to the bus now or end up waiting an hour for the next one."

I sped up to catch up with Tina who was almost halfway down the block. "Is it necessary to walk that fast? I didn't even get to tell your parents hi."

"No time, Liyah. C'mon. Shawn is going to be waiting for us there."

"Shawn?" I asked.

"Yeah, she called about an hour ago wanting to chill. I told her you and I was heading her way to Dave & Buster's. She asked if she could tag along. I couldn't see why not, so I told her to meet us at Port Authority."

"Oh, okay. That's cool then. I saw her one weekend when I was working, but she didn't see me."

"Really? She didn't tell me about that?"

"I told you she didn't see me, and I didn't say anything to her."

"Why didn't you say anything?"

"Didn't get a chance to."

"Don't sweat it then. C'mon, I see the bus coming." We sprinted to the bus stop, making it there at the same time as the bus, got on and paid our fare. I was thankful I had some change at the bottom of my bag because I didn't have time to go to the bank like I usually did. Once we were seated, Tina asked, "So, what's been going on? We haven't really talked since that night we went to the club. You never even called to let me know you made it home. I didn't know until I got in and your car was gone."

"Sorry about that. I was so tired when I got in that night that I went straight to bed," I lied to Tina. I didn't know how to tell her about what happened between Jess and me, although there's really nothing to tell. I mean, it was just a kiss. But Tina is my best friend and Jess is her ex. I initiated the kiss, so either way, it was wrong. Had the shoe been on the other foot, I might've told her, but since nothing like that would ever happen again, I opted not to. It's like it never even happened.

"No worries. As long as you were all right Liyah," she said giving me a sideways hug. "So spill it. What or *who's* been occupying all your time? I miss my best friend."

I laughed at her, "I miss you, too. And since you asked, I did meet someone." I smiled at her knowingly.

"Oh shit, Liyah! What's his name? Where'd you meet him? Is he in school? Have you gone there with him?" she rushed out at me, adding a wink when she asked the last question. I laughed. "C'mon, girl! Spill the beans." I shared with Tina how I met Kevin going to K-Mart to get batteries for my toy and she busted out laughing at me. I told her how I never called, but he saw me at the mall one day and asked if I wanted to go to dinner that evening.

She cooed in with "Oohs," while smiling at me. I continued telling her about my date with Kevin, our first kiss that evening and how we had been inseparable ever since. Whenever we had a free minute, we were spending it together.

Tina said, "Yeah, but did you give him the booty?"

"No!" I laughed. "We haven't gone there and he hasn't pressured or even asked me to."

"He's not a closet homo is he?"

"No! We just haven't taken our relationship to that level yet, T. Geez."

"Okay, just checking. You never know." We arrived at the George Washington Bridge and took the steps downstairs to catch the A Train to Port Authority on 42nd Street so we could link up with Shawn. During that short ride, Tina told me she was dating some female named Tremaine she met the night we all went to the club. She seemed to be glowing as she described her to me. It didn't matter to me. As long as she was happy, I was happy with the girl.

Finally reaching our link-up spot, we walked out onto 42nd Street to see if we could spot Shawn. She saw us before we saw her and started calling our names. We turned to find her behind us heading in our direction. She had been waiting in the lobby of the Port Authority and saw us walk out the double doors.

"Anybody hungry," Shawn asked.

"We can eat when we get there. I love the teriyaki steak with a nice TNT to chase it," I smiled. She smiled back at me.

Tina chimed in, "That does sound good."

"Then what are we waiting for? Let's get there," I said, heading up 42nd. It didn't take long for us to reach the building that housed Dave and Buster's. We climbed the steps to the third floor and headed for the restaurant portion. The hostess seated us in a booth after Shawn had flirted with her to get the seat. I noticed them swap numbers, but thought to each their own. Tina and I got the teriyaki steak with fries on the side and a TNT. Shawn went with a chicken wrap and a Heineken. After eating, I was feeling loose and ready to play some games. Actually, I just wanted to race. Race car games, skid ball and TNTs were what I lived for at Dave and Buster's.

I conned Shawn into playing Daytona 500 with me. Tina tried to warn her that I could play the game in my sleep and that racing me was a pointless battle. Shawn puffed out her chest with the bravado of a champion. I just laughed and told her to get ready to eat my dust. Three rounds later, she called it quits. Tina laughed at her and said, "I told you, you didn't stand a chance." I patted Shawn on her shoulder and told her to step her game up before she tried to ride with the big boys. Tina and I busted out laughing some more. Shawn tried to front like it didn't bother her, but you could see she was a little sour about it.

We decided to go play some other games. Shawn went to play a shooting game, while Tina got into a Mrs. Pac Man game. Skid ball was calling me, so I went over there and played a few rounds. Tina came and watched me for a minute, then suggested competing in shooting hoops. Neither of us claimed to be basketball superstars, so we did horrible trying to shoot at a basket that kept moving back and forth. It began to look like we were competing to see who could do the worst. Just as the timer was winding down, I got a lucky shot in making the final score one to zero. We just laughed at how pathetic we were and went to go find Shawn.

This was only my second time out with Shawn, but I was learning she was quite the lady's ... man I guess would be appropriate considering her demeanor. When we found her she was swapping numbers with yet another young lady. After the female walked off, Shawn noticed Tina and myself standing there shaking our heads at her. She walked over to us grinning from ear to ear as to say, *"What I do?"* We laughed and decided to go turn our tickets in, in exchange for point cards. Being around just them two, I could see why they laughed so much the night we all went out. Both were laid back and out for a good time, which they both fully executed. I couldn't even remember the last time I had laughed so much.

It was getting late, so Shawn walked us back to the Port Authority so we could catch a bus back to Jersey. She stayed with us until a bus heading to Jersey came. Before we got on, she made us promise that we'd call once we got home. I promised not to forget this time, smiling to reassure her. She gave us both hugs good-bye, and then we were gone. Tina and I talked the whole way home about our evening, concluding that we had to do it again before I left to go back to school.

When I got to my car that night, I noticed that I had a new voicemail. I don't even know how I missed my phone ringing but I decided to listen to the message before pulling off. Pressing 1, my phone called my voicemail so I could listen to my message. It was Kevin. "Hey Baby. You must still be out having a good time without me." I could hear the smile through his voice sounded like he was pouting. I smiled. "I missed you tonight and hope that we are still on for Saturday. I have something to talk to you about. Nothing bad, but we do need to talk. All right? Well, I hope you had a good time and I will talk to you later." The line disconnected and I wondered what he wanted to talk about. Not worrying too much, I put my car in gear and headed home.

Saturday came, and all day I was anxious to see Kevin and find out what he had to tell me. We had spoken and seen each other briefly a few times since he left me the message, but if I asked about what he had to tell me, he would distract me and not say anything. Even if I pouted about it, he would only kiss my lips and tell me to be patient. Now that Saturday has finally arrived, time could not go fast enough.

We decided to meet at *Friendly's*, one of my favorite childhood restaurants. Over dinner we discussed the way our week had went. Kevin told me that he spent a great deal of time with his mother doing fix-it projects for her. His dad had died a few years earlier, so Kevin tried his best to compensate for his mother's loss whenever he could. I told him that I had been trying to get as many hours as I could at work before heading back to Atlanta. I wanted to ensure I had some money saved for anything my scholarships didn't cover.

Kevin waited until I was almost done with my dessert before he began to tell me what I had been anxious to know all week.

"Aaliyah, I have really enjoyed the time we have spent together. You are an amazing woman."

I blushed, "Thank-you. You are pretty amazing yourself."

He smiled, "Thank-you, but, as much as I don't want to, I have to go back to my practice in Florida." The words crashed down on me as he continued, "I will be leaving on Monday to fly back."

"Are you serious?"

"Yes. Since meeting you, the days seemed to fly by until I realized, I really needed to get back. I actually stayed here longer then I was supposed to so I could be with you."

"Kevin, I'm not ready to say good-bye. Why didn't you tell me sooner?" I pouted, not at all happy with the news. Did he really wait all this time to tell me that?

"Neither am I. I know I should have said something earlier, but I was enjoying being with you and how happy you always seemed with me, that I didn't want to ruin the moments."

"This is important. You are leaving me." I felt the tears coming to my eyes as the realization set in. I knew he was too good to be true. I just knew it.

Kevin moved his chair closer to mine, taking his napkin to wipe my face. "Please don't cry. I didn't mean to make you cry. When are you supposed to go back to Atlanta?"

"I have to be back by mid-August."

"How are you getting there?"

"Why? What does it matter?" I asked getting upset again at the fact he was leaving me. What was the point of asking me about school at a time like this?

"Look. I'll come back. I'll come back up right before you have to go back and drive down with you."

"No. It's ok. I know you have to get back to work. I don't know why I am acting like I didn't know this would happen," I heard myself say, but I was still in disbelief he was leaving me. Twice in one summer, I have been left! This was so unreal. I thought Kevin was different.

"That what would happen?"

"That you would leave me," I cried.

"Liyah, Baby, I am going to come back. I just need to get back to Florida to make sure some things are in order, but I will come back. I promise you this. I am not giving you up that easily."

I looked at him through blurred vision, "You mean it? You'll come back?"

"Yes. I mean it."

"So, technically it's just later for now?" I smiled trying to dry my own tears. I kissed Kevin on his lips and said, "Ok. I believe you." Looking around, I got uncomfortable with the attention we seemed to be getting from the surrounding tables. I asked, "Can we go?"

"Of course." He helped me out my seat after settling our bill so that we could leave. We walked to the curb and Kevin told me to follow him in my car because he wanted to show me something. I had no idea where we were going, but I followed him until we were pulling into the driveway of what seemed to be a two-story mini-mansion. I wondered what could possibly be there that he wanted me to see.

He turned his ignition off. Following suit, I did the same. I didn't get out of my car until he signaled for me to. He waited for me in front of my car and grabbed my hand to lead me to the door. Unlocking the door, Kevin exclaimed, "Welcome to my home in Jersey."

I looked around in awe. The front corridor was an open foyer with a staircase leading to the second level. There was a formal dining room on the right and a plush family room to the left. Behind the staircase there was a bathroom and an entertainment room, which led to a massive kitchen.

Kevin continued his tour, leading me down into his finished basement that looked like he could rent it out as a separate apartment from the house. There were two bedrooms, each with their own bathroom, a full kitchen, living room, entertainment room, and den. I couldn't get over it all, as he led me back upstairs to the second level where the master bedroom and two additional guest bedrooms were. Each guest bedroom had its own bathroom and walk-in closet. The master bedroom also had its own bathroom, complete with a Jacuzzi, deep walk-in closet and separate sitting area. To say the least, Kevin's home was remarkable.

After the tour, I asked, "You live here?"

Kevin answered, "Only when I am in town on vacation or visiting my mother. It makes her feel more comfortable knowing I still have a residence here in Jersey." He motioned for me to sit down with him in the sitting area.

"Wow, this place is really beautiful, Kevin."

"Thank-you. I don't allow too many to know I have a place here. Only those I feel are truly special get to see my home." I blushed. Kevin moved his chair closer to mine. "I am really falling for you, Aaliyah. You are truly a special woman. I want to continue getting to know you even after I have returned to work; even after you have returned back to school."

I couldn't stop blushing as he spoke, and once he was done, all I wanted to do was kiss him. So I did. I pulled him to me and kissed him as my response to all he was saying to me. I kissed him, knocking for him to allow my tongue into his mouth. Obliging, he let my tongue slip in to play with his. As our tongues intertwined, I grew hot and bothered.

With our lips still connected, I maneuvered around and straddled Kevin, placing my hands on his face as I started kissing him more passionately than before. He placed his hands on my back and pulled me into him. I removed my hands from his face and started unbuttoning my blouse. He pulled away ready to say something and I put my finger to his lips. I continued unbuttoning my blouse and let it drop to his lap exposing my silk covered breast.

Kevin ran the pad of his fingers up and down my spine as he took his mouth to my neck. I shivered, letting my mouth drop open so the gasp from the sudden surge of energy could escape. Trying to ensure I covered all grounds, I asked, "Do you have protection?"

"Yes," he answered, momentarily releasing my neck from his lips.

"Where?" I panted.

"Nightstand."

"Okay." Our heavy petting grew in intensity as we tugged various articles of clothing from each other's bodies. Kevin picked me up and carried me to his king size bed as he kissed me passionately. Releasing me from his grasp, I laid there on my back, wiggled out of my pants. I left my panties on for him to take off, thinking it made me look sexier. I wanted him, but I didn't want to seem overly eager.

He stood over me taking the rest of his clothing off, before coming to me and licking my belly button. I felt myself moisten from the caress of his tongue on my body. As if that wasn't enough, he then dragged his tongue up the center of my chest, pushed my breast together and started sucking on both my nipples at the same time. My breath caught in my throat as I felt one of his fingers touch my clit and begin caressing it. I squirmed under the pleasurable pressure, enjoying the moment. Using that same finger, he pushed inside me and I rose up from the unexpected sensation.

Kevin moved his finger in and out of me, working me over, still keeping his mouth on my nipples; simultaneously stimulating me. I wanted more. I wanted him. I wanted to feel him inside me filling me up. It had been so long and I didn't want to wait anymore. I whispered, "Please. I want you now."

Kevin understood and pulled back. He pulled a condom out of the nightstand, ripped the wrapper open with his teeth and put the condom on. I took my panties off not caring about him taking them off anymore. Any second longer and I knew I would explode.

I had started playing with my clit by the time he finished and spread my legs apart. Kevin held my legs up and wrapped his hands up under my butt pulling me closer to the edge up the bed. He squatted and I felt the tip of his penis begin to enter into my walls. He slowly pushed in and pulled out so that I could feel every inch of him. I felt the liquid exiting my body with each penetrating stroke as he traveled deeper and deeper into me. I couldn't stop the moans from escaping my lips.

Taking his time, Kevin just maintained his pace even though I tried to speed it up. "Be easy, Baby, and take this dick," he said as he kept stroking me.

Feeling my orgasm, I said, "Baby, I'm about to cum."

"Don't Baby. Keep taking it. Don't cum."

"Oh my god, I am going to cum. I can't …" My orgasm cut me off and rolled out my body so violently that I shook. For months I had been holding that all inside, but I wasn't done. I was a far cry from done. That was only my first and I had so much more in me.

Turning over, I put my butt in the air and told Kevin, "I'm not done yet, Baby." Spreading my lips, I demanded, "Take this pussy," and that's exactly what he did.

jess

Chapter 9

I looked to my left and saw Mieko sleeping peacefully in my arms. Like any other time before now that we've ended up this way, she came into town unannounced. Even so, this time seemed different. Last night it was storming, so I decided to stay in reading. While reading in my study, my doorbell rang. Putting my book down in a way to keep my page, I went to the door. There she stood, soaked head to toe from the rain. Her make-up was running and her expensive garments looked like rags draped around her body. Her appearance and lack of concern for it let me know that something was not right.

"Mi-Mi, what's wrong?" I asked as she stood in the corridor of the house. Before she could respond I had concluded that I needed to get her out of the wet clothes she was in before she got sick. I told her, "Hold on. Let me get something," and ran to the basement to get a towel out the dryer. When I got back upstairs, Mieko was still standing there in the same spot, stuck somewhere far from where we were standing. I called her name, "Mieko," but she didn't respond.

I walked up to her and started removing the wet clothing from her body, leaving them on the floor to be cleaned up later. She didn't stop me, nor did she try to help me. She just looked so distant. I wrapped the terry cloth towel around her body, then picked her up and carried her to my bedroom to lay her down. Mieko still hadn't said a word to me. Making sure she was comfortable, I sat there until she eventually fell asleep. I didn't know what to think about how she was acting but figured that once she felt a little more at ease, or after sleeping a little, she would talk to me.

As not to disturb her sleep, I left the room and went back to the study to continue with my book. I saw the words on the page, but couldn't get past the first sentence. Mieko really had me worried about her and what was going on. Seeing her like that made me feel really uneasy. I went to the kitchen to fix myself something to drink. I decided to go simple and just grabbed a wine cooler from the fridge. Listening, I thought I heard her stir, but when I didn't hear anything else I went back into the study to attempt clearing my thoughts. At some point, my thoughts put me to sleep.

I woke up to the weight of someone lying in my lap. Mieko was curled up on my legs in my bathrobe smelling like a fresh shower. I wiped my eyes and asked, "Everything okay?" She looked up at me like she wanted to cry. "C'mon Mi-Mi. Tell me what's going on."

"I don't feel like talking about it."

"Are you sure? You have me worried."

"Not right now, Jess, please?" she asked in a weak whisper.

"Okay. Okay," I agreed as she sunk herself deeper into me. I held her in my arms, rocking back and forth a little bit. I whispered once more, "Okay," and kissed her on her forehead. Again, I fell asleep.

Mieko woke me up, pulling my hand in hers. I was sleepwalking behind her as she led the way up to my bedroom. She pushed me down on the edge of the bed and stood in front of

me. I still wasn't completely focused but was well aware of the
robe falling to the floor to reveal the perfect naked body that was
hiding beneath it. She walked closer to me and I could smell her
scent teasing my senses. Shaved clean, Mieko looked so inviting
and irresistible.

Closing the gap between us, I drew her into me and placed my
tongue in her slit, making my way to her clit. Now fully awake,
and aroused, I applied pressure from my tongue to her clit causing
her to push forward into me to keep her balance. I moved one of
my hands to her pussy to spread her lips apart so that I could wrap
my mouth completely around her clit. Little moans started to
escape from her lips while I sucked on her hard and deliberately.

Pulling her along with me, I began lying on my back, never
removing my mouth from giving Mieko pleasure. Once I was on
my back, she began riding my tongue back and forth, and up and
down. I held her waist so that she didn't get too far away from me,
constantly stroking her with my tongue.

She seemed to be nearing her first orgasm, so I took one finger
and stuck it in her ass. She moaned out loud as her cum started to
flow over my tongue. I kept licking and sucking until she finally
rolled off my face.

While Mieko was recovering, I put on my strap I kept only for
her. I made my way back to her and climbed on top of her. Our
lips met and our tongues began dancing erotically with one
another. Still kissing, she grabbed my extension and guided me
into the opening between her thighs. As I sunk into opening deeper
and felt the pressure against my own clit, I gasped and she moaned.
The feeling was intense. Kissing her had always felt like bliss and
made my clit become engorged.

Getting a grip, I started motioning in and out slowly and
directly. I pulled out all the way to the tip then, with a steady pace,
pushed all the way back inside of her. Each stroke made Mieko
more vocal. She begged for me to fuck her, telling me that her
pussy was mine and no one else's. I sped up my tempo, did as she
asked me and fucked her into a frenzy. She started rocking into me
to heighten the impact until her muscles started tightening up

causing her to release again.

Mieko slowly turned over on her stomach, still recouping from her last orgasm. She got on her knees putting her backside in my face. This was her way of telling me it was my turn to cum. I obliged her, spreading her cheeks and guiding myself deep into her again. First I took it slow, leaving trails of kisses down her back. She attempted to force herself back on me, but I wouldn't let her change the pace. I made her slow down, teasing her, not allowing her to climax again before I did. Through her moans, she begged me to go faster. I just kept the same rhythm until I was sure she couldn't take it anymore.

Grabbing hold of her waist I sped up my stroke, slapping her every now and then, causing her behind to jerk back and forth. When I felt my orgasm coming, I gripped her waist driving her back on me harder and harder until my moans and her screams rang in a chorus of combined release.

After I regained my composure, I took my strap off and dropped it on the floor. Mieko crawled her way toward me and laid on my chest. She flicked her tongue over my nipple causing it to harden up. I warned her, "You better stop." She looked up at me as if to challenge me and took my whole nipple into her mouth and gently bit down on it. A moan escaped my lips. "All right, I got something for that."

I laid her on her back and climbed on top of her placing our clits together. I lifted one of her legs up over my shoulder and began grinding into her. She reached for me as tears filled her eyes and illicit remarks left her mouth. I kept going, only stopping after we both came again and collapsed to the bed.

Mieko made it as far as my arm before she was fast asleep. Everything was like old times. I felt myself relax and then slip off to join her in dreamland.

I woke to Mieko's kisses upon my lips. I feigned sleeping so that she would keep trying to kiss me awake. "I know you're awake, so stop pretending to be sleep," she said realizing what I was up to.

I laughed, "How'd you know?"

"You started breathing heavier," she said hitting me with a pillow.

Pushing the pillow out the way I told her, "Come here so I can give you a real kiss then." She crawled over to me and gave me her tongue. We sat there kissing for a minute, I not breaking away until she did.

"All right, Jess. I haven't brushed my teeth yet."

"That's never bothered me."

"Yeah, but you know how I am," she frowned at me.

"Yes, I know," I smiled at her.

"Let me go brush my teeth. I'm using your toothbrush."

"Are you asking or telling me?"

She thought about it for a second before jumping up, tossing a pillow at me again, and running to the bathroom yelling back, "Telling you!" I just laughed at her.

I put the pillow she threw at me behind my back and leaned against the headboard. Flashes of the night before came to my mind. I yelled to Mieko, "What was wrong last night?"

She walked out of the bathroom and asked, "What'd you say? I didn't hear you."

"I asked what was wrong last night."

"I don't want to talk about it." Before I could respond, she went back into the bathroom.

I got up from the bed and walked into the bathroom. "I've never seen you like that. You were soaked and looking spaced out. Tell me what happened Mi-Mi."

"I told you it was nothing. Leave it alone Jess. Do you still have that box of clothes I conveniently neglected to pick up?" she smiled. I could tell she was trying to change the subject.

"Yeah, in the back of the closet."

She laughed, "Oh, so you hide me in the back for when you have your little girlfriends over, huh?" She walked past me to get to the closet, pulling out a pair of jeans, a T-shirt and some running shoes. I stood there and watched her as she got dressed.

Still concerned, I asked, "Mieko, why don't you want to tell me?"

"Because it's none of your fucking business, Jess!" she snapped, visibly annoyed and frustrated with my questions. "Damn! I'm not your fucking girlfriend anymore. What happens to me doesn't concern you. It's not your job to protect me. All I wanted from you was a good fuck to get my mind off some things, and you gave me just that last night. That is all that you need to worry about doing for me anymore. Just give me a good nut and then go about your business. That's it. So just leave it the fuck alone, ok? It's none of your business and not your problem. Damn." She got up and left the room.

I was stunned and couldn't move. Moments later I heard the front door open and then slam close announcing Mieko's departure. I sat on the bed and tried not to let the tears fall. How could I love a woman that was so damn cold towards me? I swear I had the worst luck with women. Maybe I am supposed to be alone because I couldn't seem to get it right.

It all was too much. I needed to talk to someone. The only person that could possibly understand me was my mother, so I called her. She answered on the second ring, "Hello?"

"Hey, Mom. Are you busy?"

"I was about to run out to the store to get my medicine. Why? Are you okay Jesstina?" she asked sounding concerned.

I couldn't hold back the tears anymore, "Mom, why do these women play with me like this? I try to be the woman you raised me to be and they just use and abuse me? What did I do to deserve all of that?"

"Oh Baby. What happened?"

"I care too much. That is what always happens, I start caring too much. In the end, they always have the upper hand with me because I never can completely let go."

My mother got silent for a moment. Then she asked, "Is Mieko back?"

It's scary how your mother can always see through the bull and pinpoint what's really wrong. "Yeah. She just stormed out of here telling me that she wasn't my concern anymore."

"She's right, Baby. She isn't."

"But Mom, you should have seen her last night! She looked a complete mess and distant like she wasn't even here."

"I know it is hard to do, but you have to let her go Baby. She is continuing to live her life, right? Then you should be doing the same. Besides, my Jesstina is too cute." I could hear her smiling as she continued, "If you were a few years older and not my daughter, I would try ya." She started laughing.

"Eww, Mom! That's not even cool or funny!" She just laughed harder at my reaction.

"What? Your Momma hasn't been a square all her life," she continued laughing.

"Mom, please. I don't want to know," I said starting to laugh with her. She had an infectious laugh that would not be ignored, and she knew it.

"That's what I like to hear, my Baby laughing." I smiled at the phone. "All right Baby, I really gotta go get my meds. Are you all right now?"

"Yeah."

"Good. I will call you when I get back to the house. Okay?"

"All right, Mom. Go ahead and go run your errands."

"Okay, Baby. I love you."

"I love you, too, Mom."

"Keep your chin up, Baby."

"I will Mom." The line died on the other end and despite the laughter my mother and I shared, I suddenly became depressed again. I thought about calling Ty, but I already knew what he would say. He'd tell me to stop letting her back in like I do and to move on. Then he'd probably suggest I go out with some random female I haven't spoken to in forever. That's not exactly what I needed right now, another woman in my life.

Wiping my face, I decided to get up and clean up the mess from the night before. I changed the linen on my bed and took the old sheets to the laundry room. Walking past the corridor I noticed that Mieko's pile of clothing I left at the door were gone. I shook my head and continued with my cleaning regime.

I swept and mopped the corridor, and then wiped down everything in my bedroom bathroom. I tossed my toothbrush in the garbage and replaced it with a new one. Once I was finished, I got in the shower and tried to wash the memory of her touches off my skin.

I felt a little better after my shower, but Mieko was still on my mind. I needed to check on her. As much as I knew I needed to let it be, something was wrong. I needed to be sure she was okay. I found my cell phone and dialed her number. Her phone just rang until the voicemail picked up. I hung up, waited a few minutes, and then called back. The line went straight to voicemail. I cursed under my breath and left Mieko a message apologizing about the morning and telling her that I hoped she was okay. Before ending the message, I asked her to call me when she got a chance. After I hung up, I felt stupid for calling her and wished I hadn't left a message.

My phone started ringing and I picked it up without looking at the caller ID thinking it was her, "Hello?"

"Hello? Hi. May I speak to," the person paused, "Jess?"

My heart dropped when I realized it wasn't Mieko. In a somber tone, I answered, "This is her. May I ask who's calling?"

"Aaliyah."

"Aaliyah?" I asked.

"Yeah. I wanted to call and apologize to you for what happened that night," she paused again, "the night I kissed you." I could hear her but was off somewhere else wishing that she was someone else.

Nonchalantly I said, "Oh. You're cool. I figured curiosity got the best of you."

"Yeah, maybe."

"No worries," I told her, not really focused on what she was saying.

I guess she picked up on it and asked me, "Hey? Are you okay?"

"Yeah. I'm good."

"Are you sure? You sound kind of down."

"I'll be okay. Thanks for your concern, though."

"Well, if you do need to talk, I've got time. I've been told that I am a great listener." I heard what sounded like she smirked on the phone. I just brushed it off.

"You don't even know me."

"Doesn't matter. You seem like you could use a friend, and, well, I figure I owe you one after what I did." I could hear a smile in her voice, and even I smiled with the memory of that night in my car creeping into my thoughts.

"You know, I could really use an opinion that is unbiased."

"I am all ears." Taking the opportunity, I told Aaliyah about what happened with Mieko and further explained the up and down relationship we have had over the years. I mentioned Tina and my relationship, but she asked me not to tell her about that because she wouldn't be able to be impartial. Understanding, I told her about Jordyn and the current fling I was having with her. It felt so good to just talk freely for the most part without the grunts and groans of those tired of hearing the same old cries from me.

Aaliyah listened attentively, asking questions or asking for clarification every now and then if she didn't quite understand something. She made me feel so comfortable that before I knew it, it was near midnight. We had been talking for hours. Noticing the time, I didn't want it to end but knew I needed to let her go. It had been a long time since I was able to converse the way we did.

I asked Aaliyah if it would be possible for us to talk again because I really enjoyed our conversation. She asked if her number came up on my caller ID. When I told her yes, she said to save it and use it whenever I needed an unbiased ear. As long as I didn't talk about Tina, she would listen. I agreed and thanked her for taking the time out of her evening to talk to me. She said it was nothing and that she owed me. Disagreeing, I told her she didn't owe me anything. We eventually said our goodbyes and hung up.

I rested in my bed and smiled becoming completely oblivious to Mieko's muffled ring tone that had begun to play at my side.

aaliyah

Chapter 10

As crazy as it sounded, Jess turned into a great friend after I called her to apologize about the night I kissed her. I was finally in a place where I could accept the kiss for what it was; my need to satisfy some form of curiosity towards the same sex. At the end of the day I'm not attracted to females, and that is that. I just wanted to know what it was like and now I was over it. As far as I was concerned, Kevin was the wonderful being in my life, and as long as I had him I didn't need anyone else.

The morning after we consummated our relationship, Kevin got up and made me breakfast in bed. I had never had anyone do that before, and it was an amazing feeling, and spread. He had prepared scrambled eggs with cheese, French toast with honey butter, crisp turkey bacon, buttered grits, a bowl of fruit, coffee and tea because he wasn't sure which I preferred, and fresh squeezed orange juice. They say the way to a man's heart is through his stomach, but I felt like the exception as I fell for him all over again.

We talked about our plans for the future as I ate my breakfast. In between our dialogue, he would feed me fruit and I would suck the juices from his fingers. Before long, we both were aroused and we went at it again, ending up in the shower together to clean ourselves off. I didn't want the day to end, but I knew Kevin had a flight later that evening and I had to go to work.

For a while we just laid in the living room listening to music from the surround sound system he had hooked up. I asked, "Will you call me when you get there?"

"Yes, I will."

"And you promise to come back?"

Kevin smiled at me and kissed my forehead, "Yes, I promise to come back."

"You better, Kevin. I'm not playing," I told him, catching a slight attitude.

"Baby, I told you, I'm not letting go of you that easily. As a matter of fact, I have something for you." He started moving to get up and I had to sit up so he could go retrieve whatever he had for me. Kevin returned with a small white box from Kay's Jewelry store. Handing it to me, he said, "Open it," with a smile.

Slightly apprehensive, I asked, "What is this?"

"Just open it."

With a bit of uncertainty, I opened it and could feel the tears start running down my face. Wiping my eyes, I told him, "Kevin, it's so beautiful." Before me in the box was a sterling silver chain with a heart-shaped pink pendant connected to it.

Kevin took the chain out of the box to put it on me. "I knew you would like it. I got it in sterling silver because I remembered you're allergic to gold."

"Like it? I love it! And I can't believe you remembered that!" I exclaimed before wrapping my arms around him and placing a million kisses on his face and lips. He laughed and just said he was glad that I loved it. I snuggled back into his arms as the music continued playing realizing just how blessed I was. Before I knew it, it was time for me to go so I could get home, change clothes and head to work. We kissed our good-byes and I cried all the way home, both happy and sad tears.

Although we spoke often, after Kevin left for Florida, I felt a void that use to be filled by his presence. It was actually our solid relationship that gave me the strength I needed to call Jess and apologize to her in the first place. I apologized for kissing her that night and ensured she knew not to misunderstand it because I didn't get down like that. Turned out that she was completely understanding. Honestly, I learned she was a great person overall. Realizing that, I felt silly for the way I had acted toward her the night everything happened.

We developed an unexpected friendship. I guess it was convenient for us both. She needed someone she could talk to who wouldn't judge her, and as long as she stayed away from any topics about Tina, I could do that for her. I, on the other hand, needed someone to occupy my time since Kevin had to leave. Tina had been so wrapped up in this new girl she had been dating that she rarely had time to kick it with me, so I definitely welcomed Jess's company.

In the beginning I was a little nervous, thinking that Jess might try to come on to me, but she never did. Anytime we were together, she was totally respectful. My comfort level was completely up with her, for the most part. Sometimes people did stare at us, making me a little uncomfortable. She would notice and offer for us to leave and go our separate ways until the next time. Although I knew that I shouldn't worry about what other people thought because I knew myself, I was still always thankful that she would end our get together before I did or said something offensive. To be honest, I'm not even sure why it bothered me when it never did anytime I went out with Tina and Shawn, but I figured it wasn't worth giving that much thought to.

Since Jess lived in New York, I would sometimes meet her at 42nd Street in Manhattan and we would go check out a movie. Other times she'd come down to my job and we would get something to eat and just talk. I told her about Xavier and how he left me at the beginning of the summer, only to try and come crawling back later. I even told her about Kevin and how he made me feel. She seemed genuine in her expression of happiness for my happiness.

As the time drew near for me to go back to school, I quit my job. Since the summer was pretty much over for me and I would be heading back to campus soon, there was no sense in me prolonging the inevitable. Thinking about going back to school excited me because it meant Kevin would be back soon to take the long ride with me. I hadn't seen him since he left and was missing him like crazy.

With my job laid to rest and opening up my schedule, Jess and I decided to have a movie night at her place. I had never actually been to her place but knew I had nothing to worry about.

Jess picked me up at the Port Authority on 42nd Street. When I got into her car she asked me, "Is take out good? I know a nice little restaurant in China Town."

I smiled, "That sounds great. I could go for some Chinese." We drove into China Town and were lucky enough to get a parking space only a block from the restaurant. We walked and talked about the movies that Jess got for our movie night. She chose *Under the Cherry Moon,* a movie I had never seen but she swore it was good simply because Prince was in it, and *This Christmas* with Chris Brown, which was one of my favorite movies regardless to the season.

The place wasn't too crowded, so we were able to get our order within fifteen minutes. As we were walking down the street headed back to the car, someone started calling Jess's name. We both stopped and turned around. Walking up to us was this beautiful woman who had to be a model. Her hair was in a simple ponytail, but still somehow looked high fashion. She had skinny jeans on with black furry boots and a red cashmere sweater with the sleeves pushed up to her forearms. Either way, she looked like someone you'd see in a magazine, albeit a little overdressed for summer in New York.

"Who is *she* Jess?" she asked, her words filled with venom and disdain. I took that as my cue. I didn't like drama, so I stepped to the side to give Jess some room to handle her business.

Jess responded, "What do you want?"

"I want to know who the fuck she is, Jesstina."

"What does *who* she is matter to you? Aren't you the one who said you're not my concern? If you're not mine, I know for damn sure I'm not yours, so what does it matter?"

Entirely disregarding Jess, she kept inquiring about me. "Is she why you haven't been answering my calls?"

"That's none of your business."

"It is my fucking business!" she screamed at Jess.

"Look Mieko, you said I wasn't good for anything but to give you a nut. I didn't want that for us, you did." I heard the name and it suddenly clicked who she was. She was the girl that was everything Jess ever wanted in a female, but who's career meant more to her than their relationship. I knew Jess was weak for her and would eventually give in to her if I didn't intervene. Just listening, I could tell her strong resolve was crumbling.

I walked up next to Jess and wrapped my arm around her arm. Trying to pull her away from arguing with her ex, I told her, "Honey, we have to go. Remember, we have plans tonight." I turned to her ex and smiled, "It's movie night." If looks could kill, the one Jess's ex shot me would have put me six feet under.

Jess looked at me a little confused and I just smiled harder at her, hoping she'd pick up on what I was trying to do. Finally catching on, she turned back to her ex and told her, "I have to go."

"What? Is this your bitch, now? I don't give a damn about her or some damn movie night!" she screamed and without warning, I gripped Jess's arm. "I told you I'm sorry. What more do you want from me, Jess?"

I knew what I wanted. Thinking to myself, *I've got your bitch*, I was ready to go knock this girl upside her head. Fortunately, and unfortunately, Jess sensed it and pulled me in closer. It was as if she read my thoughts and was trying to tell me not to do it. "For one, I am not a bitch. If you want to see a bitch, you might want to take a look in the mirror. For two, do not be mad that you couldn't see Jess for the wonderful woman she is. Your loss is my gain. Deal with it," I snapped back.

She moved like she wanted to attack me, but before she could say anything, Jess said, "Bye Mieko," grabbed my hand and walked away. Behind us we could hear her cursing and calling for Jess to turn around and acknowledge her. We just kept it moving in the direction of the car, praying she didn't follow. As soon as we got to the car, we got in and were on our way.

Once we were on the road, Jess turned to me and said, "You didn't have to do that, but I appreciate you doing it." She refocused on the road and continued, "As I am sure you have guessed, that was Mieko, aka Mi-Mi, the ex I had told you about who stormed out my home a couple of weeks ago. She hasn't called in a few days, but I stopped answering her calls after that night we talked. I knew I needed to let her go, but seeing her tonight caught me off guard. If you weren't here, I might've given in to her."

"I noticed. When you said her name, I figured I better step in and help you out, especially since she seemed persistent in getting what she wanted."

"Yeah, she is like that sometimes. She is a woman who is used to getting her way. Hell, she is especially used to getting her way with me."

I laughed, "She didn't tonight!"

Jess started to smile, "Yeah, I guess you're right, huh?"

"Indeed I am," I smiled with her as we continued the ride to her place.

We pulled into her garage and I noticed Jess had a motorcycle. It was covered, so I couldn't see what kind it was. To me bikes were sexy, but I could never see myself on one. Honestly, I never really knew any females who rode, so seeing the bike was a bit of a surprise. You only really see that kind of stuff on TV. I asked, "You ride?"

She looked at me perplexed, but then must've realized I was talking about her bike. "Yeah. Do you?"

"Oh, no, no, no. I like looking at them, but I can't see myself on one. Too scared," I half smiled.

"It's not really that bad."

"I'll have to take your word for it."

"It really isn't. Want me to take you around the block real quick?"

"No, that's not necessary." I could feel the butterflies starting to flutter around in my stomach as my nerves started to get the best of me.

"C'mon. I'll take care of you," Jess said pulling the cover off her bike revealing a Kawasaki Ninja. With the flawless paint job and everything looking shined to a "T," it was definitely a sweet ride. To me, more so than the Ashton Martin she drove around in. Just looking at the two alone, I was amazed that someone as young as us could be as established as she was. She handed me a helmet. "Safety first."

Somewhat reluctantly, I started putting the helmet on as my nerves shot through the roof. "I'm not sure about this, Jess."

"Don't worry. I won't even go fast. It will be like riding a bicycle." She revved up the engine and motioned for me to get on with her. "Lean into my back and wrap your arms around my waist." Thinking I was doing exactly what she said to do, I gripped her knocking the wind out of her. "Hold on! Not that tight," she gasped.

I loosened my grip slightly, "Oops, my bad."

"It's okay. Hold me just like that. I've got you," she smiled. In my mind, I prayed she really did.

Jess slowly rolled out her garage onto the street. Once she hit the pavement, she picked up speed and we floated around the block. As soon as we started it seemed over. I got a complete rush from it. It wasn't nearly as bad as I thought it would be. When it was all over, I wanted to do it again. She took me around one more time before parking the bike back in her garage. I admitted, "That wasn't as bad as I thought it would be."

"I told you I had you," Jess smiled at me. Out of nowhere, I felt myself blush. I hadn't blushed like that in front of her since the night we kissed. She didn't need to see that, so I tried to cover my face.

"So," I said, preparing to change the subject, "You want to get this movie night started?"

"Yeah," she replied, "because I really want you to see *Under the Cherry Moon*. It's a classic." I followed her into her home as the garage door closed securing her bike, car and us behind it.

Walking into her home was anything short of magnificent. We walked into a massive kitchen with the fixings any master chef would've been pleased with. I commented, "Wow! This kitchen is huge!"

"Yeah. I can throw down when I want to," Jess replied confidently.

"Oh, you can cook?"

"I can do a little somethin' somethin' every now and then," she smiled before asking, "would you like to go on the grand tour?"

"Sure!" I followed her out of the kitchen. She led me upstairs and worked her way back down. On the top floor was a spare bedroom with a separate bathroom. On the same level were the master bedroom and private bath. On the main floor, the front door opened into a hallway that led to the living area with the staircase leading to the second floor. The kitchen was also on the main level, as well as a beautiful study full of books. "Wow! So many books," I exclaimed.

"Shhh. Don't tell anybody but I am an avid reader," Jess whispered, then broke into a giggle.

I smiled, continuing to look through her collection. "Wow. You have a lot of classics. Do you have *The Song of Solomon*?" I noticed everything in her home had a way of making me say *wow*.

"Yes. Have you ever read it?"

"No. I have been meaning to, but I keep putting it off. I hear it is a really good read."

"It is. If you want, you can borrow my copy."

"That's okay. There is no way I would finish it before I had to go."

"That may be true, but the offer still stands. Just let me know. You can always mail it back to me if you don't finish it before you leave."

We left her mini library and finished the tour off in her finished basement that had been turned into the ultimate entertainment room. There was a large flat screen HDTV mounted on the wall, comfortable black leather seating all around, and a few end tables to set drinks and popcorn on. The place was set up with surround sound and multiple electronics to add to the entertainment value, including a Blue Ray Disc player and a Nintendo Switch game console. It was definitely the spot to be in.

Jess started setting up the movie and asked me which I wanted to see first. I, of course, told her *This Christmas*. She set the system up so we could watch the movie. Before pressing play, she ran to the kitchen to make some popcorn and brought back two bottles of water. We got comfortable on one of the long sofas, sitting on opposite ends with the bowl of popcorn in between us, and watched the movie.

By the end of it I was still bouncing around. It was a little late to still be in New York, but I was nowhere near tired. Jess asked if I wanted to call it a night, but I told her to go ahead and put the next movie in because I knew she really wanted me to see it. While she was doing that, I took a moment to call Kevin and check on him. I told him I was still at Jess's and that we were about to watch *Under the Cherry Moon*. Through the phone, I could feel him smiling as he reminisced about his first time seeing it and *Purple Rain*. Changing the subject because it was making me feel extra young, I asked him if he would be up that coming weekend to go with me back to Atlanta. He promised he would and that I had nothing to worry about. From the corner of my eye, I could see Jess patiently waiting, so I told Kevin I loved him and that I would talk to him later. He said the same and we got off the phone.

"I apologize about that," I smiled at Jess.

"It's cool. Is everything good?"

"Yes."

"Are you ready for the ultimate viewing pleasure?" she asked grinning like a big kid.

I laughed at her, "If you say so."

"I know so!" she declared as she started the movie up.

When the credits were finally rolling, I didn't know whether to be deeply amused or appalled. I enjoyed the movie, but the storyline was somewhat out there and the acting was just wrong, but Jess was all into it. She knew the lines as if she had written them herself. I had to muffle a few of my laughs when she would really get into it. The best part of the movie was actually watching her. It was really cute.

As Jess cleaned up, I looked at the time on my cell phone. It was well after midnight and we had a long trip ahead of us. Her trip was even longer because she had to turn around and come back home. I walked up the steps to the kitchen where she was cleaning the few dishes we had created.

"Hey, Jess. It's a little later than I thought it was."

She placed the last dish in the drainer and wiped her hands on a nearby dish towel. "Aww, you're ready to go?" Jess pouted. It was so adorable and I felt myself smiling harder than I should have.

For the first time all night, I really took a look at Jess. She had a pair of washed out jeans, another rocker t-shirt with the sleeves rolled up on her shoulders and white socks on. Her hair was in corn rolls that fell roughly to her shoulders, a style I would have never imagined on her, but that I definitely thought looked good on her. All her piercings were in and she only wore a sports watch on her left wrist. At about 5'7" with beautiful hazel eyes, she was gorgeous. I see why Tina fell for her. I'm not even into girls, but I couldn't deny her attractiveness. I looked at the tattoo on her right arm and noticed a name in script.

Trying to snap back, I finally replied, "Well, it is late," but my focus was still on her arm. I started to imagine that it was one of her exes' names. It was probably the one from earlier at the Chinese restaurant. Still I asked, "What does your arm say?"

Jess walked closer to me and I felt my temperature rising. Here we go again. This was the way I felt the night I kissed her. It wasn't a good sign, and though I knew I needed to just get us on the road, I didn't. I touched her arm and read *Mita*. "It's what they call mi madre. She's my world. That is why I have it wrapped around a globe like the Universal Studio's logo."

"Is she dead?"

"No!" she exclaimed, "No."

I felt bad that I had even asked. "I'm sorry. I didn't ..."

Jess cut me off, "No. You're okay. I just don't want to think about something like that. I don't know what I would do if I didn't have my mother around. She is who keeps me grounded." I smiled at her feeling the pride and love she had for her mother. It was sweet and an attractive quality. The way a man treats his mother is a good sign of how he'll treat his woman. But Jess wasn't a man. Even considering thoughts like that was bad and I knew it. It was more than evident I felt fascinated by her. That said, it didn't explain why I was steadily moving closer to her.

Before my nerves got the best of me and logic kicked in, I kissed her. I kissed Jess again ignoring the alarm going off in my head and the little voice screaming, *What are you doing?!?*

Jess pulled away, "Whoa! Aaliyah, I don't think you want to do that." She moved away from me to the fridge and took out a bottle of water. Twisting the cap, she placed the bottle to her lips. I knew she was right. I really needed to get a hold of myself, but as I watched her drink, I kept wanting to be the bottle. This was nuts. Regret was going to set in, in the morning. I knew this, but I wasn't worried about it. Not at that moment, anyway. All I knew was my current want, and it was her. I'd deal with the consequences later.

I made my way over to her and removed the bottle from her lips. Placing the bottle on the counter, I kissed her. Jess tried to release herself from me but when she realized I wasn't letting go, she gave in and wrapped her arms around me. As she reciprocated I felt myself getting excited. The little voices in my head were still screaming, but another voice overpowered them telling me to go for it, but what was I going for? Beyond kissing, I didn't know what else to do.

This is a bad idea. This is a bad idea. I kept telling myself that, though other thoughts prevailed. *But oh my god, I am wet. What the hell? Why am I so turned on? Why won't I stop?* Suddenly I felt Jess's hand in my pants and her finger enter my pussy walls. My knees buckled under me as the sensation made me weak. I released her lips as I gasped and my eyes rolled to the back of my head. I grabbed her wrist, guiding her finger as deep inside of me as possible. She pulled her hand out my pants and licked her finger. I could feel the muscles of my walls gripping and then relaxing, missing the pressure her finger had been providing.

Jess instructed me to take my pants off and I did it without hesitation. She pulled my panties down and lifted me up on the counter of the island. Squatting down eye level with my pussy, she pulled me to the edge before sticking two fingers inside me. I moaned as she fucked me with her fingers. To give me more balance, I laid my hands at my sides flat on the counter and started helping Jess dig into me. I was so far gone. "Oh my god! I am about to cum!" I exclaimed. She didn't stop. Instead, she added another finger and started pounding into me even faster. There was nothing I could do to stop the tidal wave that released from my body onto the counter and her hand.

Little trimmers rolled through my body while I tried to catch my breath. My pussy was still vibrating from the release it just had. I kept whispering, "Oh my god, oh my god," looking at Jess looking at me. Her eyes seemed to turn from hazel to green with lust.

"May I taste you?" she asked. Before I could even respond, she was in my pussy deep with her tongue. She paid such close attention to my clit. That was one of my most sensitive spots and she was yielding no mercy to it. I felt like I was going to combust all over the place the way she worked her tongue in me and around my clit. Without thinking, I grabbed her head pushing her deeper into my pussy.

Once it started getting too much, I tried to pull away, moving further back on the island. Never missing a beat, she just followed me. When she felt I had gotten too far and was making her strain her tongue too much to reach me, she would forcefully pull me into her tongue sending a chill all the way up my spine. I swear she was sucking and licking my pussy for a good hour, causing me to have multiple orgasms on top of multiple orgasms. That's the best way I could describe how she was making me feel. I felt myself grabbing my nipples with one hand, squeezing tightly and then letting go, intensifying some of my orgasms even more.

I wanted to feel Jess's mouth on every part of my body, but at the same time, I didn't want her to move from where she was. Finally, I just couldn't take it anymore and I came for the last time. She didn't waste a drop catching it all on her tongue as I watched. I fell back completely spent.

Half dazed, I could feel myself being lifted and carried somewhere. I was laid in a soft place where I drifted off to sleep. When I woke, I was laying in Jess's arms as she slept. I silently cursed myself asking what in the world did I just do and how I ended up with Jess like this. I needed to leave but didn't know where I was or how I got back to the familiar. She must've sensed I was awake. Opening her eyes she smiled at me. I frowned. "Jess, I need to get home."

Taking in the look on my face, she said, "No problem," and started getting up from where she was laying. I found my clothes on the nightstand next to me folded neatly. We got ready in silence. Actually, the rest of the time we were together we were in complete silence. I didn't know what to say. I mean, I shouldn't have done any of that, but I didn't regret it either. I was so confused.

Jess dropped me off at home and I kissed her on the cheek like I always did. I got out of the car asking her to call when she got home. She said she would and waited until I got in the house before pulling off. I went to my room, closed the door behind me and laid spread eagle across my bed wondering what the hell I just did and what would happen next.

jess

Chapter 11

We didn't say anything the whole time I was taking Aaliyah back to Jersey. What do you say after something like that happens? She had only come over to watch a few movies and we ended up going there. I knew deep down I wanted her in that way, but I also knew she wasn't into females. I knew she didn't get down like that. Yet and still, I kept going. I should've had more self-control. I should've just taken her home after that first kiss. But I didn't and I wasn't sure what to say to her or what it all meant for us both. That's all I could think the whole drive to Jersey. What happens now?

When I dropped her off, she kissed me on the cheek like nothing even happened. Aaliyah played her part, asking me to call like any other time I had dropped her off home or at her car. A part of me was crushed and wanted more than that. Like a kiss to let me know she felt something for me too, and this wasn't all a mistake. The logical part of me, though, said to take it for what it was because she wasn't lesbian or even bi. Hell, she has a man, a man she loves. It was at best an accident that would never happen again. She was leaving for school soon and going back to Atlanta. What did I look like chasing a taken straight female in Atlanta? It was just more experimentation. Damn, I should have stopped it.

The entire ride home my thoughts raced back and forth about what happened between Aaliyah and I. It felt so good and so right, but I knew it was so wrong, so I beat myself up all the way home. Once I got in, I looked at the kitchen island and saw flashbacks of just hours ago when she was there moaning in my ear. I could still smell her scent and taste her on my lips. I needed a shower.

Heading to my bathroom, I pulled my clothes off, dropping them as I moved along. I turned the water on and got in, letting the streams beat down on my head. My thoughts stayed focused on Aaliyah. Kissing was one thing, but tasting her, knowing how she sounded when she was climaxing, all of it was too much. I got out the shower, and without drying off, climbed in bed. I buried my nose deep into the pillow she had been laying on, inhaling her lingering scent. She continued to haunt my mind until I eventually fell asleep, opting not to call her like I promised to. I still didn't know what to say or how to act anyway.

When I woke, I half expected a call from Aaliyah asking whether or not I had made it safe, but I only had voicemails from Ty, Jordyn, and Mieko. Ty was calling to tell me about everything that I had missed by not going out the last couple of nights. Seems like a few people you'd never imagine to be an item were, while others had public breakups of which some led to fist fights and the cops being called. I was glad I wasn't around for all of that, though I still seemed unable to avoid potential drama. Since I would see Ty at work, I didn't call him back. Jordyn called to say she'd be coming to the store to return my book and to ask me something. She said she preferred to ask me in person and left her message at that.

My last missed call was from Mieko. She sounded like she had been crying and was still crying throughout the whole message she left. She apologized for how she had been acting lately and said that she had a lot going on that was making her crazy. That was basically what I could decipher from the message. Most of it was inaudible and wrapped so heavily in tears that I couldn't make out the words. I called Mieko back to make sure she was okay, but her phone went straight to voicemail. My heart still softens for her, so I left her a message saying I hope she was feeling better and not to worry about the other stuff. I told her I still loved and cared for her and for her to give me a call so that I knew she was all right.

Looking at the time, I realized that I needed to start getting ready for work. I got up and threw some boxers and a sports bra on before heading my way downstairs to make something quick to eat. Since I had showered right before falling asleep, I skipped that part of my routine and put on a pair of jeans, a t-shirt, and my black Timbs. I looked at my hair taking note to make an appointment to get something done with it during the upcoming weekend. Walking out the door I fastened my watch and bracelets around my wrists. As the garage door was opening, I got on my bike, revved it up and proceeded toward work.

Ty was already there when I got to work. He greeted me, "Well good morning Sunshine."

I couldn't help but smile back at him, "Morning Ty."

"So, how did the movie night go? Did she like that tired Prince movie you think is so wonderful?" he laughed.

"We ran into Mi-Mi."

His laughter stopped, "Don't tell me she showed up at your house."

"Nothing like that. I took Aaliyah to the spot in China Town. She saw us there."

"What happened? I know she acted a damn fool. I don't understand her. She doesn't want to be with you, but she doesn't think anyone else should be with you, either."

"Yeah." For a minute I had flashbacks of the day she cursed me and left me dumbstruck and looking like a fool, just because I was concerned about her well-being. How could I care so much for someone who treated me like crap? "Yeah," I repeated, "I don't know what it is. She wasn't too thrilled about seeing Aaliyah."

"What did she do?"

"Nothing. Aaliyah stood her ground when Mi-Mi tried to lay into her. Aaliyah played the role as if she was my girl and told Mi-Mi that her loss was her gain." Ty started smiling at me. "What?"

"Nothing," he said as he continued to smile. "So what else happened?"

"We kept it moving and got out of there."

"So outside of that, how did the rest of the night go? You still haven't said if she liked the movie or not."

"Well, I'm not sure. I never got around to asking." My thoughts trailed off again, this time to the night before.

Ty must've noticed because he asked, "So what *did* you get around to?" snapping me back to the here and now.

"She kissed me again."

"Is that all?"

"Umm, not exactly."

"Jess, stop fucking with me. Did you steal that poor girl's cherry?"

"It wasn't like that, Ty." As I tried to begin my explanation, Ty's eyes grew wide.

"Oh my god, you didn't Jess. Tell me you didn't."

Watching Ty's reaction made me feel even worst about not stopping everything before anything happened. "It wasn't supposed to go down like that. I promise." I felt ashamed and lowered my head a little.

"Oh my god. You really did it," Ty mused, realizing the reality of the whole situation. "Was it good?"

"Really? That's what you ask me?"

"Stop, Jess. I've known you too long. Was it good?"

I sighed deeply and whispered, "One of the best."

"JESS!" Ty suddenly screamed, "What are you going to do?"

"What can I do? When I dropped her off, she acted as if nothing ever happened. Besides, she leaves this weekend. And she's straight with a man!"

Ty sat there shaking his head at me. "You really got it bad. You really like this girl."

"Why do you say that?"

"Look at you. Look at how you're acting. I have known you my whole life. I can tell when you are falling for someone."

"It's not even like that Ty." That's what I told him, but the truth was that I did really like Aaliyah. I could talk to her about any and everything. She wasn't your average pretty girl and she could make me laugh. She was so intelligent and open-minded, unlike what I thought after our first encounter. I may have liked her as more than a friend, but I tried so hard not to let anything jeopardize the friendship we'd built.

Ty grunted at me and said, "Whatever." Just then, a customer came in and I used that as my scapegoat to get away from whatever Ty was about to say next. It was only temporary, but a needed break from the seriousness of the conversation. As if I didn't have a care in the world, I greeted the customer and asked if there was anything I could do to help.

Throughout most of the day, Ty would give me a look that said our conversation from earlier wasn't over. He could be rather determined when he wanted to be, so I avoided him as best as I could. Around early evening, though, customer traffic died down giving him the opportunity he needed to pick up where we had left off.

"So seriously, Jess, what are you going to do?"

"What do you mean?"

"Don't play dumb. What are you going to do about Aaliyah?"

"Nothing."

"Nothing? So you are going to pretend like nothing ever happened?"

"Exactly. That is how it seems she wants it and honestly it is probably what is best."

"Are you sure?"

"Yes," I quickly answered.

"Why don't I believe you?"

"C'mon Ty, it is what it is, okay?" I pleaded with him to drop the subject while picking up a bunch of paperwork.

Ty sighed, "Fine," taking the stack of papers I had just picked up away from me. "If that's what you want, then I'll leave it alone. I'll be in the back doing inventory."

"All right," I said trying to make myself look busy with some receipts that had been mixed into the inventory sheets. It was best to pretend like nothing ever happened. That's what I concluded and what I was going to try and stick to. The situation already had enough potential to turn extremely ugly. Drama was written all over it and I tried my best to keep away from that. Yes, the best thing to do was to forget it ever happened.

The bells over the door rang, so I geared up to play my part in customer service. "Welcome to *The Pink Pussy*. Can I help you with anything?" I looked up and saw Jordyn standing there looking at me. "Hey Jordyn," I smiled, "How have you been?"

"Really good," she smiled back. "Did you get my message?"

"Yeah, I did. I figured since I would see you, it wasn't necessary to call back."

"Oh, cool, no problem. Well, here is your book," she said handing me back my book. "I really enjoyed it, thank-you."

"So, are you a fan?" I asked putting the book under the counter.

"Yeah," her smile broadened, "Ms. Zedde has a new fan."

"She is an awesome writer."

"I agree. I so wanted to be in Jamaica having a whirlwind romance," Jordyn laughed.

Joining in with her laughter I agreed, "I completely understand. So, do you want to borrow the next one she wrote? It's called *A Taste of Sin*. It's even better than the first one."

"No. I will support and buy my own. Thank-you very much."

"Hey, just trying to look out for you," I smiled at her. Recalling the message she left on my voicemail I asked, "So, you said you had something to ask me? What's up?"

"Oh yeah," she said remembering, "I wanted to know if you would go to a get-together with me. It's nothing serious, just a few friends getting together for a good time. I understand if you say no."

Considering recent events, spending time with Jordyn might be the perfect distraction I needed. Dressed in a cute baby-T tied in the back exposing her flat stomach, hip-hugging, boot cut jeans, and black sandals with a little heel, she was an attractive woman who didn't necessarily demand attention but definitely got it. Her hair was pinned up revealing diamond studded earlobes and flawless skin. This probably would be more of date than our previous encounters, but she was not only eye-catching but also enjoyable to be around. I really dug her company the last time, so I obliged, "I'll go with you."

"Really?"

"Yeah. When and where?" Jordyn gave me all the details and I told her that I would pick her up and we could ride together. She agreed and told me she was glad I didn't turn her down. She also assured me that she didn't expect anything extra from it. I thanked her for understanding and respecting my position before she left to go about her business. Watching her exit I smiled. Jordyn really was a likable person, and not too bad to look at either. The perfect distraction. I was sure I would have a good time when we hooked up that Sunday.

The rest of the week flew by and before I knew it, it was Sunday morning. I hadn't talked to Aaliyah much considering she had been preparing to drive back to Atlanta. Her boyfriend had gotten into town Friday, or maybe it was Saturday, either way, kicking it one last time was out of the question. Feeling the need to call her, I located her name in my phone and pressed talk. After one ring she answered, "Jess! I was just thinking about you and was going to call."

I smiled to myself at how excited she seemed to be about hearing from me. I laughed, "I guess I beat you to it."

"Yeah. I wanted to let you know I was leaving today."

"Today?"

"Yeah. We are actually about to get on the road. We want to try and make it by tonight."

"Awww," I whined, "I wanted to see you before you left."

"Me too, but I got so busy trying to make sure I was ready to go back, I lost track of time. And then Kevin got here and there just wasn't enough time after that. I apologize."

Even though deep down I felt Aaliyah purposely avoided me the last few days, I sucked it up. "It's okay, Aaliyah. I know you've been getting ready to go back to school. I wish we could've linked up one last time, but I understand. Next time, right?" I forced myself to smile as if she would be able to see it through the phone.

"You're right. Maybe when I come home for break or something we can link up."

"I'm going to hold you to that."

She giggled into the phone, "Okay. Well, I have to get going. Don't be a stranger, Jess. My number will still be the same."

"The same goes for you."

"I won't. Thanks, Jess."

"For what?"

"For being a good friend. I'll talk to you later." The line disconnected before I could even reply. I put my phone back in my back pocket and tried to figure out if Aaliyah really wanted to continue our friendship or whether she was just being polite. She seemed sincere. I started to wonder if that night together meant anything to her. I wondered if the events of that night ever crossed her mind. Blowing wind while shaking the thoughts out of my head, I reminded myself that it was only experimental fun for her. *That's it*, I mumbled to myself. *Experimental fun.*

I looked around and realized I needed to clean up. For the past week, I had just let my home go. It was finally getting to me, so I started picking up randomly strewed clothes to take to the laundry room. Dropping those off, I went to the kitchen and washed the dishes that had piled up in the sink. I placed the last dish in the drainer and wiped my hands on the dish towel. My phone started to vibrate in my back pocket. I pulled my phone out and looked at the number. It was Mieko.

I answered, "Hey Mi-Mi. You okay?"

"Yeah," Mieko barely whispered.

"Are you sure? You don't sound like it."

"Are you busy?"

"Something like that. I am cleaning up before I get ready to go out this evening. Why? What's up?"

"Oh. Okay." Mieko grew silent for a minute before saying she had to go and feeding me the dial tone. It irritated me, being the second time in less than a few hours I had been hung up on, but I was even more concerned about what was going on with Mieko. A part of me wanted to call back, but another part recalled my mother saying she wasn't my problem anymore and I needed to realize that. As much as it pained me, I slid my phone back in my pocket and continued with my cleaning.

When I was done, I had enough time to hop in the shower and get dress before needing to head to Jordyn's. As I was drying off, I looked through my closet to pick out something to wear. I was in the mood to dress up, so I pulled out a pair of black slacks and my dark purple button down I got from Express for Men awhile back. My hair was freshly re-braided. Generally, I liked my hair out, but the braided look had kind-of grew on me. Adding black shoes, a silver grey tie, grey do-rag, and a black hat, I was almost set. I opted to wear a silver link chain my mother got me for Christmas one year and some diamond studded earrings I bought when *The Pink Pussy* started turning over a profit. I sprayed and stepped through a light musk before grabbing my wallet and keys, headed for the garage.

Just as I was pulling out the garage, my phone rang. Jordyn's name flashed on the display. I answered and told her I was on my way and should be to her place in twenty minutes. My phone rang again and Mieko's name popped up. Making a mental note to call her when I got in that evening, I let my voicemail take her call.

Twenty-three minutes later, I was in front of Jordyn's apartment. She had been waiting for me on the steps. She ascended toward the car and the dress she had on flowed in the wind. Looking gorgeous, she had on a long dress with blended shades of purple, grey, and black. It was a spaghetti strapped number that accentuated and gathered at her breast area. It put me in mind of a modern-day Juliet. I couldn't hide my smile. Getting out of the car, I ran around to open the door before she got to it.

She gave me a quick peck on the lips before sliding into the passenger seat. Feeling good, I got back in on the driver's side. I told Jordyn how beautiful she looked. She thanked me and said I didn't look too bad myself. You would have thought we planned it, both of us dressed in shades of purple, grey and black, but it was a complete coincidence. I smiled harder as I pulled off so we could make our way to the party.

We pulled up to the address for the get-together and it was already looking live. The address brought us to what looked like a miniature mansion. I pulled up to valet, hopped out leaving the keys in the ignition, and went around the car to escort Jordyn in. "Shall we?" I asked her, letting the gentlewoman in me shine.

"We shall," she smiled while grabbing my hand.

I escorted Jordyn to the door, where someone called her name out. "Jordyn! You made it."

"Yeah, I made it," Jordyn smiled and hugged the other female. She turned to me, "Jess, meet my friend Toya. This is her and her girl's place. T, this is Jess. Be nice," she giggled.

Toya giggled with her, "Why would I not be nice to this fine specimen of a woman. Jess, welcome to my home." She smiled and winked at me, and then turned her attention back to Jordyn. "Kristen and everybody are inside already. Go on in and enjoy yourself."

Jordyn grabbed my hand and started heading for the entrance. We walked in and the place was packed. I whispered to her, "I thought you said it would be just a little get-together, nothing serious?" She just looked at me with a sly grin and hunched her shoulders. I sighed and decided to take it all in stride. With so many women concentrated in one place, it was probably impossible not to run into someone I didn't want to see. I kept my head on a slight swivel expecting to see Mieko appear out of the shadows and go off on Jordyn.

I don't think Jordyn noticed as she introduced me to random people and we moved throughout the space. We made our way to an area with various seating all around. Luckily, we found a spot and took a seat. A female dressed in a French maid get-up came over and asked if we wanted any champagne. Both Jordyn and I took a glass. The waitress of sorts left and we fell into conversation. I slowly relaxed, letting go of the tension of possibly bumping into Mieko. Jordyn told me that Toya's girlfriend was big time and always gave extravagant, sometimes over the top, get-togethers that were by invite only. I told her I didn't think I knew her because I couldn't recall getting any invites to a house party in this area before.

Moving onto stronger drinks, her a sex on the beach and me my usual Long Island, we discussed *Bliss* in more detail. Every now and again, we were interrupted by her friends coming over to say hello or a waitress asking if we needed anything. We'd eventually dismiss everyone and continue talking.

Jordyn said something that made us both laugh and I guess we were pretty loud, because those in the general area turned their attention our way. Jordyn apologized as I caught the glare of someone I wish I hadn't noticed coming our way. Jordyn jumped up with a big smile as they both approached us. I smiled just praying that things didn't go left instead of right.

One of the females grabbed Jordyn in a hug, "Hey J! Been a minute Baby girl."

She obliged and agreed while, my ex, Tina, and I stood face to face. Attempting peace, I said, "Hey Tina. Nice to see you again." She grimaced at me.

Jordyn turned to me, "You already know Tina? Do you know Tre, too?"

I smiled, "Yes, I know Tina, but I don't think I have had the pleasure," I reached out my hand to who I figured was Tre, "Tre, is it?"

"Tremaine."

I corrected myself, "Tremaine."

She shook my hand. "What's up ..." she paused.

"Jess."

"Jess," she smiled. "Are you taking care of our J?"

"As best I can."

Jordyn cut in, "Stop that. Jess and I are just friends, so you can knock off the big brother act."

"I am just looking out for you Baby girl," Tremaine told her. Tina just stood there not saying anything. She leaned in and whispered something to Tremaine. "You are right, Baby," she told Tina.

Tina turned to Jordyn and told her, "It's good to see you out J. Tre and I will see you a little later. We just got here and still haven't run into Toya or Kay."

Jordyn smiled and hugged both of them saying she'd see them later. Tremaine said it was good meeting me before they disappeared into the crowd. "It was nice seeing them. They are such a cute couple," Jordyn commented once they were gone.

"Yeah," I said, finishing the last of my Long Island and exchanging my empty glass for another glass of champagne from a passing waitress. After drinking half the champagne, I looked at Jordyn who was looking at me.

"You okay?" she asked.

"Yeah," I quickly responded. "Was a little thirsty. Kind-of ready to go."

"Aww, but I was enjoying your company."

"You can always leave with me. I did bring you."

"But I'm not ready to go home. My roommate is there with her boyfriend. I am not in the mood for them right now."

"You can come to my place. I live alone, so I welcome the company." I felt my slight inebriation taking over for me because generally, I would not have invited Jordyn to my home.

She smiled, "Are you sure?"

"Yeah," I responded, it was too late to turn back, right? I finished the last of my glass and took her hand. I smiled at her, "C'mon." She took my hand and followed me. On our way out we stopped to thank the hostesses for having us and went on our way. The moment we reached my home, we got as far as the hallway outside the kitchen before I had Jordyn on her back calling my name.

aaliyah

Chapter 12

I let my phone shut and slid it back into my pocket. I honestly could have seen Jess before I left since I had finished all preparations earlier in the week, but I didn't want to have that awkward moment we were bound to share. She knew I had a man and that nothing could ever become of what we did ... what *I* did. The truth was that I came onto her, again. She tried to stop me and not cross that line, but I wasn't taking no for an answer. I should be ashamed of myself. I am.

What would I say to her if we were face to face? Jess has always shown me the utmost respect and I always found a way to take advantage of that and the attraction I knew she felt toward me. She probably thinks I used her and that wasn't my intentions. I never meant for things to go down like that, but I also never thought I would be attracted to another female. Shaking my head, I knew I had to let it go. Maybe when I came home we could go back to being friends like we were before everything happened. Yeah, I would like that, but for now, it's probably best to just not think or worry about it. What is done, is done.

"Are you ready, Babe," Kevin asked me taking me from my thoughts.

"Huh?" I asked by reflex.

"Are you ready to get on the road? We have a long drive ahead of us."

"Yeah. Let's get going so we can keep our time table," I said taking my seat on the driver side of my car. Kevin and I agreed that I would drive first since I didn't really like driving at night. We'd drive to Virginia before pulling over to get something to eat, which should be our second time gassing up. After that, we would switch and he would drive the rest of the way. It was good to have him riding along, especially since my mother didn't like me making the long drive alone anyway. It eased both her and my father's mind ultimately. After Kevin was comfortably in his seat, I revved up my Jetta and started heading for Route 80.

We made it to Atlanta in record time. What usually took me two days to accomplish alone was completed within 13 hours. At our first stop for gas, Kevin took the wheel, pretty much driving the rest of the trip. I fell asleep. I really tried to stay up, but long car rides have always put me to sleep, especially when I wasn't the one driving. He woke me as we were exiting off a ramp heading to Peachtree.

"Where are we going?" I asked, still groggy from my rest.

"To get a room. It is too late to try to go to the school now."

I yawned, "You're right." We pulled up to one of the Marriotts downtown and got a room for the night. As soon as we got to the room, Kevin laid down on the bed. I told him, "Baby, go take a shower so you can get some sleep. I know you're tired from the drive."

"Yeah," he said getting up heading for the bathroom. Turning the TV on, I flipped through the channels to find something to watch. I felt my phone vibrating in my pocket and pulled it out to see who was calling. It was actually a text message from Tina asking me if I made it yet. I texted her back that Kevin and I just made it and are staying in a hotel for the night. She texted back that I better be getting some "booty", her words, not mine, 'because having sex in a hotel is the best'. I laughed at her in reply. What is that even supposed to mean? I decided not to give it too much thought and went back to channel surfing.

Kevin came out of the bathroom with a towel wrapped around his waist, steam at his back, looking like an Adonis. He smiled at me as he used another towel to dry his head off. "See something you like?" he asked.

"Maybe," I replied with a sly grin.

"Maybe?" he raised his eyebrow at me in question.

"Yeah, maybe," I laughed. "I mean, you are looking *kind-of* tempting," I said slightly grinning while looking him up and down.

Kevin walked toward me, stood me up, pulled me close and whispered, "Well, I see something I like." I smiled into his kiss as he started to undress me. It had been a while since we had been able to be together like this, and tomorrow after I dropped him off at the airport, there was no telling the next time I would see him. I grabbed him closer and kissed him harder as he laid his body on top of mine, his erection rubbing the inside of my thigh.

"Hold on, Baby," I stopped him before we went any further. "Let me take a quick shower."

"Really?"

"C'mon, Baby, it was a long drive. Let me freshen up." Exaggerating his frustrations, he rolled over and sighed. I jumped off the bed. "Thank-you my Adonis," I told him before giving him a quick peck and disappearing into the bathroom. When I finally came back out, Kevin was laying there, still in his towel, knocked out.

I climbed on the bed next to him and began whispering in his ears about all I wanted him to do to me, but he didn't budge. I tried kissing his lips, but still, I got no response from him. Mumbling to no one but myself I said, "I know what will wake him up." Pulling his towel to the side, his member laid there still looking as hard as it felt before I took my shower.

I slid down until I was eye level with his dick and flicked the tip with my tongue. After a few licks, I held him in my hand, and slowly slid my mouth down until I could feel him in the back of my throat. Sucking in, I slowly raised my head, gliding my mouth up his shaft, and then slowly went back down again. I did it again, and another time before I could feel him getting even harder, filling my mouth even more.

Kevin's hands found my head, and I heard him curse while guiding my head up and down. Determined to feel him inside me, I abruptly stopped giving him head, climbed on top of him and pushed his stiffness into my wet and waiting warmth. Once he was fully inside me, my whole body tensed up from the welcomed invasion. I tightened and relaxed my walls a few times before I started riding him slowly, finding my rhythm. The more I rode him, the more he moaned. It wasn't long before his hands were wrapped around my waist and he was directing the tempo. Without warning, I violently came all over him.

After that much-needed release, I was good. Unfortunately, my man was still fully erect, and that was not going to work for me. I rolled off him, laying on my back as my release continued to flow out of me, and spread my lips apart. "C'mon, Daddy," I beckoned him and he slipped right back into my hallow cave. He worked me slowly, digging deep, then pulling all the way back until it almost felt like he pulled out, and then he fed my body every inch of him again. I was in heaven but begged for him to go faster and to go harder until he reached my soul.

After climaxing this time, he laid beside me, spent. I still had some extra energy since I slept the majority of the drive and decided to give him some more pleasure of my own. I climbed on top of him, kissing his lips softly. I slowly trailed down from there with my tongue licking a path to his chest. I nibbled on each of his nipples before continuing my journey south.

 Kevin's breath became more ragged as I moved past his well-defined abs to right above his erection. I smiled up at him, "Seems somebody is ready again," and flicked my tongue across his tip. With care, I wrapped my mouth around his mushroom top and guided him deep to the back of my throat, taking my time even more than earlier. Shielding my teeth with my lips, I began to move in an up and down motion. I knew he liked it when I took him as deep as he would go, then pulled all the way back like I was going to release him, before plunging back down on his full extension. Grabbing my head for the second time, Kevin moaned with ecstasy, gesturing for me to go faster, but instead, I continued my pace. Even though he held my head as if not to let me go until I finished this time, seconds later, he cursed and I knew it was over.

I rolled over satisfied with myself. Looking at Kevin falling back to sleep, I smiled just taking him all in. He slightly opened his eyes, mumbling while trying to get under the covers. Once he was settled, I snuggled up close to him, breathing in his after sex musk. Hours from now, I knew he would be gone and it would be a while before I saw him again. After such a wonderful session, my emotions had gotten the best of me and I cried myself to sleep, unsure of if our relationship would last and really work out.

The next morning I woke up in Kevin's arms and my tears were long gone. The world just seemed perfect. I understood, though, eventually that perfection would end because we would have to get up and start the day. By the end of it, I would be back at Morris Brown and he would either be in Florida or almost there. With this being my final year, I doubted if I would get much time away from the school other than the big holidays. Running a practice, Kevin wouldn't be able to just take off either, especially after all the time he already took off during the summer. I was relishing in this moment.

Kevin moved a little then lifted his head high enough to kiss me, before letting it drop back to the pillow. He mumbled, "What time is it?"

Looking at the digital clock in the room, I told him, "8:30. We probably should get up."

"You're right," he yawned. I kissed him on his lips before climbing out the bed heading to the bathroom. I needed to pee, and after the episode of lovemaking we had the night before, I also needed another shower. While I was showering he came in and said he was going to run and get us something to eat real quick. I told him okay and continued to wash my body. When I got out, I was greeted with a bouquet of flowers and breakfast. He was good for doing sweet things like that. I thanked Kevin before he went into the bathroom and showered himself.

By the time he came out, I was dressed, full, and ready to go. We made sure we had everything we came in with before heading to the lobby to check out. We loaded up in my Jetta and headed to the campus. It was a couple of days before Freshman Orientation, so there really wasn't many people on campus, just staff and those of us deemed as Residential Assistants, also known as RAs, for the upcoming school year. The previous year I was encouraged by my financial advisor to look into it because it would cover the room and board expenses my scholarships did not. I went through the process and was actually selected as an RA for Gaines Hall, the honor dorm. I was excited because the rooms there were the best on campus. Xavier lived there junior year, being an honor student himself. I ended up in the Towers after my off-campus housing fell through. The roommate situation was less than desirable, but feasible since I was always in Xavier's room anyway.

I parked as close as I could get to the front entrance and told Kevin I would be right back. I didn't want to make him leave the air-conditioned car for the Georgia heat if my room was closer to the back entrance and we would have to move anyway. I walked into the building looking over my shoulder out the glass window at Kevin when I bumped right into Xavier. I must've thought him up from earlier because there he was. Standing about 6'2 and probably weighing in close to 200, maybe 210 pounds; his build was every bit the athletic football player he was. Although, when you looked past that, he didn't look the part, preferring to wear a nice pair of slacks and a collared polo tucked in, over jeans and a T-shirt, any day. He had smooth caramel skin, grey eyes and wavy brown hair that would turn into little curly ringlets around his head when he allowed it to grow out. When he smiled, his cheekbones stood out and he had a perfect set of teeth.

Despite the gorgeous specimen of a man he was, I didn't really care too much for athletes. I was more taken by intellectuals. Actually, I would be all over a brother with intelligence, thus Xavier and I ever hooking up. Outside of the pain he put me through this summer, he was a really smart and sweet guy. Well, then again, would a sweet guy hurt me the way he did. Thinking it over, I rolled my eyes. *To hell with Xavier!*

"Hey Baby," he said to me, trying to wrap his arms around me and kiss me.

"Don't do that, Xavier," I told him while trying to push him away. He was a bit stronger than I remembered.

"Baby, come on. We haven't seen each other the whole summer, and this is how you act?" he asked reaching for me again.

"I said stop. Don't act like you didn't break my heart this summer. Was she worth it? Was she worth hurting me for?" I could feel myself about to lose my cool and that was the last thing I wanted to do. He didn't deserve that much emotion from me. I pushed past him heading toward the front desk to check-in. The female sitting behind the desk looked like one of my former classmates. I think we worked on a project together freshman year, but I couldn't be sure.

"Hey Aaliyah," she greeted me, obviously she knew who I was.

"Hey," I said, trying to be nonchalant, "I'm here to check-in."

"Here you go," she said as she handed me a clipboard, "Fill out the paperwork, sign here for your key and you should be set. There is a welcome-back function tonight in the student lounge downstairs for all the Gaines RAs just to cover the basics and brainstorm as a group. Should be a good time. There will be snacks, but you probably want to hit the cafeteria up before then." I took a moment to go over the paperwork, then signed for my keys and thanked her for her help.

I went to locate my room and realized it was down on the lower level where the lounge was. I would've preferred to have been on the top or main level, but I shrugged it off and headed back to the car. As I was leaving, Xavier tried me again and I told him to give it a rest so that I could at least get moved back in. He finally took the hint and I went out to the car to get Kevin.

Thankfully, by the time Kevin and I loaded ourselves with my stuff and headed back into the dorm, Xavier was nowhere to be found. I said a little prayer of thanks and led the way to my room. In about three hours, we had not only moved all my belongings into the single room but also fixed it up to my liking. I smiled and sat on the bed satisfied. Kevin sat next to me and kissed me. It was intense and made me want him right then, but he abruptly pulled away.

"I have to go."

"Go where?" I asked.

"My flight is in about four hours, and between Georgia traffic and lines at the airport, I need to get to the airport." I frowned but understood what he was talking about. I grabbed my keys and we headed back to the car. I cranked my car up and was on my way to Hartsfield to drop Kevin off.

It's a good thing we left when we did. I'm not sure what was going on, but the traffic was really bad on the way to the airport. It had completely opened up by the time I was heading back to the school. After parking my car back at the dorms, the shower was calling my name, so I took a quick shower and decided to take a nap before the social hour of sorts later that evening. I set my alarm so not to oversleep, curled up and drifted.

My alarm went off waking me from what had the potential for becoming a nightmare. I was out to dinner with Kevin when Xavier came in the restaurant acting belligerent. It was clear he had, had way too much to drink. He got in Kevin's face, screaming at him that I was his woman and that he'd better leave me alone. I was trying to make Xavier leave, but he wouldn't budge. Kevin got up to confront him. That's when the gunshot went off, but I don't know who had the gun or who was shot. The alarm went off at the same time the gunshot did, waking me from the dream.

I prayed that wasn't a premonition of things to come and got up to use the bathroom. Passing the lounge I saw that it was already set-up for the evening event with a table full of pre-typed nametags. I felt a presence behind me and turned around seeing the female from when I checked in earlier. She was already wearing her name tag that read "Naomi." I whispered, "Naomi, that's right."

"Hey Aaliyah," she said and then asked, "You are going to be here this evening, right?"

"Oh, yeah. I set my alarm and everything so I didn't oversleep."

"Cool."

"Yup. I'm going to go change and then I'll be right out."

"Great! See you in a few."

"Yup." I went back to my room repeating her name over in my head. Naomi was my biology partner freshman year, but she'd changed a bit since then. Back then she seemed really shy and kept to herself for the most part. She wasn't ugly or anything. She was taller than me at 5'9 and her brown skin was free from any blemishes. She was slim with a runner's physique sporting toned arms and legs, and long pretty black hair. I had heard she was on the Track and Field team for the school, but being the non-athletic type I was, I tried to stay away from physical activities like that.

Yeah, she was definitely attractive from what I remembered, but she didn't seem to like attention from guys, or from anyone for that matter now that I think of it. The only reason we ever spoke was because we were paired up for a biology project. She could do circles around me when it came to biology. I had to struggle to get the "B" I earned. Now, her hair was cut short with baby fine curls around her head and she seemed a bit more approachable than she was freshman year. Confidence seemed to exude from her making her hard to ignore. *Good for her.*

I changed into dark blue jeans, a wraparound top and put my flats on. I wasn't going anywhere but to the lounge, so no need to get too dolled up. I put a little eyeliner and lip gloss on before going back out to the lounge. On my way down the hallway, I texted Kevin back and told him I loved him. He'd gotten back to Florida and had sent me a text to let me know he made it safely. I put my phone on vibrate and slipped it into my pocket with my room key.

There were more people in the lounge than earlier by the time I walked in. I went to the table with the nametags, located mine and found an empty seat. In a few days the Fresh Meat, I meant, the new freshmen class would arrive. I laughed to myself at my joke, remembering being that incoming freshman as I waited for things to get started.

Naomi brought things to order, going through the agenda for the evening. It was pretty much letting us know to try and get our class schedules, IDs and financial aid situated before the freshmen arrived. We each were handed a list of prospective residents we would be responsible for and suggested ways to stay engaged. It was a lot of good information, and I took notes like I did at every meeting I've ever attended.

Once business was complete, things were opened for refreshments and socializing. Naomi walked up to me and asked, "So, what made you decide to be an RA our final year?"

I sipped from the cup of juice I had poured before telling her, "Finances. My financial advisor last year said it would offset the last bit of expenses my scholarships didn't cover."

"Smart."

"Yeah. I can't believe I was selected for Gaines. I was certain I would be in the Towers."

She laughed, "You got lucky then. I've been doing this RA thing since sophomore year. This is my second year in Gaines. I was in SAQ the first time."

"No wonder you disappeared. I never really went to SAQ."

"I didn't disappear. I was usually in the science building."

"Yeah, that really isn't my specialty," I commented.

"My bad. I forgot you had a hard time freshman year in biology. I would have tutored you if you asked. I did that on the side."

"Really? You seemed to keep to yourself, so, you know," I hunched my shoulders, letting the statement linger in the air.

"Yeah. I was shy back then, huh? Atlanta was a new place for me, so, I didn't know anything."

"Me too! I'm originally from New Jersey. Freshman year was the first time I was ever away from home, let alone Georgia. I just needed to get away from home, though. Just not the best situation," I said latching onto our commonality.

"For real? I'm from New York!" she exclaimed. "That's what's up." All this time we were from the same area and never even knew. We continued our conversation for another hour while I helped her clean up after the crowd had dispersed. She was definitely different from the female that was my bio partner, but it was a good different. She was animated and could talk her behind off. We had both found an old friend, and that, to me, was a good way to start senior year.

jess

Chapter 13

Since the party, Jordyn and I started spending more time together. She would visit me at work on nights she wasn't busy, and when we were both available we'd go to the movies or to my house and read to each other. I really thought that was different when she suggested it, reading to each other. I never considered that I would enjoy it as much as I did, either.

Jordyn was wearing on me, and more and more we were acting like a couple. She stayed over so much I gave her a drawer and she had her own toothbrush in my bathroom. To the naked eye, we were together, but she knew what it was, as did I. I still wasn't looking for a relationship. Jordyn understood and never pushed it. I dug that about her. I was still dealing with Mieko and the unrequited feelings I had for Aaliyah. Until I dealt with all of that, being official was the last thing I wanted to do.

"So, are we going to Atlanta Pride this year? Because we are going to be out in the cold if we don't hurry up and book a hotel,"

Ty said to me, snapping me out of my train of thought. He was looking online at all the events happening during Atlanta Black Pride. It happened every year during Labor Day weekend and I usually went, if for no other reason than to make sure Ty didn't get into any drama. That said, by the end of it each year I was always glad I did. It also gave me time to see a friend of mine that moved down there to go to school. The last few years she'd actually started going to the parade in Piedmont Park with us.

But, Aaliyah was there, too. What if I bumped into her? Would she be happy to see me? Or would she act like she didn't even know me? What would I do if she rejected me like that? Just thinking about the possibilities made me feel like it was probably not a good idea to even take the chance and go this year.

"I don't know. It's the same thing every year. Don't you want to take a break this year?"

Ty snapped his head around so quickly and looked at me shocked. "What?!? We ALWAYS go to Pride, especially the major ones. Hell, I thought Atlanta was your favorite."

"It is."

"So, what are you talking about? I wasn't really asking before. It was meant to motivate you and get you excited about going. You know you have to book early, so we need to get our rooms now. If anything worth it is still available, anyway."

"You already know the rooms are booked. We book early every year. So your concerns are unfounded. Either way, though, I'm just not sure if I am really up for it."

"Who are you and what the hell have you done with my best friend?"

"I'm serious, Ty."

"Jesstina Antionette Rodriguez."

"Woooooow! Really? The full government?"

"Yes, ma'am, because you are seriously tripping right now."

"What if I run into her?"

"Her who? Mieko?"

"No. Aaliyah."

"Aaliyah? Jess, c'mon now, she isn't even gay. What would

she be doing at Pride, huh?"

"She lives in Atlanta."

"She's not going to be at Pride, Jess. So, you are going with me whether you like it or not. I am booking a flight for us right now as we speak."

"Ty, I don't know."

"Doesn't matter. It's done. You're welcome." I looked at him and shook my head. He was every bit the stubborn ram his sign indicated, but I loved him and knew he was probably right. Atlanta was big and would be full of Rainbow Children. Why would Aaliyah be out and about during Pride? She's more likely to stay in until it's over cuddled up with her man. I felt a twinge of jealousy, but then I let it go. Why was I getting jealous, anyway? I really needed to learn to let go if something didn't want to be held. Not just Aaliyah, but Mieko, too.

"You're right. I need a vacation anyway."

"There's my best friend! Damn, thought for a minute I was gonna have to put in a missing person's report with NYPD," he laughed.

Laughing with him, I told him, "No, I'm here and ready."

The rest of the night was like any other night in the store. A few ladies came in to purchase sexy lingerie for their line of work. One was my favorite dancer Spice from *Black Ice*, a strip club that catered to mainly men of color. The women that worked there were crème de la crème. Their bodies were flawless and came in every shape and shade of brown. Every now and then I'd go to watch the beautiful women and have a drink. Many of the women flocked to the men in hopes they'd make it rain over them. Spice, though, made it her business to come dance for me whenever she was working, only asking for payment if it was to my liking. It always was, too.

She was really petite, probably only about 5'2 and 110 lbs. She had these cute little red freckles that spread across her nose and cheekbone area complementing her redbone complexion. Her small breasts were perky and her backside commanded attention. Spice kept her dark auburn hair cut short in a flip style most of the time, but sometimes she would smooth it down like Toni Braxton use to in her heyday. She was no model, but she was more than worth looking at.

I greeted, "I guess this means you won't be working tonight, Lady Spice?"

She smiled at me, "Depends. Will my favorite customer be dropping by?"

"I thought about it."

"You should. I can always use a good tipper," she winked at me.

"I'm sure you are tipped well every time you grace *Black Ice* with your presence," I smiled at her. Her female friend seemed a little exasperated by our flirtatious dialogue. Trying to help her out, I straightened up, "Will this be all for you?"

Spice ignored her friend and kept going, "Is it all you are offering?"

I could feel myself slowly becoming more aggressive in my response as I answered, "For now, but if you aren't busy, maybe I might have a few things for you later." I promise I'm not a pimp, but I couldn't let her think I couldn't go toe-to-toe with her.

My comeback must've caught her off guard as she visibly turned a shade redder than what she already was. Most didn't expect me to play the game, but sometimes it was nice to tease the females as much as they thought they were teasing me. She finished her transaction and told me to watch myself because next time she might take me up on my offer. I just waved and told her and her companion thanks for shopping at *The Pink Pussy*.

Later that evening, more like morning, I laid in my bed really wishing Jordyn was lying next to me. It was pretty much fall now and her classes were starting up. Being together so much I had learned she was in medical school with hopes of one day being a full blown doctor. This was her final year of formal schooling before she had to take up a residency somewhere, so, she was trying to start the year off right and that meant she had to actually sleep at night. I grinned with the remembrance of her telling me that when she was around me her hormones had a mind of their own. Still, I wished she would come over.

Knowing it was late, I called Jordyn anyway. "Hello?" she answered her voice a faint whisper and heavy with sleep.

"Hey, Babe. Were you sleep?" Dumb question, I knew, but it was the first thing I thought of.

"Jess, it's four in the morning, Baby. Of course, I'm sleeping. I have orientation in the morning."

"Oh, I apologize. I was just missing you and your company."

"I miss you, too, Baby, but I have to get up in a few hours. How about I come over tomorrow after I'm finished with everything?"

I sighed letting my depression be heard through the line as I replied, "Okay."

She ignored it. "Okay. Baby, I'm gonna go back to sleep. I'll see you tomorrow."

"All right, good night Babe." Jordyn said goodnight before disconnecting her end of the line. I dropped my arm to my side and just laid there trying to figure out what I was going to do with myself.

I was tempted to get dress and head to a bar, but I really didn't feel like driving anywhere. I just really wanted company. Raising my phone back up and locating the number I wanted, I hit talk and waited for someone to pick up.

"Hi, Baby! I was just thinking about you!" she said like my call was the best surprise ever. I could hear a lot of noise in the background bleeding through the phone. She must have been partying, and when she partied she drank. Her cheery disposition was probably alcohol induced.

"Hey, Mi-Mi. Are you in town?"

"Yeah, at the club right now."

"Want to come over? I really could use some company."

"For you? Of course, Baby! I'll be there in twenty minutes." I hung up realizing that I probably should have just grabbed a book from the study or tried sleeping, rather than filling the spot Jordyn couldn't at that time. But I'm single and a grown woman and I still love Mieko, anyway. Even if I regretted it later, I'd deal with that bridge when I crossed it.

Mieko called when she was down the street and I met her at the front entrance. When she came through the door, she kissed me like she hadn't seen me in years. I held her in my arms and accepted her affectionate greeting. As our tongues intertwined, I could taste the wine she must've been sipping on before coming to see me. The Merlot taste was so strong I felt like I was having a glass myself.

I lifted her up and took her to the bedroom, never stopping myself from drinking the liquor from her lips. When we got to the bedroom I laid her down, lying on top of her, still kissing her. I unbuttoned her jeans and forced my way into them searching for her prize. The liquid seeping out of her pussy welcomed me like an old friend and I sighed as my finger made its way into her slippery cave. Mieko spread her legs open and I applied pressure behind my hand using my knee. I wiggled my finger around inside of her and watched as her breath deepened into a low groan of ecstasy.

My own pussy was beginning to ache and desire some attention, too. Ready for skin-on-skin contact, I stuck two more fingers into her hard making her scream from the unexpected invasion, cuming all over my fingers. I pulled my fingers out and stood up off the bed. While she wrestled her clothes all off, I removed my basketball shorts and wife beater. I was dripping as I climbed back on top of her and slid my pussy over hers. Electricity flowed through me as our clits slid against each other becoming reacquainted with one another.

Looking at me intensely, Mieko whispered my name, egging me on as I made love to her. I rose up bracing myself on the bed while rubbing up against her. Suddenly getting the urge to watch her ride me, I flipped her over so that I was on the bottom. If there was one thing she could do, she could ride. I told her to ride me and grabbed her waist dictating the pace, gasping at the depth of what I was feeling as she grinded on me. She started to bounce, slamming into my already sensitive clit. As she bounced, my clit grew more and more sensitive with each compression of our pussies together. I grabbed her waist tighter and thrust my hips forward as I felt my orgasm release itself from the hold I had on it. It was feeling so good I wanted to delay what I knew was coming, literally.

Mieko smiled knowing I would be momentarily predisposed. She kissed me and began making a trail down my body. I held my breath as her movements brought her lips closer and closer to my lower ones. She kissed my lips like she did the ones on my face before spreading them with her fingers and flicking my clit with her tongue. My whole body tensed, from head to toe. She paused and admired what the slight touch had done to me, then went in for the kill and enveloped my clit in her mouth completely.

It had been a while since anyone had pleased me this way. Jordyn wasn't a pillow princess, but she also wasn't one for giving head, though she loved to receive. I loved to give, so it never bothered me. But feeling Mieko's tongue work its way around my clit and in and out my whole, I remembered what I had been missing. I put my hands in her mane and held her head in place, encouraging her to lick my pussy and make me cum. Empowered, she sucked on my clit and hummed. The vibration drove me crazy. She heard my moans getting louder and knew I was nearing my peak yet again. Sliding her finger into my opening, my dam broke and I came all over her fingers and tongue. Damn, that was so good.

Mieko got up smiling and satisfied. She said, "I'm going to the bathroom to clean up," before leaving me there in bliss. She didn't mind cunnilingus, but she had to wash her face afterward. I didn't care. I was in afterglow heaven at that moment, but when I heard the water turn on in the bathroom, I got up and went to my closet. Although I was with Jordyn more regularly, I never got rid of the strap I only used with Mieko. You'd think the thought of Jordyn would stop me from continuing any further than I had already gone, but my sex got the best of me. I put the strap on and decided to go in the bathroom after Mieko.

I walked in behind her and let my extension rub between her thighs. Realizing what I had done, her legs slightly shook with anticipation while I separated them. I guided myself inside of her and gently pushed her over the sink. I kissed her below the center of her shoulder blades, licking a trail down her back as I found my rhythm. Reaching a hand around her, I grabbed her right breast and started tweaking her hardened nipple. She lifted her left leg and rested her knee on the sink allowing me to get deeper inside of her. She turned her head to kiss me as I stroked her into a tantric high.

Because my clit was already engorged and overly sensitive from earlier, though, I wasn't sure how much longer I could hold out. I pulled all the way out to her surprise and dismay and moved her to being bent over the closed toilet seat, and then slid back inside her. I fucked her until she squealed from her own euphoria giving me the okay to let go of myself. My own cum mixed with hers and trickled down my thighs.

I was done.

We both were and made our way to the bed. I dropped the strap on the floor and climbed into the bed with Mieko finding her spot in my arms. In seconds, I was knocked out.

The next morning I woke up to a note from her.

Good morning Beautiful. Sorry I couldn't stay but I had a flight to catch. You already know how that goes. I really enjoyed being with you and can't wait to see you again. I love you.
~Mi-Mi

I rolled on my back and whispered to myself, "Of course." Deciding to get up, I grabbed all the sheets off the bed, my clothes from the night before and dragged them down to the washing machine. As the evidence of Mieko and my relations were cleansed with liquid detergent, I washed the strap and put it back up. I disinfected the bedroom and bathroom before hopping into the shower to wash her memory down the drain. Jordyn was coming over tonight and I didn't need Mieko lingering in the air while I was with her.

aaliyah

Chapter 14

"Are you kidding me? Weight training?" I exclaimed when I finally received my schedule for the semester. "Do I really need to fulfill the physical education requirement? Can't it be waived?"

The counselor looked at me and stated plainly, "All graduating seniors must have at least one semester of physical education, or be affiliated with one of the athletic teams for the college. Looking over your transcript, Miss Jones, outside of the electives on your schedule, this is a requirement you are currently missing. You can postpone it until next semester, but either way, you will have to complete the requirement if you want to graduate."

I sucked in air, trying to come up with a way to get out of this situation. Sports and any physical activities like it just weren't my area of expertise. Give me numbers, ask me to prepare a brief, all of that I could do, but ask me to do sit-ups or lift weights and I'm looking for the exit. I exhaled my breath.

"I recommend sticking with weight training now and getting it done Miss Jones," the counselor advised, looking over the rim of her glasses at me. I looked over my schedule again. Everything else listed was fine, but the weight training stood out to me as if highlighted and underlined.

Accepting defeat, I sighed and agreed, "You're right. I mind as well get it over with now." I slid out of the seat in front of her desk and headed for the door. "Thank-you Mrs. Michaels for all your help." She told me I was welcome and I left, letting the next student in line have their turn with her. Maybe they'll fare better than I did. I can't say why, but I absolutely did not like physical activity, so I was unsure how I was going to get through this semester. On top of that, I had it three times a week for an hour.

Sinking deep into my thoughts, I left the administration building and went back to my dorm. Sauntering into the building pass the front desk, I didn't even notice Naomi sitting there when she said, "Hey Aaliyah!" It was like I heard her, but because I was so in my head, I didn't hear enough to respond. I just kept walking toward my room.

When I finally got there, I sat on my bed and looked over my schedule again. Everything was what I expected for my final year, loose end classes and my senior project. Everything but the weight training, of course. It hadn't disappeared, it really was there. Blowing wind, feeling another episode of defeat coming on, I laid down and decided to call Kevin. The phone rang until his voicemail picked up. I left a message about my class schedule frustrations, that I missed him and for him to give me a call when he got a free moment. Turning over, I fell asleep.

The sound of knocking on my door woke me from my nap. The campus was pretty empty still, so I couldn't imagine who was knocking. Drowsily I got up and made my way to the door to stop the intrusive banging. Without asking who it was, I opened the door with sleepy, annoyed eyes. Standing there was Xavier. "Hey Beautiful," he smiled.

My annoyance intensified as I asked, "What do you want?" I really wasn't in the mood for him at that moment.

"Baby, are you still mad?"

"Are you kidding me? Please leave," I said ready to close the door in his face.

"C'mon Liyah," he said stopping the door. "Don't be like that. I messed up, I know, but I want to make it up to you. Let me show you and treat you like the queen you are."

"Whatever, Xavier. Don't you think you are a little late? Because I think you should've done that when you had me." I was not happy at all with how things turned out between us. We had been dating all through college up until his phone call at the beginning of the summer. I imagined building a life with him after we graduated. I loved him … love him. Despite my words, I was realizing that I still had feelings for him. That could be the only reason I was still entertaining him.

"Let me explain. Can I come in?"

"For what?"

"I just don't want to have my personal life out there like this. I am still in the hallway. This is your business, too, and I know you don't like too many people in your private affairs."

He had a point and knew me well. I shifted to the side, "You can come in only long enough to say your piece, and then you have to go."

"Fine. I can deal with that." He walked passed me in an attempt to sit down.

"Is it really going to take so long that you feel the need to get comfortable?"

"Ouch. You are cold work, Ms. Jones."

"I just don't want you to overstay your welcome." I rolled my eyes, "Can you get to it, please?"

"What? You have something to do? Your man coming to get you?" he laughed.

"That's none of your business, and stop stalling."

"Fine," he said, finally getting to the point. "I just wanted to tell you that you are beautiful and I love you. This summer I had so many females coming at me and my teammates talking about how I was whipped and needed to explore my options."

"Tell me when I am supposed to feel sorry for *you* dumping

me."

"Stop Liyah! I'm being honest. I let what others thought get the best of me and ended up losing you. Nothing was worth that, and I see that now. I actually saw it a month or so ago and called you. But when you said you were going on a date, I got blindsighted. I knew my lady wouldn't step out on me. I didn't expect for you to actually move on."

"Well, I did. And because you were too insecure, you lost me. That is no longer my problem."

Xavier moved in my direction, and I moved away out of reflex. "Wow, I can't even touch you?"

"No, I think you should be leaving now."

"Liyah, I am so sorry. Please let's start over," he pleaded. I knew the longer I remained in his presence, the more my resolve would dissolve. He needed to go.

"Please leave." I moved toward the door to escort him out of my room. Opening the door, I repeated, "Please leave." He looked me over one last time, trying to make eye contact, before finally exiting. I closed the door behind me and slid down to the floor. There I sat as the tears flooded my eyes and I cried. Cried for what it was, what it could have been, and what it wasn't anymore.

An hour or so later I finally got it back together. I needed to clean myself up, so I grabbed my shower caddy and headed for the showers. No one seemed to be around as I headed down the hallway to the bathroom. I walked to the shower I had determined to have the best pressure and put the water on. Stepping into the heat, I allowed the flow to clear my mind of any lingering thoughts of Xavier and my class schedule. The warmth surrounded me and took me to a calm place where total relaxation was the theme. My hands traveled the length of my body, finding their way to my thighs. I hadn't had any since the night before Kevin left and I'd forgotten my toy back in Jersey. With no one else around, now felt like the perfect time to explore me.

Sliding my finger between my lower lips, I tapped on my pleasure button. I jumped a little caught off-guard at how sensitive

I was. I guess the lack of sex and the heightened emotions from earlier really did a number on me. Even so, I knew I needed this release, so I continued to get reacquainted with myself.

As the shower water rained down on me, I tickled my clit, gliding my finger over my wetness. Closing my eyes, I applied more pressure as I swirled around and across my hot spot and let my thoughts drift to when Kevin and I were together last. I shivered as I thought about his hands gripping me and him sliding deep inside me as I stuck my finger inside my pussy. Working myself over, I imagined my legs wrapped around his waist as he bounced me up and down, and up and down again. Finding release, I tightened the grip of my thighs around his waist.

Kevin gently led my feet back to the ground before he slowly got on his knees in front of me and buried his tongue deep in my already flowing river. Arching my back and thrusting forward, I pushed his head deep into my valley. I egged him on to devour his pussy and make me cum again. Maintaining his tongue play on my clit, I felt two fingers move deep inside me, finger fucking me from moaning to calling out in extreme pleasure. As I reached my plateau and my orgasm came down, I called out Jess's name.

My eyes opened wide as the realization hit home. I covered my mouth in disbelief that I called for Jess while I was cuming. If anything, I should have been calling Kevin's name, not some female. This was unreal. I couldn't help but think about what was going on with me.

I quickly washed up and got out of the shower. I felt like I needed to hide. From who, I couldn't tell you, but I knew the bathroom shower was not where I needed or wanted to be.

Once I got in my room, I called Kevin to remind myself of the man I loved and to find some solace. He didn't answer. Of all the times not to answer, he would choose now. I dropped the phone on the bed and screamed into my pillow. My mind kept going back to calling out for Jess.

I had to find a distraction. Despite just taking a shower, I decided to do something I never did. I threw on some sweats, grabbed my iPod, and left my room. To avoid running into Xavier,

I chose to go out the side door instead of the main one. On my way out, I ran into Naomi.

"Hey Aaliyah!" she exclaimed when she saw me. "What are you up to?"

"I need to get out my room, so I decided to go for a run. You?"

"Me, too. I try to run a few times a week on my own," she said while she stretched a bit.

I frowned my face and told her, "Not me. I'm not really into all this physical activity stuff, but today it just seems like a good idea."

"Really? Is everything okay? You did look upset when I saw you earlier." She stopped stretching and looked at me with concern.

I vaguely recalled what she was talking about. I was really in my head when I first got in the dorms mulling over the whole weight training thing. "Oh, that?" I decided to say, "It was nothing. Just a class I have to take I've been avoiding."

"Can't be that bad."

"For me, it can be."

"Want to talk about it?"

"Not really."

"Okay." Naomi turned toward me like she wanted to say more. I could tell she was thinking of something but chose to keep her thoughts to herself. Instead she asked me, "Well, do you mind if we run together? It's always better to run with someone, for safety."

Thinking it over, it did seem like a better idea to have someone to run with. A whole lot of people would be upset if something was to happen to me, including me. And considering I wasn't much of a runner, it sounded like a great idea to have a little bit of company. "Okay, but I'm not a great runner."

"That's cool. We can run at your pace." We started running toward SAQ, all the way past the apartment complexes to the Papa John's parking lot. We crossed at the corner, ran a block toward the block the Towers was on, and then ran up Mitchell pass the Towers. We ran through campus to the AUC library, around Clark Atlanta and back up toward Morris Brown on MLK. I was dog tired since the closest I got to this much activity was sex, but Naomi didn't look phased at all. She guided us toward the stadium and pushed me to run up all the stairs leading back to the dorm. I thought I was going to die!

I didn't, but by the end, all I wanted to do was lay down. Naomi told me to walk around to get my heart rate back to normal. Following her advice, I cooled down. Her room was closest to the main entrance, so she invited me to her room to get a bottle of water and to chill for a bit longer. She said I looked like I was going to pass out at any second, so she wanted to keep an eye on me.

Naomi's room was neat, with everything looking like it all had its own assigned spot. While I sat there, she took off her shirt and threw it in a laundry basket she had in a corner. To say the least, I was a bit jealous. I wished my body looked like hers. "You work out a lot?" I asked.

"Yeah, comes with being an athlete."

"You're an athlete?"

"Yeah, since freshmen year I have been on the Track and Field team."

"Wow, you just do everything, huh? Like a renaissance woman, or something."

She smiled, "I wouldn't say that, but coming from a not so great background, I wanted to ensure I could afford to go to college. I am only able to pay because of the athletic and academic scholarships I've received."

"I feel you completely. My family tried, but I knew they couldn't afford to put me through college. I decided long before I was even in high school that I had to do what I could to excel academically. In my mind, it was the only way to open up doors of opportunity."

"Exactly! The same with being into sports. Both that and academics are the reasons I will have a degree at the end of this school year." I smiled at her, nodding my head in agreement. "Well, you look like the color has come back in your face," she smiled.

"Great!" I smiled again. "Thanks for being so concerned. I

really appreciate it." I stood to my feet and reached my hands up to the ceiling in a stretch.

"It's cool." She grabbed a towel and washcloth she had hanging in her wardrobe and put on shower shoes. "Well, I am going to go head to the shower. I would say stay as long as you like, but I'm sure you probably want to take one, too, and go relax."

"Yeah, you're right. After all of that running, I am not smelling too fresh, so I am going to go do the same." I thanked Naomi for running with me and pushing me to finish. Despite how much it sucked, I felt really good about myself and the fact I didn't quit. I left Naomi's room beaming all the way to my own, proud of my accomplishments.

jess

Chapter 15

"Hello?" I yawned into the phone.

"Hello? Jess?" It sounded like Aaliyah, but I hadn't heard from her since she left for school, so it couldn't have been her. I had to be tripping or had way more to drink last night then I thought. I really needed to wake up.

"Yeah, it's me," I said into the receiver.

"Hey Jess, long time no speak."

Still unsure of who I was talking to I asked, "Umm, excuse me, but who is this?"

There was a pause before the caller answered, "It's Aaliyah."

I sat straight up and tried to play the shock and surprise in my voice off, "Aaliyah? Hey! Wow, wasn't expecting a call from you."

"Yeah, I know I'm a horrible friend."

"No, I didn't mean it like that. Just, we haven't really talked since before you left. I'm sure it's because we've both been busy," I said, forcing a smile into my voice. As happy as I was to hear from her, I was skeptical about why she was calling.

"Probably. Senior year is quite a different beast, but I am managing. How have you been?"

"Oh, I've been good. Staying busy at the store. How's everything for you? How's Kevin?" I cringed a little pushing that last part out. I only asked because I wanted to give her the sense that everything was good between us. That said, I know how I feel about Aaliyah. I have finally come to terms with that, and because of it, I would rather there not be a Kevin or anyone for that matter. But even if he was out of the picture, it doesn't mean I would be since she doesn't like women. At least, that's what she says. Past situations imply otherwise. I don't know. She had to be one of the most confusing females I have met up to this point.

"Umm, everything is good. He's in Florida handling business. I'm throwing myself into my studies in his absence. Still getting harassed by Mieko?" I almost missed what she said because I was so deep in my own thoughts. But, by her nervous laughter, it was obvious I wasn't the only one hesitant to ask about certain subjects.

"No, I'm not. Everything is good." After I answered, we both fell silent for a moment. I wondered what she was thinking and what made her call me. Even though I had my concerns, maybe it was a good thing she called, since she'd been on my mind even more than usual lately. In another week I'd be in Atlanta for Pride and I did want to see her. At least I was hoping to see her. I broke the silence and told her, "I'll be in Atlanta for Black Pride in a week or so. It would be awesome if we could get together while I am there."

"Oh really?" her voice squeaked.

"Ah, yeah. Ty and I come down every year."

"Oh. That's cool."

"So, would that be cool with you?"

"What?"

"Seeing you. Will I be able to see you while I am there?"

She pushed out, "Suuuure. Of course you can."

"Are you sure? You seem hesitant."

"Yeah, yeah. Why wouldn't I be?" Before I could respond she continued, "Just call me when you get here."

I asked again, "Are you sure?"

"Yes, Jess. I am sure. It would be good to see you."

"I'm glad to hear that. I miss my friend," I smiled into the phone. This time it was genuine.

"Me too." For a beat, we both didn't say anything, and then Aaliyah said, "Well, I need to go. I have RA duties to attend to."

"RA?"

"Residential Assistant. I have desk duty in my dorm."

"Sounds fun."

"Not really, but it's helping pay my room and board, so I can't complain." I could sense she was probably grimacing on the other end of the line, but content. She added, "But I do need to go."

"I understand, go and handle your business. It was really good hearing from you, Aaliyah."

"The same."

"See you soon."

"Yup, just call me." She hung up and despite how awkward the exchange was, I felt good about it.

I stretched a bit and got up out of bed. Claiming that today was going to be a great day, I headed to the bathroom to shower and get ready for it. I pulled out a pair of jeans, a black button-down shirt, and a red graphic T-shirt I loved. I pulled my hair back and braided it all together. My hair was really soft and slippery, so I tightened it with a black rubber band so it wouldn't unravel. I grabbed my Timbs and phone and headed downstairs.

As I hit the landing, my phone started ringing. I looked at the ringer and it was Jordyn. Smiling, I answered, "Hello Beautiful."

She replied, "Hello, yourself, Gorgeous."

"Well, thank-you. How are you doing today?"

"I'm good. Taking a break from studying. What are you up to?"

I held the phone to my face with my shoulder as I put my boots on. "Just got dressed. Not sure what I am about to get into, though. Thinking I might go see mi madre."

"Aww, that's sweet…"

"Damn," I cursed as my phone slipped and fell to the ground. Yelling loud enough for Jordyn to hear me I said, "Hold on! I dropped the phone. Give me a second." I finished with my boots real quick and picked up the phone. "I apologize for that. I was putting my Timbs on when the phone dropped."

"That's okay. I was just saying how sweet it is you are so close to your mom. I miss mine. I am way overdue for a visit home."

"The holidays are around the corner. Thanksgiving is only like two months away. Can you go home then?"

"No," I could hear her groan. "I have a huge project like paper due by the end of the semester. I won't be able to go home until Winter break."

"It won't be that long. Besides, you still have me here in N.Y." I smiled into the phone.

"That's true." She paused as if contemplating the statement before speaking again. "Anyway, I was calling to see if you had any plans for Labor Day weekend. I was thinking of going to the Jersey Shore for the holiday."

"Aww, that sounds like fun, but Ty and I are going to Atlanta."

"Atlanta?"

"Yeah. Ty and I go to Atlanta for Pride every year. I was thinking of sitting it out, but Ty talked me into it."

"I see."

Sensing the change in her voice, I asked, "What's wrong? You sound different."

"Nothing."

"No, seriously, what's wrong? It sounds like your whole demeanor just changed."

"It's nothing. You're good."

"Okay," I said, brushing her evident attitude change off. "Well, I'm excited. Got a few friends down in Atlanta that I haven't seen in a while."

"Like who?"

"Like my girl Naomi, who went down there for college, and Aaliyah, too, who actually called me today out of the blue."

She zoned in on Aaliyah. "Aaliyah? Isn't that the girl from this summer? Your ex's friend? The one from the club?"

I didn't like where this line of questioning was going. Jordyn sounded like she was heading down a path I wasn't in the mood to travel.

Honestly, I don't understand how females want you to be honest and truthful to them, but then throw all that honesty in your face. I braced myself for impact. "Yeah. I haven't seen her since she left."

"Jess, why do you need to see her? She played you. She's not worth your time."

"Don't go there, Jordyn. She's my friend and I want to see her."

"Bullshit, Jess! That girl doesn't even want you! Why are you wasting your time? You have me right here and you are seriously going to Atlanta to see some chick who doesn't even want you? Are you serious right now?"

"Jordyn, you don't want to do this. I was having such a good day and we were having a great conversation. I am not about to let you ruin it. I'll hang up before I let you do that." I could feel my blood pressure rising. I really wasn't trying to argue with her about this. "We were friends before all that mess and are still friends after. You should not be concerned about any of that, anyway. You are making it into more than what it is."

"No I'm not and why shouldn't I be? I am the one who is there for you. I am the one spending time with you. I am the one who is fucking you. What the fuck, Jess?" She paused before saying, "Fuck it! Fine! You run to her, but when she hurts you *AGAIN*, don't come over here. I don't have anything for you."

"Are you kidding me right now, Jordyn? First of all, you knew what you were getting into when you first started kicking it with me. I never sugar coated that with you. Don't think just because you have a toothbrush at my house that you can stake any claim over me. We are not a couple, so you really have no reason to be tripping so hard right now."

"You know what? Fuck you, Jess!" Jordyn hung up the phone before I could get another word out. I closed my eyes in frustration. I don't even understand what she's so upset about. I know she can get a little jealous, but she has just gone way off the deep end.

Exasperated, I walked in the kitchen, grabbed a Budweiser Black Crown and then went to my study to try and relax my mind. My thoughts were racing so badly, that sitting in one spot wasn't helping at all. She completely killed my vibe. I called Ty so I could vent and be done with it, but he didn't answer his phone. I left him a message telling him how Jordyn was tripping because I was going to see Aaliyah in Atlanta. It didn't dawn on me until after I hung up that Ty probably was going to agree with Jordyn about seeing Aaliyah.

Under my breath I said, "Whatever," as I got up. I grabbed my wallet, keys and made a beeline for the garage. Usually I would ride my bike around when I really needed to clear my head, but solitude was not my friend right now. I got into my Ashton Martin as the garage door went up. Making a left, I resolved that it was going to be a *Black Ice* night.

Black Ice was a real upscale establishment with valet parking for those who could afford the extra expense. I handed over my keys and warned the valet to be easy on my clutch. It was still a little early, but I drove out here hoping that Spice was working tonight. Watching her dance could always lift my spirits. She always focused on me, unlike the other females who were busy vying for the attention of the dudes in the spot. I could really go for her attention as a distraction right now.

Despite being early, it seemed like there was a lot of us needing some extra attention today to keep from thinking of whatever we were running from. I grabbed a table in a corner and ordered a Long Island Iced Tea. Looking around the club, I didn't see Spice anywhere. It was disappointing that she seemed to be nowhere to be found. I sipped on my drink, sunk into my chair and played on my phone.

Before I knew it, I was looking at the bottom of an empty glass. "Would you like another drink?" a person from beside me asked.

I looked up to the waitress standing by for my answer. "Yeah. Another Long Island would be good. Can I ask you something?"

"Sure."

"Do you know if Spice is working tonight?"

"I think so. I think she's in the lineup that starts in a few."

"Okay. Thanks."

"No problem. I'll be back shortly with your drink." She left and I turned back to my phone. There wasn't anything happening on social media, but I was still trying my best to find something to keep my mind off earlier. Just when I felt myself easing up, the screen flashed. It was Ty returning my call, and I knew already what he was going to say. I didn't need that at the moment, so I let it go to voicemail.

Putting my phone down, I sipped my Long Island and scanned the club. The DJ changed the music and started playing *Pour It Up* by Rhianna as he introduced the first dancer of the night. "Coming to the stage, the sensationally sexy Chyna Doll! Get out your seats and make sure you show her some love!" A chocolate female with full lips walked onto the stage with an outfit that left little to the imagination and what seemed like 8-inch platforms.

She was the same female that was with Spice the night she came to the *Pinky Pussy*. Sex appeal dripped off her like rainwater rolling down your skin. I didn't recall her being that sexy that night at the store, but she was commanding my full attention. Then again, it may just be this liquor talking. I smirked and took another sip of my drink.

I got out of my seat, pulling out a few bills on the way to the stage. She was crouched down with her back to the audience, bouncing her backside up and down to the tempo of the music. I could only imagine what I would do to her at that very moment if the chance was given. I reached out to get her attention. She looked my way and started crawling toward me. When Rhianna started singing "All I see is signs, all I see are dollar signs," right on beat, she thrust her pelvis against the stage, making her bottom perfectly rise and fall in front of me, before finally getting to me. She turned around and leaned forward raising her butt in the air. Before I knew what was going on, she lifted herself up and did a split in the air. Entranced, I stayed at the stage tossing bills until the song finished and she left.

I went back to my table and took the last of my drink to the head. After watching that dance, I really could use Spice's attention. As if she heard my silent request, she appeared in front of me, "Hey Sexy. I heard some chic was looking for me, I'm glad to find that it was you."

Smiling, I looked up at her and told her, "Yeah, I came here to see you tonight. You always make a sister feel wanted." I took in her soft pink lace boy shorts and matching lace top. Her little petite body was pulling the attention of onlookers, but her focus was solely on me.

"Is that so? I like that you came to see me," she said flirting with me.

"Yeah. Are you available for a lap dance?"

"I can do better than that for you." She reached out her hand and said, "Come with me."   I grabbed her hand as I stood up and followed her through the now packed club toward the VIP area. I'd never been to this part of the club before, but it was set-up with individual rooms for private dances. "Over here," she pulled me into one of the open rooms, closing the door behind her. "Just relax."

I looked around the room, taking it all in. *Black Ice* didn't spare any expense when it came to VIP. The room was set up like a scaled down 5-star hotel room. I took a seat on a couch in a seating area off to the right side of a nice plush four post king size bed against one wall. There was also a bathroom connected to the room, which seemed to be the equivalent of a mini spa.

Spice walked to a sound system hidden in the wall opposite where I was sitting. The sounds of Jill Scott singing *'Don't want this thing, but can't let go. Even though, I need it so'* began playing around the room as she slowly walked toward me. I watched her body sway before me, dictating the movement of my eyes. She turned around and laid her body against mine, rubbing on me erotically. My hands caressed her silky skin and took her essence into my senses.

I've always found the fact that she was so petite cute, but in this moment she was pure sensuality and sex. The more she grinded on me, the more I wanted to devour her. She stood up and straddled me, grinding down on me sending chills through my body. Whether she realized it just then or not, it was going to go down, but not here.

I pulled her ear close to my lips and whispered, "May I have you for the evening?" She smiled at me and kissed me. I sucked on her tongue before pulling away from her. "Not here." Something about having her in the club just made me feel some kind of way.

"Okay." She got up and asked, "Please wait here?" I nodded and she disappeared into the attached bathroom. Sitting there I went over in my head whether I should be doing this or not. I resolved to pump my breaks a bit and ask some questions. At that moment Spice came back out dressed, "Are you ready?"

A little sober from my lust filled inebriation, I told her, "More than you know I want you right now, but I need to know if you are good health-wise." I was dead serious. She looked at me inquisitively. I stared back at her. Like I said, I was dead serious. No matter how much I wanted it, Spice's lifestyle had me a little concerned. No pussy was good enough to possibly put my health in jeopardy.

Spice opened her purse and handed me a piece of paper. It was medical papers giving her a clean bill of health. "Does this help?" she asked.

"How old is this?"

"Check the date yourself." I looked and noticed that it was dated for earlier in the week.

"Look, I meant no disrespect…"

She cut me off. "None taken. I understand your concerns, but trust, I am very selective about who I give my full attention to," she winked at me. "You still want to get out of here, or what?" I got up and again grabbed her outstretched hand.

I smirked, "Indeed I do."

aaliyah

Chapter 16

As much as I loathed this part of my week, I headed to my weight training class with plans to put the least amount of effort possible into it. That's what I had been doing all week without consequence. I mumbled to myself, "Thank goodness it's Friday." Even this overachiever couldn't push herself to do more than the minimum. For the whole period I planned to ride the bicycle, slowly peddling with the least amount of resistance.

I watched others take the class seriously, especially Naomi, who was an unexpected surprise on the first day of class. I guess I never did tell her it was weight training that was giving me so much heartache. Anyway, she was really into it. As she interchangeably lifted dumbbells, her muscles flexed. Sweat visibly showed through her shirt at her collar and armpits. I couldn't understand how she could work herself to the point of sweating. Riding the bike kept me perfectly dry by the end of class.

Naomi put down the dumbbells and walked over to me. "Is that all you plan on doing today?"

I looked at her and said, "Yeah. This is what I have been doing every class this week and Coach Barr hasn't said anything. I don't really want to be here, you know, so this is my happy place."

She shook her head at me. "I really think you should take it more seriously. I know Coach. If he hasn't said anything as of now, know that it's coming."

"But I just don't like physical activity like this. I told you that. I am not the least bit athletic. I know you remember that time we ran together. By the time we were done, it felt like I was going to die," I told her as I continued my pace.

"Yeah, I remember, but I can help you. I don't mind helping you out, Aaliyah. It could be just like freshman year," Naomi smiled.

"No, I am fine with this right here," I motioned to the bike I was peddling on.

"If you say so," she said as she hunched her shoulders and walked over to a leg machine, piled on some weights and started opening and closing her legs against the resistance. I shook my head at her but was secretly jealous of her dedication. I mean, she had to be dedicated because her body was flawless. I looked at my arms. By no means am I considered fat, but I am definitely not the poster child for fitness. Regular people like myself were just not built that way. I shook off the thoughts and just kept peddling.

At the end of the class, I was ready to bolt out of there. Before I could make it, though, Coach Barr called my name, "Aaliyah, I need you to stick around a moment. I need to speak to you."

In my head I cursed and turned around towards Coach Barr, "Okay." I took a seat on one of the benches while I waited.

When the last student left, Coach Barr came and sat next to me, "Is everything okay with you, Aaliyah?"

"Why do you ask that?" I fiddled with the dry towel I had in my hand.

"Well, you have been coming to this class for a little while, and I have yet to see any effort from you." I looked down at the towel in my hand. What am I supposed to say? I hate anything physical and that this weight training class was not my idea? I couldn't say that, so I didn't say anything. "Look Aaliyah, if nothing is wrong with you, you are going to need to pick up the effort. You are heading down a path that is going to lead to you failing my class."

I looked at him flabbergasted, "What?!? I'm coming to class and working out. What does it matter what I do as long as I am doing something?"

Coach Barr tone changed as he cut my rant off, "Miss Jones that is enough. Just like any other class, you need to show effort to receive a passing grade. Either you get it together or repeat this class next semester. The choice is yours." With that, he got up and left the room.

"Shit!" I yelled as his words started to sink in. This man just told me I was on a failing path. At weight training. Failure is not an option. Not only would it ruin my grade point average, I just don't want to have to try this all over again next semester. It was now or never. "Ugh, what am I going to do?"

I got up, made sure I wasn't forgetting anything, and headed to the locker room to shower. The whole conversation was a complete buzz kill and I really had no idea what I was going to do in order to make it through the rest of the semester. So deep in thought I walked into the locker room and sat on one of the benches with my head in my hands.

"Is everything okay Aaliyah?" I heard the familiar voice of Naomi ask.

I looked up whipping the few tears of frustration that had escaped my eyes. "Oh, hey Naomi, I didn't think anyone was still here."

"Well, I was about to head to the dorm but saw you with your head down. Is everything okay?"

"Umm, yeah, it'll be okay."

"What will?"

I honestly didn't know what to say or if I even wanted to tell her what Coach had just got finish telling me. "It's nothing. Don't worry about it."

"C'mon Aaliyah. Aren't we friends?"

"Yeah."

"Then tell your friend what's up. What did Coach Barr say? I saw you stayed behind with him."

I took a deep breath, nothing to lose with telling her, right? I looked at Naomi and told her, "He told me that if I don't start showing more effort he was going to fail me." I stared at her waiting for her to say something like 'I told you so,' since she kind of did tell me the same thing in class not too long ago.

"Coach Barr has always been that way. He really takes his job seriously." I grimaced at her. She continued, "Well, my offer still stands. If you need some help, I can help you."

"No, I will figure it out. I don't want to slow you down. I see how into it you are and I'd just be a burden."

"Aaliyah, I am offering to help you because I want to. If I had any concerns or reservations I wouldn't offer."

Our eyes locked. Naomi had a stern look on her face; she meant business. I sighed and agreed. Who better than her to get me through weight training anyway? Hell, she got me through Biology. Besides, if the consolation prize was even looking half as good as her body did, why not. I thanked her before she left and finally hopped in the shower. I couldn't wait for this semester to be over.

Despite the messed up morning I experienced, the rest of the day went fairly well. I listened as my professor went over what to expect for next week prior to dismissing us to either our next class or the weekend. For me, the end of the class meant the weekend. I grabbed all my belongings, putting them in my book bag and headed out of the classroom. One of my classmates caught up with me before I got too far to ask to borrow some notes. We walked and talked heading toward the student library so that she could just photocopy the notes. It was a lot easier that way. Besides, I didn't mind sharing my notes, I just wasn't giving them away to anybody.

Once she got her copies and we went our separate ways, I went to my dorm. Xavier was standing at the front desk talking to whoever was on duty. I sighed wishing I had taken the chance and checked if the side entrance was open. Ready to just get the interaction over with I tried to pass by him unnoticed.

"Aaliyah!" I heard him call from behind me. I kept walking like I didn't hear him. He ran to catch up to me. "Hey, Aaliyah, wait up." I took a deep breath and rolled my eyes. Just when my day was starting to go well again, now I needed to deal with this. Xavier caught up to me and started walking with me, "Didn't you hear me calling you?"

I snapped, "I wasn't trying to hear you calling me."

"Ouch! What's got your panties in a bunch?"

"Shut up, Xavier." He just laughed, disregarding my attitude.

"You know, even when you are acting like this you're gorgeous, right?"

I stopped and looked at him, "What do you want Xavier?"

"Just to talk to my favorite girl, that's all."

"I'm not your girl. As a matter of fact, I'm not even your friend, so say what it is you want so you can leave me alone."

"Liyah, why are you still being so cold towards me? I apologized to you for what I did this summer. I told you what was going on and why. Why can't you just forgive me?"

"Are you kidding me?" I looked at Xavier as if he'd grown two heads. "Are you seriously kidding me right now? You hurt me, Xavier. You broke my freaking heart, and because now you figured out how good you had it, I'm supposed to just fall in line? Fuck you, Xavier. I don't have time for this." I turned and walked off determined that the next time I stopped it would be behind the closed door of my dorm room.

I made it to my room without any further interruptions. Xavier was smart enough to know not to try and follow me. I sat on my bed, picked up my pillow and screamed into it. Why did he feel like everything was just okay because he apologized? I loved him so much and so deeply and would have done anything for him. Obviously the feelings weren't mutual, or else we wouldn't be having these types of interactions. I would be laid up with him somewhere reading a book while he's watching ESPN or something with his head in my lap. He brought this reality on himself, not me, and he needed to realize that.

I was done giving Xavier attention or the space to occupy in my mind. Shaking my head, I pulled my phone out of my book bag. Whenever I have classes I turn the ringer off so that it doesn't accidentally go off in class. Keeping it in my bag also keeps me from getting chastised by one of my professors for being on the phone during class.

The screen indicated that I had a missed call from Kevin and a voicemail. That brought a smile to my face. I was certain the voicemail had to be from him. Considering how up and down my day has been going, hearing from my man was the perfect way to bring me out of the funk I was in.

I quickly checked the message and swooned when his voice started coming through the phone, "Hey Baby. I am going to guess you are still in class. When you get this message, give me a call. I have a surprise for you!" The way he said it made me laugh. He laughed too into the phone, "Really, I hope you are having a wonderful day. Call me when you can, Beautiful. I love you." The message ended and I couldn't stop grinning from ear to ear. What could the surprise possibly be? I was so anxious!

Looking through my contacts, I scrolled to Kevin's number and hit send to dial it. The phone rang a few times before he finally answered, "Hey Beautiful, hold on a second. I was just about to walk out of the office."

"Oh, no problem, take your time," I told him just happy to be speaking to him. I hated that we were so far apart and I couldn't see him when I wanted. And between our two schedules, we couldn't always talk on the phone like we did during the summer, anyway. It was hard, but he was worth it in my book, so I sucked it up.

"Are you still there," he asked as he came back on the line.

"Yes! So what is this surprise you were talking about?"

"How bad do you want to know?" he asked. I could tell he was smiling.

"I can show you better than I can tell you," I said flirting with him over the phone. I was long overdue for some loving. Thinking about it made me make a mental note to go to *Tokyo Valentino* to pick up a new toy. There was no telling when I would see my man again and I needed something to keep me until then. Thinking about it slightly changed my mood. "When will I get a chance to again? I really miss you," I pouted.

"Aww, Baby. I miss you, too. How about I come up there Labor Day weekend?"

Getting excited, I said into the phone, "Don't play with me, Kevin."

"I'm serious. That was the surprise. I was going to take a few days off around Labor Day to come spend some time with you, unless you are going to be too busy for your man?"

"NO!" I yelled. He just laughed. "No, I would love for you to come up here. I miss you so much. It has been forever since I've seen you and I need you to extinguish this fire."

"Fire, huh? I definitely have something for that."

"I know; I'm waiting for your hose to put this fire out," I responded as I licked my lips; the exchange was starting to excite me. I wanted Kevin next to me, touching me, playing with me. I trailed my hand down and unbuttoned my pants. The ache in between my thighs was calling for some attention.

His voice deepened as he asked, "Is that so? How exactly would you like me, I mean, *my hose* to put it out for you?" Unzipping my pants, I went exploring with my fingers until I was touching the slickness that I felt developing. I caressed my pleasure button, which was exceptionally sensitive, knowing I had to do something about it. My breathing became more labored as I got acquainted with myself, slightly more focused on what I was doing than the phone. I heard Kevin ask again about putting my fire out.

As I was about to explain to him just what I wanted, there was a knock at my door. "Shit!" I exclaimed, pulling my hand out my pants. Who the hell could be knocking on my door of all times at that very second?

"What's wrong?" he asked.

"Someone's knocking at my door." The knocking continued as if the person on the other side of the door was determined to get me to open the door.

Kevin sighed, "Go ahead and get it, Baby. I will be there soon and I will take care of you."

"But I don't want to. I was enjoying where this was going."

"It's okay. Get the door, I need to go anyway. I pulled up to the house a few minutes ago but have been sitting outside this whole time. It's raining and I have a few things to take out the car I don't want to get wet."

"You already have something here wet," I said slyly.

"I know, and I wish I could take care of that." The knock came again so loud that Kevin heard them through the phone. "Go ahead, Baby. I will talk to you later."

Pissed off, I obliged and got off the phone. I was so furious with whoever was on the other side of that door, that I flew up and opened it. "WHAT THE HELL DO YOU WANT?!?" I yelled before I realized who was at the door. Naomi was standing there with an exasperated expression on her face. She looked at me, looking down before quickly looking back at my face. Her face turned flush. I looked down and realized my jeans were still open. I quickly turned around and zipped myself back up, pulling my shirt over the top of my jeans. *That was awkward*, I thought to myself.

When I turned back around, Naomi was back in frenzy mode. "Aaliyah, you need to come with me. We have a situation involving one of the students living in your section."

"Okay, okay," I said grabbing my room key and throwing on some shoes, before running with Naomi down the hall to see what was going. I guessed play time would have to wait.

jess

Chapter 17

"Good afternoon passengers. This is the pre-boarding announcement for Delta flight 1920 to Atlanta. We would like to invite our Medallion members, those passengers with small children, and any passengers requiring special assistance, to begin boarding at this time. Please have your boarding pass ready. Thank you."

Finally, the boarding announcement came over the sound system. I nudged Ty who had been sleeping since we got to the airport, putting me on watch duty. "Wake up, Ty, they're boarding."

"Already," he yawned and stretched.

I thought to myself, *We've been here for two hours, what do you mean already?* Maybe I was jealous because he got to sleep and I didn't. I never get any sleep before traveling since I tend to spend the night before packing. With most things, I strategically map out my plan of attack to make execution seamless. When it came to packing, though, not so much. I always found myself spending all night and morning packing, and end up with more clothes and shoes than I could possibly need. "Story of my life," I mumbled to myself.

"Huh? You say something J?" Ty asked, bringing me back into the here and now.

"Nothing. Just thinking out loud." I stood up and stretched myself. "Let's go ahead and board now. I want to find our seats and stow our carry-ons before they begin boarding the general population."

Ty and I boarded the aircraft and found our seats fairly easy in First Class. We got comfortable as a flight attendant checked on us and took our drink requests. Once she left, I took out my phone and made a quick call to my mother to let her know I was on my flight about to head to Atlanta. No matter what, I always called my mother to let her know when I was leaving the area and when I was back.

After I got off the phone with her, I called Jordyn. Since telling her I'd be in Atlanta for Labor Day weekend, things had been a little tense between us. I'll never understand why she was so in her feelings over the possibility of me seeing Aaliyah. First, she and I were friends, maybe with a few extra benefits, but that's it. There were no labels between us. Second, Aaliyah and I were just friends and nothing more. She doesn't even like females and Jordyn knows that. I just didn't understand.

After a few rings, her voicemail picked up. I was tempted to just hang up but decided to dial back my petty meter and leave her a message letting her know I was on my way out of town and that I'd let her know when I was back. Just as I was finishing my message, an announcement requesting electronics to be switched to airplane mode filled the cabin as flight attendants were walking through doing final checks for seat belts. I shut my phone down and put it away.

Ty closed the magazine he was reading while I made my calls. "J, I am so excited! I don't know, but I feel like we need this vacation right now."

"Yeah," I agreed with him. "To think I almost canceled this

year. Nay would've been pissed," I laughed.

"That wouldn't have happened. I wouldn't have let that happen."

I laughed even more at how serious Ty was, "Oh really?"

"C'mon J, this is the biggest Pride we go to *every* year. No way was I going to let some chick keep us from attending."

"Who?"

"You know who I'm talking about, don't play dumb Jess."

I sighed. I knew exactly who he was referring to. Aaliyah was the reason we almost didn't make the trip this year. She definitely wasn't winning any cool points with my friends. "Aaliyah's not that bad, Ty."

"I never said she was, but she had your nose so wide open…" he stopped and looked at me funny. "Or maybe she still has your nose wide open," he half stated, half asked.

"What are you talking about now?" Again, I knew he was referring to the possibility of me getting to see her.

"Just stop. You cannot be serious about seeing her."

"Why not? She's my friend. It's not anything more than that."

"Not because you don't want it to be. I've known you just about all my life, Jesstina and I can tell when you have it bad for someone. I don't understand why you put your energy into someone who doesn't even want to admit she likes women, especially when you have someone in your life that actually does and wants you! I swear, you lesbians make things harder than they need to be."

"Jordyn and I have an understanding."

"That girl really cares about you, J. Open your eyes and let her in. I know Meiko messed you up bad, and then Aaliyah came along shaking things up, but Jordyn has been good to you and for you. You know I'm right. Leave that girl alone, there is no need to seek her out while we are in Atlanta."

I sat there and listened to Ty go in on me, all the while thinking it's not even that serious. I got it that I liked Aaliyah, but I was smart enough to know that ship had sailed. It seemed I was the only one who saw everything for what it was; not what it used to be or could have been, but what it was in this moment. Besides, I was not at a point where I wanted to give Jordyn all of that, I just wasn't. I shook my head; this conversation was over as far as I was concerned. "Got it, Ty, I'll keep all of that in mind." I took out my headphones, turned up my iPod, and looked out the window at the clouds. I could tell Ty was huffing and puffing at me, but I really didn't care. I just wasn't in the mood to continue the conversation anymore.

Ty and I didn't talk to each other the rest of the flight. The pilot finally came over the sound system for the jet and announced our descent into Atlanta. I felt a few butterflies as I thought about being in the same place as Aaliyah. Trying to quiet it down, I reminded myself that she was just a friend, nothing more.

I put my headphones away and prepared for landing. Once we were rolling toward our gate, I called Nay to let her know we had touched down. She let me know she was already there and would be waiting for us by luggage claim. I hung up the phone, turning to Ty asking if he was still mad. He, in essence, said it was my life and I could do what I wanted to do with it. I rolled my eyes realizing he was still in his feelings. As far as I was concerned, I hadn't done anything wrong and that everybody really needed to just chill when it came to my friendship with Aaliyah.

Nay was standing off to the side of one of the carousels when we finally got to luggage claim. She looked up from her phone and noticed us coming. Walking up to us she smiled and said, "It's so good to see you guys. I always look forward to ya'll coming down. It gets lonely without your family around." She hugged me, and then hugged Ty who gave her an over exaggerated amount of attention.

"Seriously, Ty?" I asked looking at him crazy.

"What? I'm glad to see someone with some common sense," he retorted back to me. I rubbed my head. His attitude was really starting to irritate me.

Nay interjected, "Whoa! What's going on between you two? What's all the hostility for?"

"Nay, talk some sense into your girl. She has freaking lost her damn mind over some straight girl!"

I chimed in, "That's not true!"

Nay laughed, "So it's about a girl? Figures. C'mon Ty, you know our girl can't help herself."

"But Nay, you don't understand! She's trying to see the girl when she has a perfectly fine one at home."

"Well, it is Pride, and if I know Jess, she didn't come down here with any ties."

I rolled my eyes, "Ya'll are really funny. I am *not* that bad."

Nay laughed, "Yes you are, but that's okay. IT'S FREAKING PRIDE! And my family is here!" She hugged both us forcing a reconciliation between us, at least for the moment. I welcomed it because this vacation would be awful if Ty and I were feuding. We hadn't feuded in years, but the last time we did, we didn't talk for months. I didn't really want to go through that again.

We joined in laughing with Naomi and grabbed our bags off the conveyor belt. She dropped us off at the Westin on Peachtree Street before heading back to the AUC. I made a mental note to get up to her campus and check out the college student scene before we left Atlanta. We all agreed to get together later that evening to hit up this spot called The Hideout that was kicking Pride Weekend off on a Thursday.

Once I was checked into my room and finally alone, I called Jordyn again. This time she answered, "Hello?"

"Hey, it's Jess. I was just calling to let you know we made it down here safely."

"I know," she said stiffly, "I got your message from earlier."

"Are you still mad at me Jordyn?"

"No, it's cool. You are a grown woman, Jess. You do what you want to do, no need to answer to anyone. Especially not me, not like I'm your girl or anything."

I couldn't help but roll my eyes in frustration. Why did women have to be difficult for no damn reason? Rubbing my left temple I spoke into the phone, "Please let's not go there right now. I just wanted to check in and let you know we made it."

"Okay. You made it. Glad to hear it. Have a great vacation. Bye." The phone connection went dead. She hung up before I could even say good-bye myself.

I mumbled under my breath, "Fucking women," and pulled out my charger to plug my phone up. I then remembered that I hadn't called Aaliyah yet to let her know I made it into Atlanta. I scrolled to her number and hit the call button to connect with her. The line just kept ringing until finally, her voicemail picked up. I couldn't deny I was a little bummed when she didn't answer the phone. I left her a message letting her know that I was in Atlanta staying at the Westin downtown on Peachtree. If she got a moment, I asked her to give me a call or to text me when she was available. The message took and I put my phone on the charger so it would be fully charged for tonight's shenanigans.

It had already been a really long day since I didn't get any sleep the night before. Taking my toiletry bag out my luggage I headed to the shower to wash some of the wear and tear off my body. After a short, but much needed hot shower, I dried off and laid on the bed in the buff. It was only a matter of time before I had drifted into a deep sleep.

There I stood in the room not knowing where I was. Four walls and a door surrounded me, with not much else. I walked through the door running into Meiko screaming at me, but I couldn't understand what she was saying. She was crying and pointing at me, pushing me, and screaming some more. Eventually, she pushed past me and disappeared. I was left in a completely vacant space. Even the door I had come through was gone. What in the world was going on? Just when I decided to turn around, there was Jordyn looking at me with sheer disappointment. I opened my mouth to speak, but nothing would come out. She simply shook her head at me and walked away. I tried to use everything in my being to scream her name, to get her attention and ask what I had done. Why did she look at me like that? She just kept walking until I couldn't see her anymore. I felt like I was losing my mind. First Meiko and then Jordyn, what or who would be next?

Rubbing my head, I turned around and saw a figure walking toward me. I couldn't tell who it was until it was way too late. Aaliyah walked up to me and smiled. She just stood there staring at me and smiling like she knew something I didn't. Again, I opened my mouth to speak, but nothing escaped. Aaliyah put her finger to my lips and laughed while shaking her head at me. I reached out to touch her and with a bang, she combusted into a sprinkling of dust. Even after she was gone the banging, continued. Brandy's *Best Friend* started to play as I searched for the banging.

"JESS, OPEN THE DOOR!!! I KNOW YOU'RE IN THERE!!! WHAT ARE YOU DOING?!?" I suddenly woke, realizing Ty was banging on the door of my hotel room and blowing up my phone.

I jumped up, grabbed a robe, and ran to open the door, shouting "Stop banging! I'm coming," at Ty.

Opening the door, I rubbed my eyes as he gave me the business, "Jess, you're not even ready!"

I closed the door behind Ty and sat on the bed, still rubbing my eyes, "What time is it?"

Ty flipped the light switch on as he answered, "It's after 11. You know Nay is going to be here any minute to pick us up. You need to be getting up and ready."

"All right. I'm getting up," I said, still wiping sleep from my eyes. I pulled out what I had planned to wear that night and disappeared into the bathroom to get myself together. Since I had already pre-staged everything, it didn't really take long to get dressed and ready to go. I sprayed on my *Guilty* by Gucci, one of my favorite colognes to wear when going out since it had citrusy and woody undertones, and a lingering effect. As the night wears on, it actually smells better.

Interrupting my thoughts, Ty knocked on the door, "Are you done yet? Nay said she's almost here."

"Yeah, I'm coming out now." I did a once over in the mirror and decided I looked good enough for a Thursday night event and left the bathroom.

"Well, whose panties are you trying to get into tonight?" Ty snickered as I walked into the living area of the room.

"Haha," I laughed, "Whatever, Ty. It's Pride and one does not half-step during Pride."

"Is that right?" he asked with a raised brow and commented, "I'll remember that," as he looked down at his phone. "Nay just texted that she's downstairs. Let's go before someone tries to give her a ticket or something. I am texting her to circle and that we'll be down there by the time she comes back around."

"Sounds good, let me just get my wallet and we can head down." We took the elevator down to the lobby and it looked like Queer Central with all the Rainbow Kids filling the space. I smiled because it always felt good to be around so many of my own. As we got outside, we saw Nay pulling up. We ran to the car and hopped in, making our way through the crowded downtown streets to The Hideout.

aaliyah

Chapter 18

"Ugh, why is she calling again? She is so persistent!" Since Jess has been in Atlanta she has called me at least five times, and each time I let her call go to voicemail. Who was I kidding, I couldn't meet up with Jess. What if everything just seems okay because I knew I wouldn't bump into here on the street like I could back home? What if I see her and the same thing happens again? I am definitely not into women, but whenever I'm around Jess, I just don't know. It is best for us both if we just do not see each other. I've come to that conclusion, why can't she figure it out, too?

I called my voicemail box and listened to her voicemail. After listening to it, I deleted it. Laying my phone back down on the stand next to my bed, I went back to watching the rerun of *A Different World* that was playing on my TV. I remember when I was still in Jersey and would watch this show as a child. I could not wait to get to college and have friends like Fran, Whitley, Jalisa, and Denise; and a boyfriend like Ron. I really had a thing for Ron back then because deep down on the inside, he was a sweetheart. His exterior persona was just a façade.

Being here now, though, it really isn't like on television; college life is not really that eventful. I am in my senior year, and most of what I remember has to do with my nose being stuck in the books and my failed relationship with Xavier. My youth had slipped away from me and I would never get that time back!

In the middle of my mini mid-life crisis, my phone started to go off again. A little perturb I stated, "Jess cannot be serious right now! Obviously if I did not answer the last time she called, why call again 5 minutes later?" Even though I was completely irritated, I figured enough was enough. With total frustration, I answered the phone, "Hello?!?"

"Hello, Liyah?" the voice on the other end of the phone inquired.

"Kevin?" I asked.

"Yeah, Baby, who else would it be?" The sound of his voice completely turned my mood around and I began to smile like the Cheshire cat.

"Hey Baby," I purred into the phone. "How have you been?"

"I have been good. Is everything okay?"

"It is now that I am speaking to you," I grinned even though I knew he couldn't see me.

"Are you sure? You sounded like something was bothering you when you answered the phone."

"Oh, it was nothing that mattered. I have really missed you," I said trying to get him off the subject. Honestly, all I wanted to do was talk to him, not waste time on things that weren't important. "Tell me about your day."

Taking the hint Kevin replied, "It has been a long day. My last patient just left and I am finishing up the record update now. I decided to take a break and check in on you."

"Aww, you were thinking of me?"

"I'm always thinking of you."

His response made me smile from ear to ear. "I can't wait to see you. By the way, what day are you flying in? I know we discussed you coming up for Labor Day, but I haven't seen an itinerary or been given any idea as to when you are going to be here? Are you trying to surprise me?" I asked playfully into the phone.

"Aaliyah, about that," Kevin spoke, his tone completely different from just a moment ago.

Deep down, I already knew what he was about to say, but a portion of me was hoping I was wrong. Hesitantly I asked, "What about it?"

"Something has come up and I'm not going to be able to make it up." I am pretty certain after that he said something about being sorry, but I just tuned him out. Kevin and I have not seen each other in months. I really was looking forward to spending time with my man. I needed him now to help drown out all the craziness going on, especially with Jess in town. I needed confirmation of everything I kept telling myself about moving on and having a man. Lately, though, I wasn't so sure.

Thinking on my feet I responded, "Okay. Well, I can come down there."

"NO!" he responded almost like he was panicking a little. Seemingly recovering, he said, "No, you can't come here."

"Why not? What came up?" I was starting to get an uneasy feeling and thinking that Kevin was hiding something from me. Is there someone else? Is he cheating on me? *"Not this again,"* I thought to myself. *"That's what I get. That's just what I fucking get!"* I felt the tears building up in my eyes.

"Something came up with my mom I need to take care of. Nothing but the family could or would keep me from coming to see you," I heard Kevin say through the phone.

I wiped my tears with the back of my hand, trying to calm myself before speaking, "Your mom? Is she okay?"

"Yeah, she is, just forgot about something I needed to do for her."

"Oh, okay." I asked, "Anything I can do?" trying to mask the guilt of my thoughts with concern.

"No, Baby. I just really apologize that I have to go back on my word. I promise I will make it up to you."

"I understand, I do. Do what you need to do."

"Thank you for understanding, I know it's not what you wanted to hear right now," he stated apologetically.

"You're right, it's not. I was really looking forward to seeing you," I pouted.

"I will make it up to you Aaliyah."

"I'm going to hold you to that."

"Good," Kevin said before letting me know he had to go. He was still at work and needed to finish updating the record for his last patient. We said our 'good-byes' and 'I love yous' before hanging up. I put my phone down and just screamed out my frustrations. Granted, I really did understand why he couldn't come up, it didn't mean I wasn't upset. Actually, I was extremely upset. Thrusting my head into my pillow, I let out another scream for good measure.

A minute or so later, there was a knock at my door. Whipping my eyes, I dragged myself off of my bed to answer my door. Through the door I asked, "Who is it?"

"Naomi. Is everything okay in there? Heard a scream that sounded like it came from your room."

Opening the door I frowned, "I didn't think I was that loud."

"You were. Are you sure you're okay?" My frown deepened. "Hey Aaliyah, what's up? You can talk to me if you need someone to talk to."

"It's not that important. I'm okay," I said kind of looking away so I didn't make eye contact with Naomi. I was on the brink of tears because honestly, I was really pissed at Kevin for canceling on me, family situation or not. I also felt selfish for feeling that way. Before I knew it, the tears were coming down my face and Naomi was hugging me as I let it all out.

After I had a good cry, I ended up telling Naomi everything. Since she started helping me with my weight training problem, we had become fairly close. She wasn't necessarily on the level of Tina, but she was the closest friend I had in Atlanta, so I told her everything. Well, everything regarding Kevin, anyway. I told her how I met him and the summer we spent together. Told her how he had graduated from Morehouse and was a dentist in Florida so that is why I didn't get to see him often. Even told her that with my past experience in previous relationships that I felt like he may be hiding something from me and that was the real reason why he couldn't make it up here. My paranoia was starting to get the best of me and I just really needed to see him in order to calm my mind of the negative thoughts that were creeping in.

She sat there and listened intently for however long it took me to spill my guts out into the open, not interrupting or saying anything more than, "I can understand that," and "Okay." Once I was done she declared, "You need to get out of this room."

"I don't know about that, Nay. I'm not really in the mood to be around people." I tried to refuse, but it didn't seem she was going to take no for an answer.

"Fine," I finally gave in, so here I was now, out with her at some poetry slam being held at Apache Café. I had heard of it before, but never really took the time to look into it. Standing outside of it now, about to go in with her, it didn't really look like much. Even so, there were a lot of people standing in line along with us waiting to get in. I was starting to have second thoughts, "Hey, Nay, maybe I should just go back to campus."

She looked at me and defiantly told me, "No."

"No?" I questioned.

"Yes, no. After everything you told me, leaving you cooped up in your room to your own demise is probably not the best possible choice for the evening. Here you can enjoy a different atmosphere and listen to some spoken word to help get your mind off of all of that. I promise one night out of your room is not going to kill you."

I looked at Naomi and could tell two things. One, she was being sincere, looking out for her friend who obviously was going through a lot. Two, that she was probably just as stubborn as I, making leaving not an option. Taking a deep breath, I said, "Okay. You're probably right."

The rest of the time we were in line we huddled close to stay warm. Despite the *HOTlanta* name, Atlanta could get a little cold at night when you were only wearing jeans and a simple short-sleeve

T-shirt.

We finally were granted access inside and WOW! What a difference the inside was to the outside. While the outside looked like an abandoned warehouse to me, the inside was completely opposite. The space reminded me of basement parties with good friends, ebbing and flowing together. Stepping into that vibe relaxed me, even with all the people that seemed to be filling the space. My head began to bob as the track coming through the speakers caught my attention. I wasn't even sure who it was, but I made a quick note of the lyrics *'it's a special affair better act like you know who I am'* in my phone to look up later.

Naomi and I were able to locate a spot to sit that had just opened up and quickly took it over before someone else did. It was off to the side with a decent view of both the stage and the crowd that had gathered in front of it. It was good timing, too, because the show was beginning. It started with a poet who had a way with words, spitting metaphors with ease. In awe, I listened to all the performers remembering when I use to be able to bring words together and to life like that. It had been a long time since I had really written anything, but sitting there was inspiring me. Maybe I'd look into picking up the pen again. Well, maybe after I graduate, I don't want to lose focus when I am so close to the end.

As I looked over to Naomi to thank her for bringing me out, I noticed I had caught the eyes of someone who was looking me dead in mine with suspicion. My breath stalled as I whispered to myself, "Jess."

"Huh?" Naomi asked looking at me inquisitively.

"Oh, nothing. Just," as I gathered my thoughts to respond, Jess was quickly approaching. I was trying to speak, but my voice fell away as she drew closer.

"Jess!" she exclaimed once Jess was in front of us, greeting her like an old friend.

Jess had been grimacing but smiled and greeted her back. "Hey, Nay." She looked at me, "Hello Aaliyah."

Naomi looked at me. Then she looked at Jess, asking, "You two know each other?"

Before I could answer, Jess replied, "Kind of, we met over the summer. She's Tina's friend."

"Tina, Tina?" she asked, eyes wide in amazement.

"Yeah."

"Wow, small world."

"How do you two know each other," I asked, reminding everybody that I was still present. They both looked at me, and then back at each other.

Naomi spoke first, "Jess and I go way back. We grew up together back up North. You could say she is one of my best friends." She smiled and beamed with pride.

"Oh," was all I could think to say at that moment without seeming like I was prying or cared.

"How do you two know each other," Jess piped in.

Again, Naomi spoke first, "Aaliyah and I go to school together. Freshman year we were Bio partners and now we are both RAs at the college. She was having a rough night so I figured a night listening to some spoken word could pull her out of her funk."

This time it was Jess's turn to say, "Oh." She continued saying, "Well, don't let me interrupt. We'll get up later, Nay. Aaliyah, it was good seeing you again." Although she didn't say anything else after that before leaving, I could sense this was definitely not the end.

Naomi repeated out loud, but more to herself, "Small world, indeed."

As she digested what just took place, I excused myself, asking her where the bathroom was. I really just needed to think somewhere and going to the bathroom was the perfect cover. She gave me directions, asking if I wanted her to come with me. I told her no and to hold our seats and that I would be right back. Once in the bathroom, my phone started vibrating in my hand. I looked at my phone and saw I had a message from Jess, "Hey Aaliyah, can we talk?"

What I had been avoiding this whole time, I somehow walked right into. At this rate, my life was going from bad to worse. I contemplated just walking away right then and there. Just walking right out the door, finding a cab or something, and texting Naomi that I wasn't feeling well and had headed home. Who would stop me?

No one.

Just as no one was stopping me as I texted Jess back asking her where she was. Everything in me said to go with plan A. Hell, even plan B was a better option; go back to enjoying the atmosphere and act as if nothing happened. Those options were too easy, so I sat there taking the one I had done so well with evading up until that point. *"Damn you!"* I cursed Kevin in my head for canceling on me. Here I was now knowingly making bad decisions.

I got a text back from Jess, "I'm on the patio." For the second time, I contemplated just walking away, but my feet led me to the patio. I hesitated at the entrance trying to give myself more time before facing her. Through the door I could see her back. She was standing in the corner just looking into the night, probably going over what she planned to say to me. That's the same thing I was doing, stalling and trying to get my mind right.

Taking a deep breath, I headed on to the patio. I had no idea what to expect or what she would say. All I knew was that I was ready to get it all over with. Even so, I was also praying I didn't repeat the mistakes of my past with Jess. Seeing her was surreal and making it hard to ignore her existence as I had been doing since leaving Jersey.

jess

Chapter 19

I slid my phone back into my pocket after texting Aaliyah I was outside. Truth be told, I didn't know if she would really show up. I stood there hoping she would, though. Since I made it to Atlanta, I have obsessed over her and just wanted to see her. She didn't have to do anything but sit there allowing me to be in her space. As crazy as that sounded, that was all I wanted, a few moments of her time.

That's what I thought until I saw her with Naomi. They were sitting and whispering to each other, smiling, enjoying the evening. I must have watched too long because Aaliyah caught my gaze. Trying to be cool, I walked up to say hello, but also to find out why of all people, she was with Nay. Neither of them had ever mentioned each other, so why were they together now?

Walking up, Aaliyah just stared at me, Nay never the wiser didn't even notice me until I was already there. They say they know each other from school. Even though that was absolutely plausible, my head couldn't wrap my mind around it.

Sensing that someone was behind me, I turned around to see

Aaliyah approaching the corner of the patio I was standing in. She was more beautiful than what I had remembered and she wasn't even dressed up. Honestly, she looked like she was dressed for a relaxing evening with a good friend. Just a simple T-shirt and blue jeans get up that fit her in a way that accentuated all her curves. *Were Nay and Aaliyah good friends? How good?* I thought.

"Well, I'm here," I heard Aaliyah say, pulling me out of my head.

"Yeah, I didn't think you would show, considering I have been trying to get in touch with you since I got here."

"Yeah," she responded, "I've been busy. Naomi just happened to catch me when I could use a friend. I honestly wasn't planning on coming out tonight."

I looked at her wanting to ask more about her and Nay's relationship to each other but decided to postpone that. "Nay said you were having a rough night. Is everything okay? You know I have always been good at listening," I smiled. She gave me a half grin back. "We are still friends, right?"

"Yeah, we are." She sighed, "I've just been busy; that is all. Is that why you asked me out here?" Her half grin disappeared and seemed to be replaced with irritation.

Before speaking, I took a deep breath, "How do you and Naomi really know each other? Like, how did you two meet?"

"Are you serious, Jess? That's why you brought me out here? To interrogate me? She told you how we know each other. Anything more is none of your business."

She had slightly raised her voice, so anyone who was within earshot started to look in our direction. An audience was not what I was going for or needed, so I told Aaliyah, "Please calm down. I am just asking because I thought you were …" I stuttered. I decided to change my approach, saying instead, "I just wouldn't expect you and Nay to hit it off. She doesn't really allow a lot of people into her circle that she hasn't…" I trailed off. What was I saying or insinuating about my friend? Jealous or not, she didn't deserve for me to cause speculations of her intentions if there were none. She definitely didn't deserve that from me when I called her my friend. I stopped, *Wait. Am I jealous?*

"Jess, what are you talking about?" she looked at me confused.

"I," I started and then looked at Aaliyah. For months I wanted to see her and just get my friend back. But that's not really it. I wanted her and despised the fact that everyone but I could seem to have her and be close to her. Everybody could be in her world but me. I opened my mouth, "I'm jealous." As the words slipped past my lips, I realized I couldn't pull them back in.

"Jealous? Jealous of what?" Not only was her tone one of utter disbelief, so was the expression that took over her face.

"Of you with Nay. Of you with Kevin. Of you with anyone that isn't me." It was frustrating wanting someone who seemingly didn't want you, but if that were true, why was she there with me now. She was not obligated to see what I wanted. If she didn't feel something, too, she wouldn't be standing in front of me, right? Obviously, I am not alone in my feelings. Straight, gay or bi, females were all the same when it came down to that.

"Umm, Jess, you know it's not that kind of party here, right?" her voice had softened a bit. I could tell she was pitying me. At least, that's what it seemed like. "We've discussed this before. This summer was a misguided mistake. I had a lot going on then, and you were a good friend who got mixed into it. For that, I apologize, but there is nothing between you and me."

I could hear her, but I knew I wasn't listening anymore. My thoughts were scrambled, and all over the place. My inner voice was fighting to be heard, to warn me of the consequences of the actions I was contemplating taking. Alarm or not ringing in my ears, I moved forward, grabbing her into my arms and placing my lips on hers.

Aaliyah just needed to feel me, understand what I feel for her. She was always making the move, she needed to know I wasn't afraid to make those moves, too. Before she could truly react to the situation, I slipped my tongue past her lips and beckoned hers to dance with it. Surprisingly, and thankfully, she did and I pulled her into me, getting even more lost into the moment.

Then she abruptly stopped, pushing and pulling away from

me. "No, Jess, no." What was going on? *No, Aaliyah. Please…please…feel me*, I thought as I felt the tides of the moment changing. As I felt her stop reciprocating.

I wanted to grab her back into me and hold her even tighter, but my inner voice finally got my attention. Releasing her, I apologized, "I'm sorry Aaliyah, I just… I was…"

"I've got to go," she said, cutting me off. "I really have got to go." With that, she left the patio, never looking back for a second to see if I was watching. I was. I watched her until she disappeared into the crowd inside. That's when I noticed the eyes cutting my way and the voices whispering. The patio suddenly became stuffy, and I took that as my cue to make my own exit.

Heading back inside, too, I looked for Ty. That was the first time since seeing Aaliyah I had even thought about him, but I knew he was probably enjoying himself since he hadn't sought me out.

I ran into Nay first. Trying not to come off weird, I asked, "Have you seen Ty?"

She said, "Yeah, we were just sitting down talking." I wondered what about, but didn't ask.

"If you see him again, can you let him know I went back to my room?"

"Are you cool, J? Everything okay?" she asked, genuinely concerned. "You want me to give you a ride?" Just then Aaliyah appeared.

I answered, "Yeah, I'm good. I'll just catch an uber, you stay and enjoy the rest of the show. I'm going to text Ty, but if you do see him, just let him know in case he misses my text message."

"All right," she said, still looking concerned but knowing better than to press the issue any further. We said our 'goodbyes' and I got out of there as quick as I could.

Once I was in my room, I grabbed a glass and poured myself a drink. After the night I had been having, I earned that drink. I turned the TV on and flipped through the channels looking for something to catch my attention. Given the hour, nothing was on, so I turned the volume down and streamed a playlist from my collection.

At some point, I must have fallen asleep. In the distance, I could faintly hear a ringing. The ringing kept up, becoming louder and louder. Waking up, I realized it was my cellphone. I reached for it, thinking it must be Ty letting me know he made it back to his room. Roughly, I spoke into the phone, "Hey, what's up?" my voice laced with sleep.

"Hello," the voice came through, "Jess?"

"Yeah, this is her." It wasn't Ty.

"Hey, Jess. It's Aaliyah. We need to talk."

"What?" I heard who it was, but the combination of sleep and alcohol in my system made it incomprehensible. "This is who?"

"It's Aaliyah. Can we talk?"

"Nah, I don't think so," I sat up, trying to get my bearings.

"Please? We really need to talk. I've been thinking about tonight. I've thought about this summer. We never talked about it at all. We need to talk."

"Nah, Aaliyah. You decided that. I'm not doing this with you."

"Let me come see you."

That inner voice of warning was speaking up, but it might as well been speaking a different language as I probed, "Come see me when?"

"Now. Where are you? I'll come to you."

"Stop, that. You're not coming to see me."

"I will if you answer me. Where are you?" she asked again.

"Whatever. I'm at the Westin in the Governor's Suite."

"The Governor's Suite?"

"Yeah, why?"

"Nothing. Okay. I'm on my way."

"Yeah, okay," I said before hanging up. I was fed up with Aaliyah's games, so I wasn't expecting anything. If she needed to talk, fine, but I was over it. *I'm not a lost puppy desperate for an owner.*

I stood up, got another drink and waited. About 20 minutes later, there was a knock at my door. I got up to answer the door, astonished she'd even come, especially after tonight. When I opened the door, it wasn't her. It was Ty, "Hey chic, you okay?"

"Yeah, why are you asking?" He gestured to the drink in my hand. "I'm good," I said, taking a sip.

He slanted his eyes at me before saying, "Did you know Nay was at Apache tonight?"

"Yeah, I saw her."

"Oh. Okay."

"What?"

"I saw Aaliyah at Apache tonight, too. After I saw her, I ran into Nay again who told me you had left."

"Oh, you did?"

"Don't play with me, Jess. You saw her, didn't you?"

"Look, Ty, I'm really not in the mood. I'm glad you made it back safe. I'll talk to you later."

He looked unsatisfied with my retort, but agreed, "That's fine, just don't overdo it, Jesstina. I love you."

"Yeah, a'ight. I love you too." I closed the door and went back to sitting in front of the TV.

After an hour and several drinks had passed, I called it quits. I whispered to myself, "I don't know why I even care. I knew she wasn't coming." I cleaned up and went into the bathroom to shower. Putting my phone on the counter, I hopped into the welcoming heat of the water. When I got out, I checked my phone. Nothing. Calling it a night, I put on a t-shirt, a pair of basketball shorts, and went into the bedroom.

As I was laying there, I received a text from Aaliyah stating she was five minutes away. "Sure you are," I said out loud. "Sure you are." I turned over and fell asleep again.

Banging on my door woke me up. "You've got to be fucking kidding me!" I exclaimed as I jumped up to answer it, perturbed by the intrusion. Swinging the door open I inquired, "Can I help you?!" My tone was clearly all business, blended with bitter annoyance.

"Hey Jess," she said, standing there looking smaller than she did earlier that night.

"Aaliyah?" I said her name, questioning if my eyes were

actually seeing what I thought they were seeing.

"Yeah. I apologize for taking so long to get here. Honestly, I was having second thoughts," she smirked innocently.

"I really didn't think you were going to show." I leaned into the door jam, thinking I must still be sleeping.

"Well, I did."

"Yeah."

"Are you going to let me in?"

"I don't know if that's such a good idea, Aaliyah."

"Jess, if you're not going to let me in, why did you let me come out here?"

"I didn't tell you to come here."

"No, you didn't," she said as if she was thinking that maybe she made a mistake and should not have come. "Well," she said as if determined to go through with whatever plan she had concocted, "I'm here now and we need to talk. Don't be childish, Jesstina. Let me in." A little caught off guard by hearing my name and not my nickname coming from her, I moved out of the way as she squeezed past me and the door and took a seat at the table.

"Okay. You're here. What's up Aaliyah?" I sat in a chair on the opposite side and end of the table from her.

She grimaced, "Why are you acting like that?"

"Like what?"

"Like I'm some sort of disease or something. Am I bothering you?"

"Aaliyah, look, it's late. If you aren't going to start talking, I'm going to have to ask you to leave." I stood up and started heading back to the door.

"Jess, please sit down." I stopped, looked at her, and then took my seat and waited. She looked at me as if she expected me to say something first. I didn't. I just sat there and looked at her and waited for her to speak her piece.

She started, again, "I apologize for… for this confusion that is between us. I think you are a wonderful person."

"Thanks," I said under my breath, rolling my eyes and sighing.

"I'm being serious, Jess."

"So am I. Is there a point you are trying to get to?"

"Ouch. If you are trying to get under my skin, you are doing a great job of it. I am just trying to clear the air between us."

"Spare me. If you wanted to do that, you would have answered my calls. Or here's one, you would have called me!" Slowly my emotions were starting to get the best of me. It was imperative I maintained my composure. Clearing my throat, I told her, "You are only here now because you unexpectedly ran into me tonight. Admit it."

Fidgeting, she answered, "You're right." I rolled my eyes again. "I was trying to avoid you. I've been avoiding you since we…," she paused and took a deep breath, "since we went there this summer."

"I noticed."

"I didn't know how to confront you or the situation. I'm not into girls. Yet, I did that with you."

"That's why I tried to pretend like it never happened. The only thing I was trying to be was your friend, Aaliyah. You came on to me not just once, but twice. TWICE! Actually, if you want to be honest, three times because you definitely responded to me tonight. Then you pushed me away, like every other time. What the hell, Aaliyah? I may be a lesbian, but before that, I am human and I've got feelings. Feelings you continue to toy with."

"That was and is never my intentions." She looked down, focusing on whatever she was doing in her lap. "I hated that I had done that to you."

"Is that so? Because you left me dazed and confused. The more I tried not to think about it or you, the more I did. The more I wanted you and yearned for you. I can't even focus on what's right in front of me because of you. And that's not even your fault. It's mine."

"No, it is my fault." She got up and walked to where I was sitting. "It really is mine. I should've said something sooner, but the whole thing had me so confused. I had never felt like that before and I took it was just because I was going through so much. I've never even looked at women before, let alone been attracted to one. To deal, I told myself it was because my ex had hurt me so bad, and you were so nice, things just happened, I guess. I'm so sorry Jess."

As I listened to Aaliyah try to explain what she'd been experiencing and apologize to me, I could feel the tears sliding down my face. *Why does this shit always happen to me?* She noticed my tears and touched my face. I pulled away from her.

She started, "I really am sorry, Jess. Please believe me that none of this was my intentions. A part of me wishes I could take it all back," she hesitated, "but another part doesn't."

I looked at her, wondering what part she was referring to and what she didn't wish to take back. "What part is that?"

"The part that likes you."

I smirked, "Whatever. It's time for you to leave, Aaliyah." I directed her to the door, ready to open it for her.

Now it was her turn for tears. While I opened the door for her to exit, she reached up and grabbed my face between her hands, "I like you, Jess. That scares me."

Pulling away, I spoke in an even tone, "That's really unfortunate. You've got to go." I opened the door and held it for her to walk through. She looked at me looking for a break in my resolve, but there was none to see. Defeated, she finally walked out the door without another word. I closed the door behind her and poured myself another drink.

aaliyah

Chapter 20

It's been months since Jess kicked me out of her hotel room. Somehow I imagined things going differently. I imagined that everything would be okay. How naive was that? Extremely. Then again, I'm not sure what I was really expecting. Whatever it was, I definitely didn't think that Jess would be so cold towards me. Silly me, huh?

Naomi and I continued to develop our friendship as she helped me not fail weight training. She never inquired any further about Jess and I or how we even met. Maybe for her, knowing Tina and I was friends and that's how we were connected was enough for her. Likewise, I never asked her about Jess. That night, Jess made some implications about Nay that piqued my interest. Be that as it may, I didn't want to lose another friend, so I left it alone. She never did anything to me that gave me a reason to pry or to think that she had any ulterior motives.

Knowing I should leave well enough alone, I did try to contact Jess. She completely ignored me. I even tried her back at her store and the moment she knew it was me she would pass the phone to someone else. There was no one to blame for it all but me, I had brought this on myself. *Too little, too late.*

As if I really needed more personal stress, it had been really hard to get in touch with Kevin lately. I got to talk to him, but not like I use to, he always seemed so busy with work. After the debacle of Labor Day, I could have used some time with my man. Scrolling through my phone, I found his number and hit call. Seconds later, the phone was ringing.

"Hey Baby, what a wonderful mid-day surprise," Kevin answered completely brightening my day.

I smiled, "I was just thinking about you. I wanted to hear your voice. Are you busy?"

"I just finished lunch, so I have a little bit of time. How is everything going? The semester is almost over."

"Yeah, everything is everything. I can't wait for this semester to be over. Just about a month to go and then I'll just be coasting. Next semester my main focus will be my internship. How have you been?"

"Good, the practice has been keeping me busier than usual, but I cannot really complain."

"Oh. Still busy, huh?"

"Yeah. Why? What's on your mind?" he asked, probably catching the drop in my tone.

"Nothing," I didn't want to come off as if I didn't understand that his job could be demanding at times. Before meeting Kevin, I never thought a Dentist would be so inaccessible, but I hadn't known much about the dental field either. If he was busy, he was busy. I didn't really question it because I trusted him.

I sighed loud enough for Kevin to hear me. "If that was the case, you wouldn't be sighing through the phone. Talk to me. What's on your mind, Liyah?"

"I miss you, Baby. I miss my man. Every time we are supposed to see each other, something comes up."

"I know, I know. I promise I will make this all up to you. We will see each other soon. Just be patient with me. Can you do that for me?"

"Yeah, I can do that."

"I will make time for you. Your happiness is a priority to me."

"Yeah, I know. I can't help that I miss you, though."

"I wouldn't want you missing anyone else," he chuckled into the phone making me smile.

"There isn't anyone else to miss, there's only you."

"You mean not even old boy Xavier?"

"Oh, stop that!" I laughed. "You know better than that."

He laughed with me, "There goes my Baby. I knew she was in there."

"Oh hush," I blushed.

"Soon, Baby I will be able to come to see you. Until then, just be patient."

"I will."

"Okay. Well, I need to get back. Lunch has been over for a while and I have a patient coming in soon. I will call you later tonight."

"I understand. I love you."

"I love you, too." With that, he was gone. I sat there with the phone in my hand, not sure what to do next. My next class wasn't until later in the afternoon, leaving too much time for me to think about why my world just seemed off kilter. Even though I heard his words, it felt off. I needed to shake this dread I was feeling. *I trust my man, I trust my man.*

Setting the alarm on my phone, I kicked off my shoes and laid in my bed hoping to sleep it all away. My thoughts were all over when I had a brilliant idea. I sat up, "If he can't come to me, I'll just go to him." In a few weeks I would get a few days off for Thanksgiving. Although I don't know exactly where Kevin lives, I do know where his office is. I could surprise him since he can't get away to come up here. *This could be the best option for us both to get what we want and what I need*, I thought to myself while smiling. Before long, I was napping peacefully. I couldn't wait until Thanksgiving.

It seemed to take forever for Thanksgiving break to come, but it was finally here. I left my last class, beelining for my room to get ready for my trip. The plan was to leave in the morning, probably no later than seven. It would take almost five hours to get there, so I wanted to get down there so I could spend most of the time I had off with Kevin.

As I was mulling over my plan, there was a knock on my door. Probably way more cheerful than necessary, I asked, "Who is it?" while opening it.

"Well look who's in a good mood," Xavier said.

I rolled my eyes, "What do you want, Xavier?"

"Just seeing how my favorite girl is doing."

"I'm fine," I said leaving the door and returning back to what I was doing before he interrupted. I was in too good of a mood to let Xavier take that away from me.

He caught the door and walked in behind me. "Where are you heading?"

"What do you care where I'm going, huh?" I asked not giving him any eye contact. He always had a way of just showing up at my door despite the fact he knew that we were done. I figured eventually he would get it, but now I wasn't so certain. Either way, it wasn't my problem.

Completely ignoring me, he asked, "Want to go get some food off campus? Maybe even catch a movie?"

Finally I stopped, "I don't think so."

"Why not? I'm not going to push up on you or anything, Liyah. Just chilling, like old times."

"During old times, we were together. These aren't old times, or have you forgotten?" His presence was slowly gnawing away at my great mood.

"I don't mean it like that."

"That's fine, I don't care how you meant it. The answer is no. I'm busy tonight." The space was small, so I had to maneuver a little bit to get around him to open the door. "You can leave now."

"Really, Aaliyah? It's like that?"

"Yeah, so it seems." I gestured my head towards the exit,

"Have a nice Thanksgiving Xavier." He looked at me in awe and disbelief. After a beat, he left and I closed the door. "You brought this on yourself. You didn't want me." Taking a deep breath and sighing, I returned to what I was doing to prepare for my trip.

My phone alarm went off waking me from a sound sleep. From habit, I hit the snooze button. What only seemed like seconds passed and the alarm went off again. "Ugh," I groaned. "I'm up, I'm up."

I turned the alarm off completely and laid there for a second. It was way too early to be up on a day off, but here I was, up early on a day off. I rolled out of the bed, grabbed my toiletries and went to the bathroom. Surprisingly, I wasn't the only one up. "Good morning, Nay. What are you doing up so early?"

"Hey, Liyah! I'm about to go for a run. Why are YOU up? You are the last person I expected up when you don't have to be," she laughed.

"Hush," I yawned. The truth was the truth, I am a sleeper. Sleeping in is one of my favorite pastimes. "I'm getting ready to get on the road."

"Oh? Where are you heading?"

I brightened a little bit, "To see my man in Florida."

"Very nice," she smiled at me. "Well, let me let you get to it. Have a safe trip and I'll see you when you get back." She walked out of the bathroom and I finished doing my morning routine to wake myself up more fully.

I went back to my room, packed up the toiletries, and headed to my car. Once everything was loaded up, I went over a checklist in my head to make sure I wasn't forgetting any essentials, like my wallet. I did that once when I was back in Jersey when I took what was supposed to be a short trip to the District of Columbia. Little did I know I would be visiting for longer than just a night. Luckily, a friend was also in town and let me crash with her while I waited for my mom to send me my wallet.

Satisfied I had everything, I got on the road making my way to the 75 southbound. As long as I only stopped when I needed gas, I would get there by noon. I was banking on getting there by then so I could surprise Kevin with treating him to lunch, or being lunch, both would work for me. The thought made me smile with anticipation. I wondered how his face would look, and imagined the love we would make. They say absence makes the heart grow fonder, and we were so overdue.

On schedule, I found myself pulling into the parking lot of Kevin's practice. There weren't too many cars in the lot. I figured it was possible because it was lunchtime. It wasn't really that important since in just a few minutes I would be face to face with my man, looking into his eyes, with his flawless smile being all mines. I sat in my car for a minute, taking a few breaths. *Oh my goodness, why am I so nervous.* My heart was beating a mile a minute.

"Calm down, Aaliyah. Nothing to be nervous about," I told myself before getting out of the car. I walked through the double doors and spotted the receptionist desk. Walking to the desk, I waited patiently for her to acknowledge my presence.

When she noticed me standing there, she asked, "Good afternoon. May I help you?"

"Yes," I answered, "Is Dr. Kevin Anderson available?"

"Dr. Anderson is currently with a patient. Do you have an appointment?"

"No, I do not."

"Okay, ma'am. May I have your name?"

"Aaliyah Jones."

"Okay, Ms. Jones. I will let him know you are here to see him. Please have a seat in the waiting area." I thanked her before going to take a seat. I picked up one of the random magazines strewn across the coffee table and started flipping through it.

Out of the corner of my eye, I saw a woman dressed in a simple pencil skirt dress and black pumps. She had a real modest appearance, although she was stunning in her all business attire. Holding her hand was the cutest little boy who had to be all of four or five years old. His dad was probably quite the eye candy because he was sure to be a lady's man once he was older. I smiled to myself and went back to the magazine.

The woman went to the counter and the receptionist greeted her warmly, "Hello Mrs. Anderson! Dr. Anderson is just finishing up with a patient." My ears perked up a bit when I heard her last name, but figured Anderson was a common last name. I assumed that Kevin was her son's dentist and she brought him in for a checkup. Convinced that was it, I went back to the magazine again.

Voices from the receptionist area caught my attention again causing me to look up from the magazine. Kevin appeared at the door next to the receptionist desk and I smiled, getting ready to get up and greet him only to stop full in my tracks. Curiously, I watched him pick the little boy up into his arms and kiss him on his face. He then turned his attention to the woman and kissed her deeply on the lips.

As I sat there and watched him, watching him interact with this woman and young child, it all suddenly made sense. This was why he was always so busy. This was why he never once invited me to come to see him. This was why he would cancel plans with me. This whole time, he had someone else. I looked at the woman's hand, and then I looked at Kevin's hand. Not just someone else, but a family. Kevin was married with a kid!

Under my labored breath I mumbled, "This can't be life," before I tried to quickly get out of there. In my haste, I ran into the edge of the coffee table bringing attention to myself. Everyone looked my way trying to see what happened, and I just looked at Kevin. His eyes grew wide as he realized I was there. I apologized and quickly excused myself. Once outside, I practically ran to my car. Kevin caught up to me outside, "What are you doing here?"

"I thought I was surprising my man who was always too busy to come see me. Guess the jokes on me."

"It's not what you think."

"No, it's EXACTLY what I think, Kevin. So, this is why you are always so busy, huh? This is why you can't always talk, huh?"

"Calm down. Let me explain."

"Fuck you, Kevin," I said trying to wipe away the tears that started to appear. "There is nothing for you to explain. You are a fucking lying, cheating asshole."

"Aaliyah please, just let me talk to you," he pleaded. "We are getting a divorce."

"Oh, really? A divorce? How convenient to say because it sure didn't look like it," I heard the words strain my voice. I was screaming. I did not drive all this way to be screaming like that. Calming down, well, at least lowering my voice, I said, "Fuck you, Kevin. Just fuck you." With that, I got into my car, backed out of the space and drove away as fast as I humanly could.

When I got back to school, I went to Naomi's room. I didn't know who else to go to and I wasn't even sure if she would be in her room. Lucky for me, she answered the door, "Hey, aren't you supposed to be in Florida?" Before I could even open my mouth, I barged into her room and just started sobbing. "Hey, hey, hey, Aaliyah. What happened?"

"He's fucking married!" was all that I could get out in between my cries. She just hugged me as I continued to cry my eyes out, wondering how I always seemed to get into these situations. *Why me?*

jess

Chapter 21

Since my trip to Atlanta, I have done a lot of thinking. For the first month or so, Aaliyah would call leaving messages of apologies or checking in. At a certain point, I didn't even listen to them anymore. As soon as I heard her voice I would delete the message and go about my day. That included text messages. She even called the shop and I ignored those calls, too, passing the phone off to someone else to 'assist' her. I only did exactly what she did to me. Not necessarily to get back at her or anything. I simply just didn't want to be bothered. The moment I allowed it, would be the moment she would weasel herself back in, and I was over being her yo-yo.

I talked to my mother about everything that had happened. I asked her, "Mom, what should I do? This woman makes me absolutely batty!"

"Baby," she said with so much love in her voice, "Cut her off. If she can't see my Jesstina for who she is, she doesn't deserve you."

"Ugh, I know. I just keep putting myself in these situations."

"Yes, you do," my mother agreed, "But I know you will be okay. You are stronger than you realize, Baby. You may have your father's last name, but you have the strength of the women from my bloodline. So stop letting these women feed off of your energy. Get you a good girl and leave all of these crazy women alone."

"I know, mom. I know."

"If you know, you need to act like you do."

"I am."

"Good. I love you Jesstina. It's going to be okay." I told my mother I loved her too and hung up the phone. Aside from being the wisest person I knew, my mom was also the realest and never held any punches. She would call a spade a spade and nothing else. I didn't even know how I was so fortunate to have her as mi madre, one of the few things my father did right. I followed my mother's advice and eventually, Aaliyah's calls stopped and I fell at peace.

Throwing myself into my business, most of the time I was either at work or at home. If I wasn't, I was spending time with Jordyn. We reconciled after I returned from Atlanta. We sat down and talked about the whole Aaliyah thing. I actually apologized for being blind to my own bias regarding Aaliyah and that she didn't have to worry about that ever again. Since then, we had been solid. She would usually be working on something for her classes while I sat there and read a book or looked over the numbers for the shop. Ty would try to get me to go out, but I was never in the mood. Ripping and running didn't have the same appeal it once did.

The quiet times with Jordyn grew on me becoming the best part of my day. Those nights I wasn't with her, I missed her. I mean, I really missed her like a part of me was gone whenever she couldn't come over. Even so, I wouldn't claim that I had feelings for her. Feelings were like an emotional commitment and commitments only led to disaster and loss. I knew this all too well, so the preference was to avoid it at all cost.

One night while Jordyn was at home working on her thesis statement, I found myself driving around on my bike wandering through the streets of New York. I drove past *Black Ice* and decided to stop in and at the very least have a drink. When I walked in, I immediately felt like I shouldn't have been there. Spice spotted me before I saw her and sauntered my way, "Long time no see, Stranger." She smiled at me.

I looked down and saw her standing there dressed like an extremely sexed up version of Harley Quinn. *Oh yeah, it is almost Halloween*, I thought as I took in her appearance. "I see you are still looking sexy as ever," I smiled back.

"Why thank-you," she responded before asking, "Would you like a private dance?" Before I could even answer, she grabbed my hand and led me to the VIP area. As appealing as she was, and tantalizing the memories of her riding me were, it all felt wrong. She led me into one of the rooms, closed the door behind her, and played a track on the sound system. I watched her but hadn't moved from where I stepped after she initially led me into the room. Spice noticed and asked, "Is everything okay, Love? Something on your mind?"

I looked at this gorgeously freckled redbone beauty and then diverted my eyes, "I don't think I'm feeling it tonight. I apologize for wasting your time."

"Oh?" she looked a little confused.

"Yeah, something feels off. As tempting as you are, and believe me, you are particularly tempting tonight, I can't."

She smiled, "It's just a lap dance."

"Yeah, but I don't know about that."

"What?" she smirked, "You've been cheating on me?" I could tell she was only trying to lighten the mood, but the comment hit a chord with me.

"Haha," I grinned. I apologized again and paid her for the dance I declined. She took the money and told me if I ever changed my mind I knew where to find her. I just smiled and left.

I got on my bike, taking the long way home thinking about what Spice had asked me. *Cheating on her, huh? Hmm.* Before I knew it, I was sitting in front of Jordyn's place. I looked up at her window and noticed that it was dark. *She's probably already sleeping. It is late*, I thought. I sent her a text saying I was thinking about her, revved up my bike, and went home. As far as I was concerned, there was nothing out at that hour that I wanted or needed in my life.

For Thanksgiving I decided to invite Jordyn to my mother's to spend it with my family and me. She was really swamped with school, so going home for the holidays was not an option for her, but no one should spend a holiday meant for being with family and friends alone. Thing was, though, I hadn't invited anyone over to my mother's since Mieko, so this was huge for me.

While having a lunch date with Ty and my brother Jamaal to tell them I invited Jordyn to Thanksgiving dinner, I tried to play it off as no big deal. But between the both of them, they were showing me no mercy. No one really knew me better than them, so something like this would definitely get their minds going, thinking and saying unnecessary things. Jamaal had never met Jordyn, but he had heard about her from Ty. Somehow Jordyn had worked her magic on Ty and won him over. That alone made the situation the perfect catalyst for him to play the role of my therapist, telling me what I should and shouldn't do with my love life.

I told them both, "Just stop, both of you. It really isn't that serious." I only meant to inform them that Jordyn would be joining us for the holidays, not have a counseling session.

Jamaal and Ty looked at each other, then looked at me. Jamaal responded first, "You do realize you haven't brought anyone to meet our mom since you were with Mieko, right?"

Ty chimed in, "What was that, like five or six years ago?" he looked at Jamaal for consensus. "Since then, there have been plenty of other chics come and go, but you never brought them around the family."

"You two are really making something out of nothing," I defended myself. "I only invited Jordyn over because she won't be able to spend Thanksgiving with her family. Who wants to spend Thanksgiving alone when it is about being with people you love and care for?"

Ty's eyes got big. He more stated than asked, "You love her?!"

"No, no, no. It's not even like that and you know it, Ty." I could feel myself getting flushed. I wasn't sure if it was because he was pissing me off, or because I was actually embarrassed. Either way, I was not about to give these two the satisfaction. "We are just friends."

Ignoring me, Ty spoke directly to Jamaal, "You know Jordyn has practically moved in with her, right?"

"Moving in together. Spending time with the family. Yup, it looks like our little Jesstina has been bitten again," he responded back to Ty.

"Hello!" I waved. "I am right here and can hear you."

"Listen, Sis, it's okay you know. No judgment here. As a matter of fact, it's about time. You can't be a hoe for the rest of your life."

"Whoa! A hoe? I'm not a hoe, Maal." I was astonished he even said that to me.

"J, you have been doing a lot over the years. And you've had quite a few bedfellows," Ty agreed with my brother.

"Damn, so that's what you two really think?" I asked, dumbfounded. How the hell did a conversation about me inviting someone over for Thanksgiving get to me being a hoe?

"Look, we love you, so we aren't going to sugarcoat it. You've been hot in the pants, screwing every beautiful chic you meet. Straight, bi, gay; doesn't matter," I heard Ty say. I was too busy taking it all in to even glance at him.

"Whatever," I said getting up. "I don't have to listen to you two make me feel like I'm the bad guy. Any female I have been with I have been upfront with about my intentions. If she wanted to still get down that was her choice. I didn't force any of these women to be with me. Hell! Some took advantage of me, and not the other way around." I was heated that they would both imply that I was loose or something. All parties involved have been consenting adults. *UGH!*, I screamed in my head.

"Jesstina, calm down. You are getting hyped for no reason." That time it was Jamaal speaking up.

"Oh, so I should just be okay with my brother and my best

friend calling me a hoe? Yeah, okay. Whatever," I rolled my eyes.
"I've got to go. I'll see ya'll later." I got my stuff, threw a twenty
on the table to cover my tab, and walked out of the restaurant. So
much for lunch with the men in my life.

As I was racing to my car to get out of there, I got a text from
Mieko, "Hey Baby, guess who?" with a smiley and kissy face.

Exactly the distraction needed from the nonsense I just left, I
texted back, "Mi-Mi? At least that's what it says on my screen.
Haha." It was pretty impossible to not know it was her considering
it was a text.

"Whatever," she responded with a smiley face. "What are you
doing for your birthday?"

"I don't know. I don't have anything planned, yet."

"I'll be in town. We should hook up."

I looked at her text and thought about the conversation I just
had with Jamaal and Ty. *To hell with them! They don't know
anything,* I thought as I texted back, "We can do that."

She replied, "Good. I'll let you know when I'm there and
where to meet me."

"I look forward to it." I slid my phone in my pocket before
getting into my car. I was getting those feelings again that I was
doing something I shouldn't be doing, but I just shook them off and
put my car in gear so I could be on my way.

As planned, Jordyn joined my family for Thanksgiving and
fitted right in with everyone. From my cousins to my uncles,
everyone pulled me to the side to tell me how much they liked her,
or how beautiful she was, or how intelligent she was. Everyone
told me she was a keeper and that I should bring her around more.

My mother and brother were no exception. My mom
absolutely loved Jordyn. She took out old photo albums, showing
Jordyn my baby pictures and talked about how cute I was as a little
girl. Considering then I wore a lot of dresses and ponytails, it was a
drastic change from the person I was now. Jordyn would look at
the pictures, then at me, and joke with my mother about what
happened to the cute little girl in the picture.

The moment Jamaal and Jordyn were introduced to each other they were in sync. He took hold of her and decided it was a perfect time to share my most embarrassing childhood memories with her. She just soaked it up, instigating my horror. Of course, I had to defend my honor, sharing his stories, too. Jordyn just laughed at us both.

After everything was done and most of the family had left, my mom pulled me to the side. "I like this one," she said referring to Jordyn.

"I do, too, mom," I told her, picking up some used and left behind cups. I stacked them into a tower, and then tossed them into the trash.

"No, Jesstina. I really like her. Something about this one. She is much better than Mieko. You remember how she acted around the family. This young lady fits right in with us."

I told my mother, "Don't say that. Mieko wasn't that bad," but as I listened to my mother, I was reminded of why I didn't like bringing anyone around my family. It didn't necessarily have to do with not having been serious with these other females. Truthfully, when Mieko met my family it was a bit of a disaster. My mom was old school and could sense trouble a mile away. When she met Mieko, it was obvious to me that she didn't like her. Mi-Mi was standoffish and guarded around my family. It was like she couldn't or just wouldn't relax and my mother felt her vibe. Even so, my mom was congenial, ever the perfect host, although her normal level of warmth was missing. She later told me that she didn't think Mieko was right for me. I guess she knew something I didn't. Once Mi-Mi's career started taking off, it was obvious that I was an optional accessory.

Shaking the memory away, I decided to focus the conversation and my thoughts back on Jordyn, "So you like Jordyn, huh, mom?" I smiled at her.

"Yes, she is like one of the family already. I think you should keep this one. Don't let her get away." My mother smiled at me, gathered a few dirty plates, and walked away.

Out of the corner of my eye, I saw Jordyn approaching me. I

turned to her and asked, "Ready to go?"

Jordyn looked around, "You're not going to stay behind and help clean up?"

I laughed, "My mom would shoo me away to be with my company, telling me how I was being rude."

She smiled, "I don't mind helping, too."

Just then my mom was passing us and stopped to say, "Thank you, Baby, but I've got it. Besides, I'll get Jamaal to help me. You two don't have to. Jesstina tells me you are going to be a doctor and have papers to do. Go home and enjoy the rest of your evening so you can get back to the books." She kissed Jordyn on the cheek, told her it was good meeting her and then continued about her business.

Amazed by my mom's actions, I looked at Jordyn and said, "Well, you heard the woman. I guess we are off the hook." We got our jackets and said good-bye to whoever was still there. My brother gave Jordyn a big hug and told her not to be a stranger and that if I gave her any problems to let him know before letting us leave.

Once outside, Jordyn grabbed my hand, kissed me and said, "Thank you for inviting me tonight. I really enjoyed myself and your family is so awesome. I felt like I was home."

"I'm glad," I swelled with pride. As we began our walk to the car I held her hand tighter. The whole way to the car I beamed and for the first time in a long time, I felt like I was exactly where I needed to be. When I got home, I texted Mieko that I would have to cancel for my birthday. I knew the only person I wanted to spend that day with was Jordyn, even if it meant doing nothing at all. I had found my peace.

Since realizing what everybody else was saying, I started to put more time and effort into Jordyn and my relationship of sorts. I mean, we still weren't a couple officially, but I treated her like we were, even more so than before. Both Ty and Nay told me this was a serious development when I told them I had canceled on Mieko for my birthday. I was realizing that there was no reason for me to continue the toxic relationship Mieko and I was having.

When Nay visited for Christmas she told me she was astonished and didn't think she would see the day I turned Mieko down. Neither did I, but there I was turning women down left and right, telling them my attention was already occupied. Jordyn had been so steadfast with me through all the shit I put her through. I seriously don't understand why she even agreed to my terms, but she did and has proven to be one of the closest friends I have outside of Ty and Nay. No matter if I was venting to her about Mieko, Aaliyah or just some random mess I got myself into, she remained committed and there for me. I don't know why it took me so long to see what everybody else had seen for months, but I finally did. Jordyn was the real deal.

Concluding that I didn't just need Jordyn in my life, but that I *wanted* her in my life, I decided to tell her as much. I set-up a romantic evening for Valentine's Day. I booked the Bentley Suite at The St. Regis New York on Fifth Avenue. It was definitely not easy to do considering the day, but I was able to pull it off. This room was top of the line with Bentley accents and style mixed with the elegance expected from St. Regis. To some it may have seemed overboard, but I wanted Jordyn to know just how serious I was about her. Money was not an object.

On Valentine's Day, I arranged for her to be picked up by a limo to accompany me to a private dinner for two in our suite at the Regis. Jordyn came out of her building looking like a vision. She was wearing a red, off the shoulder wide strap dress that draped and gathered over her bodice in a crisscross design. As she glided down the steps, so did the full length of her dress, seeming to wave effortlessly in the wind. The nearly sheer bottom split as she walked giving peaks to her smooth legs ending in 5-inch, maybe 6-inch strappy heels that wrapped around her ankles. She was flawless.

I grabbed her hand and helped her into the limo, sliding in behind her once she was settled. She asked, more stated, "Well don't you look gorgeous," as she kissed me.

"Gorgeous? Have you looked in the mirror? I'm going to have

to fight them off you," I laughed.

Joining in the laughter, she retorted, "You mean I would have to fight them off you! By the way, what's the plan tonight? Where are we heading?"

"That's a surprise."

"Oh? What kind of surprise?"

"Now if I told you that, it wouldn't be a surprise anymore."

"I'll still act surprised," she smiled.

"Nah, you'll see soon enough. Just be patient."

"Ugh, okay, okay. I'll stop asking."

"Would you like some champagne?" I asked holding up the complimentary bottle of champagne.

"Sure," she said picking up two glasses.

I popped the cork and champagne began spilling out just missing my suit. "Whoa! That was close. Hold the glasses up." Jordyn held the glasses as I filled them up, and then handed one to me. On the ride to the hotel, we talked about how her internship had been going and my thoughts of opening up another location.

Soon enough we were pulling up to the Regis. The driver opened the door letting us out. I tipped him and thanked him for his services, before escorting Jordyn to our suite. Once we got to the suite and our private butler opened the door to greet us, she screamed, "JESS, YOU'VE GOT TO BE KIDDING ME!" I just laughed and told her the night was just getting started.

Dinner was already waiting for us. We were seated and served a three-course meal with a vintage bottle of wine that I had recalled Jordyn once talking about. Once the last dish was removed, I dismissed our butler for the night so that I could have Jordyn all to myself. I turned on some music and grabbed her hand, beckoning her to dance with me. As I rocked in a slow two-step with her, she said, "Jess, this is amazing."

"I'm glad you like," I replied and kissed her. We kissed and danced until our kissing took over our dancing. I lifted her up and carried her to the bedroom, laying her on the bed. Her dress fell to the side exposing her inner thigh. I took that as an invitation to place kisses on her exposed flesh. As I slowly made my way to my prize, she squirmed around. Teasingly I asked, "Should I stop?"

Breathless and full of arousal, she told me, "No." She wrapped her legs around me and pulled me into her. I gave her exactly what she wanted, and continued my journey until I found what I had been searching for.

To my surprise, and delight, she didn't have on any panties. That sent shock waves straight through my clit as I took her tantalizing scent in. "No panties," I said, looking up from my post. She just gave me a silly grin, before closing her eyes and releasing a deep moan, reacting to my thrust of tongue that had just entered her secret garden.

I darted my tongue in and out of her. She arched her back and grabbed my head, pushing me deeper into her. Good thing I can swim, because she was drowning me with her juices. Reaching her limit, she screamed as she wet my tongue with her crème. I watched as her body continued to convulse until she laid there still. I climbed up her body and kissed her lips. I whispered in her ear, "I hope you don't think I'm done with you."

Opening her eyes, she smiled, "I was hoping not."

The next morning, I had ordered breakfast but dismissed the butler again before Jordyn woke so I could serve her myself. As I walked into the room, she roused and said, "Last night was wonderful and now I even get breakfast in bed. Are you okay, Jess? You are pouring on the sweetness a bit thick," she laughed.

I placed the tray on the bed next to her. "Ouch, that hurt," I stated before stealing a piece of her bacon. "I can be romantic, too, you know. Besides, it is a holiday today."

"Oh? What holiday is that?"

"Why it's Side Chic Valentine's Day!" I exclaimed laughing.

Jordyn grabbed a pillow and threw it at me. She laughed, too, "Oh, so I'm your side chic, huh?"

I stopped laughing, "Unless you want to be my main chic."

She kept laughing until she realized I wasn't anymore. "Wait, are you being serious?"

"I am."

"Really?" she asked a bit confused.

"Yes, really," I replied trying to convince her I was telling the truth.

Sitting up she probed, "What about not being ready to commit?"

"I want to commit to you." Grabbing her hand I told her, "I've already committed to you."

"And everybody else?" her voice cracked as the tears started to stream down her face.

"Already gone. Like I said, I have already committed to you. I realize that through these ups and downs, you have been consistent. You are always there for me and want nothing more than for us to just build together. I appreciate that and know you deserve the best of me."

Jordyn pulled me in close to her and kissed me with a passion had I never felt or known before. Tears still streaming down her face, she said, "If you are serious, then my answer is yes. But I don't want to be your main chic, I want to be your only one."

"Already done."

aaliyah

Chapter 22

I have lost track of how many times I have cried since going to Florida to see Kevin. Once I got back all I wanted to do was stay in my room and sleep. Nothing seemed to matter. Not even school, and finals were steady looming.

If it weren't for Naomi, I would have likely just called it quits completely those last few weeks of the semester. Those first few weeks after I ended it with Kevin she would come to get me and walk with me to my classes in between her own. During our weight training class, she rode me harder than usual just to keep me focused on my goals in the class, rather than recent events in my life. She was my life saver. I knew my ability to survive it all was in large part due to her friendship.

For Winter Break she went back up North to New York. I really considered it, but didn't want to chance running into anyone like Jess, or even Kevin. A week before the break he actually called me. Rushing to my room after a class to stand my desk duty, I answered my phone without looking at the display, "Hello?"

"Hello," I heard the familiar voice say back to me. "I can't believe you answered your phone."

I rolled my eyes at the phone, "Had I known it was you, I would've sent it to voicemail. And if you left a message, the moment I heard your voice I would have deleted the message without a second thought."

"Wow, Aaliyah. That's pretty cold."

"We know you would know something about being a cold individual, Kevin." I was ready to get off the phone with him. To rush the conversation along I asked, "Please tell me why I shouldn't just hang up on you right now because I honestly don't have time for your bull."

"You use to always have time for me."

"Keywords 'use to'. That was before I knew you were a lying, cheating asshole with a fucking family! You've got two seconds, and one is already gone."

"Okay, okay. I was calling to see if you were going home for the holidays."

"Why?"

"Because I was going up to visit my mother, and I would love to spend some time with you while I was up there. Take some time to explain my side of the story."

"Is this some type of prank?" I smirked. "Are cameras about to pop out around me? Or do you think I am that fucking stupid, Kevin?" I was so infuriated that he would even have the audacity to approach me after what happened in November. *You have got to be fucking kidding me!* "You know what? Don't even answer that. I already know." Before he even had a chance to comprehend what was happening or rebuttal, I hung up the phone. Some people are just too bold for their own good. If I ever heard from Kevin again, it would be too soon.

During the break, most of the other students did go home, though, so the campus was quiet. My dorm, in particular, was especially quiet. I spent most of my time reading or trying to get back into writing. Since going to the Poetry Slam I had been inspired to pick the pen back up. It has been a slow process, but I am hopeful and plan to attend more events in the future. Other times I just wondered the halls.

I ran into Xavier during one of my random roams through the halls. "What are you doing still here," I asked him.

"I could ask you the same," he countered.

I laughed, "Touché." I couldn't lie, but I was happy to see him, a lot happier than I had been previously. "So, seriously, why are you here?" I quizzed.

"Didn't really feel like going home. You?"

"Just not a good time to be up there, too much going on."

"Oh," he said probably because he didn't know what else to say. "Well, try not to get too bored. Just one semester to go."

"Yeah, I am definitely ready to graduate and move on to the next chapter in my life because this last one hasn't been all that great." I stuffed my hands in my pocket, thinking to myself, *Some of that was your fault.*

As if he heard my thoughts, he responded, "If I knew then, what I know now, I would not have hurt you the way I did, Aaliyah. I really do apologize for that."

"It's okay," I tried to grin. "Things happen all the time. Trust me, I know." Without warning, I felt the tears sliding down my cheeks.

"Whoa, whoa, whoa, is everything okay?"

Whipping my face, I told him, "Yeah, I'm all right. I'll be fine."

"You don't look it. If you need to talk, I have the time." Xavier gave me a hug and then escorted me toward the side door. "C'mon, let's go for a walk like we use to and get some fresh air." I didn't say anything, I simply followed his lead.

We walked up the block toward Papa John's, not really saying anything to each other. Walking together was enough given I didn't want to tell my ex that my new boyfriend is now my ex-boyfriend because he neglected to tell me he had a whole other family apart from being with me. I just couldn't see how telling him all of that would help my situation any. This, walking in silence, was a perfect alternative.

After a turn or two around the block, we headed back to the dorm. Xavier walked me back to my room. "Thanks Zay, I really needed that."

"Wow," he perked up, "You haven't called me Zay in a long time."

I chuckled, "Is that so?"

"Yeah, it is. Must mean I am not in the dog house anymore," he laughed.

I joined him in the laughter, "I guess not." I thought for a moment, and then I asked, "Would you like to come in?"

He looked at his watch. "It is a little late. Maybe next time."

"Are you sure? You could spend the night." I stepped toward him removing the space that was between us.

He stepped back, "That's not a good idea, Aaliyah."

"Why not? You have a girlfriend or something?"

"Or something."

His response just sat there in the air for a few seconds before I finally spoke. "Oh."

"I'm sorry Aaliyah, but you made it clear that you had moved on. In the midst of it, I met someone and I am really feeling her."

All I could say was, "Oh," again.

"Hey, I enjoyed walking with you tonight like old times, but I have to go. See you later." Xavier gave me a quick hug, and then turned and walked away. *Did Xavier just reject me?* It took me a minute to comprehend what had just taken place. Granted, since the start of the year, I had pushed him away, and now I was welcoming his comfort. I couldn't believe things were so bad that I was leaning on Xavier for comfort as if he hadn't done the same thing as Kevin did to me. And he rejected me. I went into my room utterly perplexed. First Jess, then Kevin, and now Xavier. In a matter of a few months, I had completely struck out.

The new school semester was a welcomed distraction from my life. I threw everything into it to keep my mind off of what had gone wrong in the first one. My internship with Atlantic Records kept me occupied most days. Anything needed, I volunteered, whether it was organizing files or handing out flyers. I was trying to keep myself busy just like the previous summer when Xavier dumped me.

Those times when I didn't have any work from school or my internship, I was chilling with Naomi. I trusted her. She was my best friend in Atlanta. Her schedule was pretty open since she managed to cram most of her course load in her sophomore and junior years. She was merely coasting through our senior year. I envied her, but at the same time, I didn't. Fewer distractions meant more time sulking over things that weren't worth the attention. Our friendship had developed to the point that we would go to the movies, open mic shows, shopping, and out to eat together often. There weren't too many things I couldn't talk or vent to her about.

Unfortunately, I still experienced those moments when I had to stand face to face with my failures in love. Valentine's Day was one of those days. While everyone was running around acting like fools in love, I was doing everything I could to avoid it all. The reminders of my inability to maintain a healthy relationship weren't a particularly favorite topic of mine.

Naomi was even busy on Valentine's Day. Supposedly she was going on some date with someone she'd recently met. She didn't say much about who she was going out with, but I also didn't care to ask. I was pretty over anything dealing with love and relationships, even a possibly budding new one for my friend. Before going, though, she stopped by my room and gave me this cute little teddy bear and card that essentially said to chin up, you will find love when it's right. The sentiment was nice, but it only made me even more depressed and over everything. Well, I told myself I was, but in my solitude, I sat there crying over the sappy romantic comedies that every channel seemed to be playing.

As my birthday approached I figured it would be another day like Valentine's Day, minus the sappy romantic comedies. I had no plans, nor did I even attempt to make any. My boss at my internship gave me the day off, so I had resolved to spend the day doing nothing. Until there was a knock at my door. Opening the door, I leaned in the door jam and said, "Yes?"

It was Naomi. She pushed past me, barging into my room. "What are you doing?" I climbed back in my bed and gestured at the TV. She asked, "Are you serious? Isn't it your birthday?"

"Yup, it's my birthday. I have no plans, sooo, yup, I'm serious."

Grabbing my wrists, she started pulling me up. "Get up! You are not spending your birthday in bed like an old woman."

I resisted, "Why not? I am an old woman."

"Lili, you are far from an old woman. Let's go."

Most shortened my name to Liyah, but one day she just started calling me Lili and it stuck. I'm not even sure how she came up with that name. Trying to return back to the conversation, yet still not wanting to do anything, I asked, "Where are we supposed to be going?"

"I don't know yet." With that, I pulled my arms from her hold.

"Then there is no need for me to get up." Frustrated, she grabbed me again, this time she seriously pulled on me. "Stop that, Omi," I protested. Omi sounded better than calling her what everybody else did, and I am petty enough to want my own name.

"I'll stop when you get up."

We went back and forth like that for a minute until I got tired of her pulling on me and I exclaimed, "Fine! Fine. I'll get up, but what you see is what you get." I had on a pair of leggings and a t-shirt with my hair in a messy bun on the top of my head.

"That's fine. You're still cute, so I wouldn't be surprised if you didn't still meet someone," she laughed at me.

I rolled my eyes at her. "Whatever, Omi."

She just continued to laugh. "What you have on is fine. I've decided where we are going and what you have on is perfect."

"And where is that?"

"To Six Flags! You aren't afraid of rollercoasters, are you?"

"Why would I be scared of roller coasters?" I inquired.

She hunched her shoulders, "Some girls are."

"Well, I'm not some girls. Let's go." It had been years since

I had gone to the amusement park. Hearing we were going to Six Flags made staying in my room on my birthday no longer appealing.

Naomi drove all the way to Austell, Georgia while I played DJ. I have a bit of an eclectic style when it came to music. Interestingly enough, she does too because she knew just about every song I played, regardless of genre, year, or artist. I was impressed. Most people weren't into the same music I was into. It made for an easy ride.

When we got there, we went on all the major rides, no matter how scary they looked or how long the line was. While I screamed like a crazy woman, she laughed and poked fun at me. We shared a funnel cake and walked from one end of the park to the other and back again. On top of it all, she literally paid for everything, whether it was the entrance to the park, food, or games I wanted to try. She said the trip to the amusement park was her treat and my birthday gift, but it felt almost like a date. *A date?* I thought. *Where did that come from?*

Once the thought was in my head, I couldn't shake it. Whenever she wasn't looking, I would look at Naomi and try to figure out what she was. I mean, I knew she was friends with Jess, but that didn't mean she was gay. The thought of her sexuality had never been a blip on my radar until now. To myself I whispered, "What are you doing Aaliyah?"

"Huh? You say something?" she asked.

"Oh," I said, realizing she heard me. I covered it up telling her it was nothing; that I was just thinking out loud. She accepted my explanation and went back to whatever she was talking about. I had missed some of it because of my own thoughts. Was Naomi gay? And was this a date?

After an extremely long day at the park, we finally headed back to the campus. I was so exhausted that on the drive back I fell asleep. Faintly, I heard someone calling my name. Naomi was trying to wake me up to let me know we were back at the school. Looking around dazed, I slowly realized where we were. Rubbing my face, I checked to make sure I didn't drool on anything before climbing out of the car. I was still slightly sleep and stumbled a bit trying to get out.

Naomi caught me and half carried me to my room. As we got closer to my room, she asked for my key. I told her it was in my pocket, but I wasn't sure which pocket. How incoherent I was, was ridiculous but I hadn't been out all day like that in a while. I was seriously tired from the day's events. In the midst of my thought process, she found my key and had walked us into my room.

I stripped down to my bra and panties and climbed into bed. It felt so good to finally lay down. Naomi asked, "Are you good?"

Groggily I said, "Yes. Thank you for spending my birthday with me. You're so awesome."

"No worries. You shouldn't have to stay on campus on your birthday when you don't have a class."

"Yeah," I slurred.

Taking that as her cue to leave, Naomi said, "Go ahead and get you some rest. I'll see you in the morning."

Reaching out for her I protested, "No. Please just stay here with me until I go to sleep." I knew I probably sounded like I was drunk, which was exactly what I tended to sound like when I was really sleepy. At that moment, I was at my limit. Through the slits of my eyes, I could see that she was contemplating whether she should stay or not. Again I said, "Please stay, Omi."

Probably against her better judgment, she agreed and was about to take a seat in my desk chair. "No!" I stopped her. "Up here." I patted the bed beside me.

"Right here is okay, Lili."

"Oh my goodness! I'm not going to bite you! Come here, Omi!" She sighed deeply, and then came and laid beside me, facing me. I whispered, "Thank-you," and got comfortable. I don't think Naomi and I had ever been that close before, but she smelled really good, like cocoa butter. Sniffing her, I told her, "You smell good."

"Thank-you. Now go to sleep."

I pouted, then obliged saying, "Okay." I dreamt that I kissed her before rolling over and finally going to sleep. I can't say if that really happened or not because I don't remember anything, truly, after saying 'okay'.

The next day, I woke up refreshed and more aware. I thought about how I had gotten to my room and in my bed. As I replayed the evening in my head, the probability of having kissed Naomi came up. *Did I really kiss her?* My life had been full of the unexpected so anything was possible.

Instead of making assumptions, I got up, put on a pair of sweat pants and a t-shirt and went to Naomi's room. She answered after the second knock. "Hey, Lili. You're up early."

"Yeah, I know. I slept really well last night since I was so exhausted."

"You were definitely exhausted last night."

"I figured, that is why I am up right now. May I come in?"

"Umm, sure." She moved to the side so that I could come in and closed the door. "What's up?"

I blurted out, "Did we kiss last night?"

She paused before answering me. "Not necessarily. I mean, you did kiss me on the lips, but it was nothing crazy."

"Oh my goodness! I didn't!"

"It was innocent. You were tired. Do you know that when you are really tired you come off as if you have been drinking?"

I pierced my lips together, "Yeah, I do."

"It was… different, but cute. You didn't want me to leave."

I felt my face turn flush and my voice squeak, "Really? How embarrassing!"

Naomi laughed, "You were okay. I'm glad to see you are back to normal now."

"Yeah, I guess so." Briefly, I thought back to my birthday and remembered my thoughts of having been on a date with Naomi and whether she was gay. "Hey, Omi. Can I ask you a question?"

"Of course. Go for it." She offered me a bottle of water before opening one for herself and drinking from it.

"Are you gay?"

Spitting her water out, she asked, "Did you just ask me if I was gay?"

"Yeah, I did. Because yesterday we went to Six Flags for my birthday and you paid for everything like when you go on a date. So, I started thinking and wondering and realized I didn't know the answer."

"A date? You thought we were on a date?"

"No, no. You are missing my point. I know we weren't on a date, it just felt like one." Naomi didn't say anything, she just looked at me peculiarly. "Was it a date?"

"No, not in that sense. Just one friend treating another friend for her birthday."

"Oh," I said, trying to sound relieved, but I couldn't tell if I really was.

"Everything okay? You sound disappointed."

"No, no. Everything is okay," I forced a smile.

"Okay. Is that it?"

"You never answered if you were gay or not. Are you a lesbian like Jess and Tina?"

"Does it matter?"

"No, but I still want to know."

"I am."

"You are what," I asked so that I was certain.

"I am gay." I fell silent for a moment. The next question in my head was a stupid one. It was totally vain and inappropriate.

Even so, I asked, "So, am I not attractive?"

"Aaliyah, why are you asking me all of this? What does my level of attraction to you have to do with anything?"

"Nothing. I was just curious." Naomi seemed frustrated and annoyed all at once. I noticed that whenever she was starting to get pissed she would rub her eyebrows as she was doing at that moment. I knew I should've left well enough alone, but I dug deeper into that rabbit hole. "Would you date someone like me?"

"No, I wouldn't. You aren't a lesbian or even bisexual. It would be a waste of time to chase a woman I could never have."

"You think I would be a waste of time?" The question slipped out my mouth easily, unconcerned with the possible consequences or answer to the question. At this point, I was on auto-pilot, dropping bombs as I went, not thinking about the damage I could potentially cause with my inquisition.

"Aaliyah, why would I pursue a straight woman?"

"I've been with a woman before, you know."

"That doesn't mean you *like* women. After being able to get to know you these last few months, I am certain that if you have been with a woman it was likely out of curiosity. Nothing more."

"That may be so, but why not be with a woman, huh? I have absolutely no luck with guys. Maybe with a woman, someone will finally want me. Not just a portion, but all of me, and understand me." I could feel the tears welling up in my eyes. *Why couldn't someone just choose me for once?*

Naomi interrupted my thoughts stating, "Being in a relationship with a woman is not necessarily different from being in one with a man. It is not about sexuality, but individuality. It's about two individuals interacting with one another and building a lasting partnership. Whether gay or straight, it is the same. If you do not understand that, you don't need to be in a relationship, male or female." I didn't know how to reply to that, so I didn't. I sat there losing the battle of holding back my tears. Realizing I wasn't going to respond, she added, "I know you have been hurt a lot lately, and maybe that is why your curiosity has been piqued so heavily. Your hurt could be clouding your feelings, desires, and judgment right now."

"I hear you," I barely said over a whisper.

"Look, Lili, I am not trying to dog you or put you down. I am just being honest with you because you are my friend, and I care about you. You shouldn't rush into a relationship no matter who the person is. Especially not now. Just date and allow yourself time to heal."

"What if I said I wanted to date you?"

"C'mon, Lili. We just went over this."

"For real, Naomi. What if I wanted to get to know you and date you? I am sitting here listening to everything you are saying, and it makes complete sense to me. At the same time, I am thinking about who has been there for me through some of the roughest patches I have experienced, and it's been you. You are my best friend. I talk to you about my life more than even Tina. Who better to grow with than your best friend?"

"I don't know if that's such a good idea. I am at a point in my life where I know who I am and what I want. I am not trying to be someone's trial companion."

"You say that, but you haven't said no. I am not trying to make you a trial companion. I am really interested in seeing where this," I gestured my hands from her direction to my own, "could go. Do you not like me, or something? Because if it's that, please just say that so I can stop embarrassing myself."

"Of course I like you, Aaliyah."

"Don't play with me, Omi. You know what I mean. Do you like me, like me?" There was a pregnant pause in which had a pin been dropped it would have definitely been heard. "Omi, do you?" I asked again.

As if wrestling with whether to answer truthfully or not, she finally responded, "I do like you, like you Aaliyah. I've had a crush on you since Freshman Bio." I blushed at her statement. "That said," she continued, "I am very well aware that right now you are in the process of healing. You need to heal. Jumping from one situation to the next is not generally the best way to do that."

"Okay. I understand that, and it makes sense. But," I hesitated, "would you like to date me? I mean, just see how it goes anyway?" I honestly couldn't get any further down the rabbit hole than I already was, so why not go for it?

"I don't know about that, Lili."

"It's not like I am asking to be your girlfriend. Just dating. A slight step up from being a platonic friend. Nothing necessarily more."

"Just dating, huh?"

"Just dating. Similar to how we are now."

"I'm sorry, but I'm going to need to think about this one. Is that okay? It is just a bit much for me to rush and make a decision on."

Although I was crushed that she didn't say yes, I whipped my eyes and told her, "That's fine. I understand."

jess

Chapter 23 (Graduation Day)

Although Jordyn's graduation was only a few days after Nay's, there was no way we were going to miss it. Being the trooper she was, Jordyn took the time to fly down with Ty and me to see our best friend achieve such an awesome accomplishment. I was definitely a proud friend. On top of that, she had been dating this female she called "Lili" and we all were curious about who she was. It had been a long time since Nay was this into someone, so this Lili chic had to really be something special.

After the graduation, we stood by waiting for Nay to show up so we could congratulate her on her graduation. I spotted her in the crowd, but couldn't see if her girl was with her since there were so many people around the graduates until they were up close.

I squinted my eyes, thinking I was seeing things. There must have been something in the water, a glare from the sun or I was just tripping because the woman in tow with Nay looked a whole lot like Aaliyah.

When Nay was finally able to get to us, she ran and hugged all of us before beginning the introductions. She turned to us and said, "Jess, Ty, Jordyn, please meet my Lili, the woman I am currently dating. Jess, you know her as Aaliyah, but as you know, I call her Lili." She then turned to Aaliyah and introduced her to us, "Baby, you already know Jess and this is Ty, our friend since we were kids, but I don't think you've met Jordyn before. She's Jess's girlfriend."

I watched Aaliyah's express when Jordyn was introduced as my girlfriend. Granted from my angle it looked like she frowned her face, but it was only for a split second. I doubted if anyone but I had even noticed it.

Despite the slight bit of tension in the air, everyone remained congenial. Nay announced her and Aaliyah would be taking a mini vacation after graduation before heading back up North. Nay never mentioned it, so I couldn't tell if Aaliyah had ever told her about us. Not knowing kind of made this whole interaction awkward. If she had, how was Nay even able to date her and be around both of us knowing we'd been intimate? If she hadn't, should I be the one to tell Nay about the fling we had considering she's my best friend? Hell, did any of that even matter?

Technically, yeah, because whether she had or not could mean possible drama down the road. My best friend with a chic I had messed around with. That just seemed like a problem waiting to happen. I really didn't like unnecessary drama, but at this point, the future really remained to be seen. For now, I'll just smile and let this hand play itself.

ABOUT THE AUTHOR

Ameehsal MindSpeaka is a poet, writer, and author of two collections of poetry *Emotional Development* and *Love Symply*. Starting her writing career as a child, she has been writing poetry and stories for decades.

All that she has learned over the years and the feedback she's received from others, she has put into her highly anticipated first novel, *Tempted*. She has a storytelling style that pulls you in and keeps you entangled in the world she creates until the last word. Through *Tempted*, she brings together and to life characters that are relatable, giving readers a sense of connection to them, either to root for them or hope for their demise.

Ameehsal is originally from Paterson, New Jersey, but chooses to call Atlanta, Georgia home since she finds herself traveling often in her line of work. Writing is something she has always loved and finds time to do even while on the go.

To keep up with her, check out her website and blog at www.MindSpeaka.com or follow her on social media:

Instagram: @MindSpeaka (https://instagram.com/MindSpeaka)
Twitter: @PoetMindSpeaka (https://twitter.com/PoetMindSpeaka)
Facebook: Ameehsal MindSpeaka (https://facebook.com/MindSpeaka)

ACKNOWLEDGEMENTS

First and foremost, thank-you to the most high. Next thank-you, to my wife, Tynesha, and family for supporting me through this and being my beta readers. Thanks Mel for getting me to done. Also, thank-you to all of my supporters who have stuck by me through the years. Know that without you, this novel would not be a reality. Thank you for reading, sharing, and providing feedback without hesitation. You all are superstars and I wish nothing but success and blessings for you.

Thanks for reading! Please add a short review on Amazon and Good Reads and let me know what you thought!

Sign up for my mailing list to be the first to hear about new books or events at www.MindSpeaka.com/contact/.

Purchase Emotional Development and Love Symply, both on Amazon!

www.ingramcontent.com/pod-product-compliance
Lightning Source LLC
Chambersburg PA
CBHW022129050726
47590CB00002B/474